There Was An Old Woman

There Was An Old Woman

Howard Engel

THE OVERLOOK PRESS
WOODSTOCK & NEW YORK

A Benny Cooperman Mystery

Published in the United States in 2000 by
The Overlook Press, Peter Mayer Publishers, Inc.
Lewis Hollow Road
Woodstock, NY 12498
www.overlookpress.com

Library of Congress Cataloging-in-Publication Data

Engel, Howard.
There was an old woman: a Benny Cooperman mystery / Howard Engel.
p. cm.
1. Cooperman, Benny (Fictitious character)— Fiction.
2. Private Investigation— Fiction. 3. Ontario— Fiction. I. Title.
PR9199.3.E49 T53 2000
813.54— dc21

Manufactured in the United States of America

ISBN 1-58567-044-8

1 3 5 7 9 8 6 4 2

For Eric Wright, Julian Symons and Justin Kaplan
who know a quotation when they see one

Cast me not off in the time of old age;
forsake me not when my strength faileth . . .

Psalm LXXI

There Was An Old Woman

Chapter One

As I went up the twenty-eight steps to my second-floor office, I heard, as usual, the sound of the running toilet. I swallowed a curse as I came to the top of the stairs and went into the washroom to jiggle the flush handle. It was a slight mechanical adjustment, but it meant the world to my sanity. The tank began to fill and I closed the door behind me. What angered me about the sound of the running water was the fact that it announced to me and to the world in general that Kogan, the caretaker, that little man of little work, was goofing off again. Kogan hated work.

When I first met him a few years ago, he was panhandling along St Andrew Street. His favourite stand was the stretch between the Diana Sweets Restaurant and the bank at the corner of Queen Street on the north side. As a panhandler, Kogan could really indulge his sense of independence. You never saw him downtown on a nice day. I imagined him off fishing or having a sunbath on a picnic table in Montecello Park. I speculated that he might be a secret millionaire, who simply pretended to be destitute for his own amusement. He certainly seemed to be a student of human nature. He knew just what to say to each of his customers to make them part with more than just a few quarters. During the cold months I'd come into the office in the mornings and find him rolled up in a corner in Frank Bushmill's *Globe and Mail*. Sometimes he'd pick the washroom, which made do for both sexes, where he would be lullabied to oblivion by the bubbling waters in the ancient plumbing. Kogan was an old rummy, but he had character written in every leathery line of his face. In his third- or fourth-hand blazer and gray flannels, he looked almost dapper.

Kogan stopped being a fixture on the streets and began working at 220½ St Andrew Street when Frank Bushmill, the chiropodist, and I convinced our landlady, Mrs Onischuk, that she needed someone to take out the garbage and sweep up the offices. I think we both had the sense that we were going out on a limb in recommending him and we both lived to regret it. It was one of those good deeds that dribbles stale beer on you instead of getting you a gold star in heaven. Not only was Kogan a hopeless caretaker who neglected the garbage and failed to sweep out the offices, but he quickly became a favourite of Mrs Onischuk, for whom he could do no wrong. When I complained that his empty bottles were turning up in my waste-paper baskets or that his lunch was sometimes left in my files, Mrs Onischuk laughed at Kogan's devilment and thought less of me for complaining. Frank told me that Kogan had become fond of the Black Bush that he kept among his medical records. What broke Frank's heart was that it was all one with Kogan whether he was drinking fine old Irish whiskey or nail-polish remover.

The bubbling noise of the filling toilet diminished to the sound of a spring freshet as I unlocked the office door and kicked off my rubbers under the hat stand. Outside it was a wet December morning, but mild enough for the time of year. I looked around. My framed licence to practise as a private investigator was still hanging crookedly behind my chair. The file drawers were closed to hide their emptiness and the desk was cluttered by the mess I had abandoned yesterday at closing time.

With the toilet finally silent, I could settle down to what, from the other side of the desk, might pass for work. I paid a few bills, wrote a cheque for the renewal of my licence, and finished a report to my one and only client, whose cat had allegedly been poisoned by a jealous neighbour. Once the paperwork was under control, I rubber-tipped my teeth the way the dentist keeps telling me I should. (God forbid I shouldn't go to my grave with a full set of teeth!) When I had once more stolen a march on plaque build-up, I made a couple of phonecalls. From one I learned that the cat had been killed with a herbicide. I added that information to the report and put it into an envelope for the "Out" basket.

It was about twenty after ten, just when I was thinking of going out for a coffee at the Di, when there was a knock at the door. It was Kogan. He opened the door, but he didn't make a move to cross the threshold. He stood there, holding a mop, as though that would fool anyone who knew him.

"You busy, Mr Cooperman?" he said.

In spite of what I've already said, I should say that I liked Kogan. He had a way about him that made him his own man. Even in the old days when he was panhandling, I always got a kick when he accepted the change I passed along to him. He didn't take money from everyone. He prized his independence at a higher price than a looney or a couple of quarters. His way of life was a criticism of everything a would-be taxpayer like me stood for. He didn't own anything and he didn't want to. His only possession, his only treasure, was his discharge pin from the Canadian army. That made him at the very youngest at least seventy. I remember him telling me about heavy fighting at Carpiquet Airport near Caen in Normandy. Maybe he felt that having risked his life there, he was all paid-up in the work department from then on. Certainly, he had always made me feel as though he had been doing me a favour when he took on his caretaking responsibilities.

"Come in, Kogan. I want to talk to you!"

I gave him hell for the way he had been letting the garbage accumulate, the way he had all but abandoned my carpet. From his fixed stand by the door, he nodded. There was no sign of dumb insolence as he shifted his weight from one leg to the other. He stood his ground and took my criticism patiently. I left the toilet for last. It was the clincher, the single item that would make him see into his very soul. Again he nodded agreement. I told him that the time had come for him to make up his mind about whether he wanted the job or whether he would prefer to return to St Andrew Street. He stood there, mute, like an old print I'd seen in a book in the library: the teacher scolding the lazy scholar. When I'd finished, he looked up again and said:

"I'm sorry, Mr Cooperman. Sorry. You see, it's my girlfriend —"

"You shouldn't let that interfere with your work, Kogan." I was warming to the role; I could almost imagine Kogan as the lazy student. And yet somewhere I had the notion that he was setting me up. The way he stood there nodding told me he was holding his completed assignment or at least a handful of aces.

"Sorry," he repeated.

"No excuses!" I said, knowing that my comeuppance was only a word away.

"She's dead," he said. "My girl-friend died and I had to look after all the arrangements. She not having any family at all."

"Kogan," I said, feeling like the father who has just shot the faithful family dog that turns out to have been defending his child from the marauding wolf now dead beneath the bloody bedclothes. "Why didn't you say something?" I don't know why I asked. It wouldn't have been Kogan if he'd told me straight out.

"You never asked. I was going to wear a black armband, but I haven't had a minute. What with the police and all."

"Police? What have the police to do with it?"

"I called them. She shouldn't have died, Mr Cooperman. Liz had a few more good years in her. Even if her mind was going."

"Kogan, why don't you leave that smelly mop out there in the hall and come in and sit down?" He slowly came into the office and took a chair in front of my desk. He left the mop leaning against the door frame, but the smell followed him. "Now start at the beginning," I said, popping a cough candy into my mouth. "Tell me about it. The whole story."

He sat there collecting his thoughts and pinching the non-existent creases in his trousers. At last he looked at me. "Lizzy Oldridge and me go back a long way," he said. "Our parents were friends before the war. I call her my girl-friend, but it's just that she needed somebody and she didn't have family..." Kogan wiped his nose on his sleeve, forgetting the buttons there were designed to prevent that useful service. "She'd been poorly for some time and needed somebody to do for her." I said a silent prayer, hoping that Lizzy had fared better than Frank Bushmill and me.

"I'd bring over something to eat and sometimes she'd let me in."

"Why were the cops involved?"

"I told you! I called them. Lizzy starved to death as sure as I'm sitting here. She had lots of money in the bank, but she couldn't get at it. They wouldn't let her have a cent of her own money to buy a litre of milk with. When she was so weak she couldn't get up, I went to the bank and begged them! But they wouldn't give me a brass thumbtack. Then they got an injunction so I couldn't even go near her house without getting arrested."

"Did you have power of attorney, Kogan? They couldn't legally let you touch her money."

"Yeah? Well, when she was well enough, they wouldn't let *her* touch it either. How do you like them apples?"

"Had she been certified incompetent or something? There has to be an explanation."

"That's why they're holding an inquest into her death right now over at the new court-house. I just come from there."

"Well, they'll get to the bottom of it. If there's been a slip-up, the coroner will discover it and we'll read all about it in the paper tomorrow or Monday."

"I guess," Kogan said.

"There's no way, Kogan, that an old woman can starve to death in Grantham. We've got all sorts of social agencies: municipal, provincial, federal. There has to be a better explanation than what you've just told me."

"I guess," Kogan said.

"You've been over there all morning?" Kogan nodded and added that he'd been there for the opening session the day before. He began to look twice as hopeless as I'd ever seen him. I forgot that he had a black belt in manipulation. "Maybe I'll wander over there after lunch to see what's going on," I said.

"I was hoping you'd say that, Mr Cooperman, but it may be all over by then. I'd get right on it if I were you." Feeling he had perhaps overplayed his hand, he added, "Which of course I'm not."

"I'll take a look, Kogan. They don't usually rise until one. I've got lots of time."

"You understand I'm not in a position to hire you, Mr Cooperman? I'd like to, but I'm a poor man."

"Get lost, Kogan. I'll talk to you when I get back."

"You ain't going to bill me for this afterwards?"

"Kogan, go fix the toilet! Please fix the toilet!"

"You know the way some of these sharp operators work: you think you've won a trip for two to Paris, France, and you end up with a subscription to a dozen magazines." I handed him a bent coat-hanger, which was as close to a set of plumbing tools as I had handy.

"You do your job, Kogan, and I'll do mine. You'll hear nothing about Paris from me."

He took the wire and gave me a grin. We had an understanding. Or at least I thought we had one, which, as I reflected later, wasn't the same thing at all. I know that he hadn't yet emptied his bag of tricks. Kogan, when his blood is up, is quite a manager. I only hope he didn't suspect how little I had in my office to occupy my time.

Kogan moved off, forgetting to take the mop with him. I didn't follow to see whether he was now restoring the plumbing to its rightful use. Let the public library serenade the literate and illiterate alike with the soothing sounds of bubbling fountains; a washroom should have more practical ambitions.

Chapter Two

The new court-house replaced the parking lot that had replaced the old Carnegie Library at the corner of James and Church. We all hated to see the library go, but we had to admit that the new one, across the street next to the police station, was bigger and better. But the old court-house hadn't done so well. It had been turned into a shelter for a bunch of boutiques and cafés serving Italian coffee. It wasn't a fair ending for a building that had heard the dread sentence of death pronounced in its courtrooms. The selling of candles that smell like soap and soap that smells of sandalwood tends to trivialize a structure that is approaching its hundred and fiftieth year in the public service. How do you put a building out to stud?

Courtroom D was an L-shaped room with pews running down to face the coroner from one direction and, at right angles, to face the jury from another. A piece of dark railing, probably rescued from the old building, formed the bar that separated those with business for the court from the rest of us. There were microphones attached to the coroner's high bench and others to pick up what the witnesses and lawyers had to say. The provincial flag hung limply to the left of the coroner, Dr Geoffrey

Chisholm, a man with steel grey hair and a gnarled red nose. Behind him, the wall was decorated with oak battens of wood running from floor to ceiling at two-inch intervals. Between these, the orange wall reminded you that this was the new court-house not the old one.

I moved into a back seat, beside a bailiff I knew, and listened. My neighbour Jimmy Dodds leaned over and identified the witness. "That's Thurleigh Ramsden," he said, looking up at me to see if that meant anything. It did, but the bell was so faint, I couldn't identify the sound. Jimmy read my face and supplied a few missing facts. "Lawyer," he said. "Ran for mayor three years ago. Stands to the right of the Tories." I nodded my thanks and began to tune in on the proceedings.

Ramsden was being questioned by Jack Webley, a lawyer I'd seen in action before, about the finances of Lizzy Oldridge. From his answers, I got the impression that Ramsden wanted to show that he had kept his distance from the affairs of Kogan's friend. His answers were brief and vague, as though he had important business awaiting him outside the courtroom. He kept trying to score social points with the coroner.

"She was, ah, not sartorially in the same class with Dr Chisholm, for example," he said with a smile directed at the bench.

"She was a sloppy dresser?" Webley asked.

"She was a poor dresser. Personal hygiene was never one of her strong points." Webley, who was wearing a polyester shirt, looked like he wanted to move on, but we both caught another attempt to get a smile from the coroner.

"How did you come to have joint signing authority over her accounts at the Upper Canadian Bank?"

Ramsden let a slow smile reveal his large, beaver-like front teeth. He sucked in air, and seemed to expand. His small eyes looked like they were about to be popped from the stretched skin of his face. His wispy moustache waved as he exhaled.

"I don't know where you got that idea. I never had any authority over any of her bank accounts."

"Yes, but she kept the bulk of her money in her safety deposit box. You had joint signing authority there, didn't you?"

"Yes, but her bank accounts were her own business."

"Do you know how much was in her savings account?"

"I have no idea. I have a great many things pressing upon my attention. I don't pretend to know everything."

"Would you be surprised to learn that Miss Oldridge had less than ten dollars in her accounts?"

"If you say so, I suppose I'll have to take your word."

"How did you become the executor of Miss Oldridge's estate?"

"Quite simply: she asked me."

"Under what circumstances?"

"It was after a meeting of a society I founded, the Guild of the Venerable Bede. Miss Oldridge was a member, a member of long standing, if I remember aright. She used to sing the national anthem at our meetings. When she was younger, she had a remarkably beautiful voice."

"And?"

"And she took me aside and asked if I would act as executor in the will she was having drawn up."

"You were one executor among several?"

"No, young man, Miss Oldridge trusted me. I was the sole executor."

"You weren't by any chance her lawyer too, were you?" Webley asked in what appeared to be an offhand way.

"No, sir, I was not!" Ramsden shot back. The coroner frowned at Webley, but did nothing with the gavel he was holding.

Ramsden was sweating under his black-and-white striped shirt. You could see his undershirt through the damp fabric. His blue blazer with a yacht club crest made him look quite the confident man about town.

"Was it at that time that she asked you to enter into an agreement whereby it took both of your signatures to gain access to her safety deposit box?"

"No. That came later, when she felt that her physical and mental powers were overtaxed. I reluctantly agreed, but only after convincing her to arrange to draw a regular allowance from her funds. She had the habit of turning all of her loose cash into term deposits, you see. She left herself short more than once. By my plan, she would have living money every week."

"Do you remember what amount?"

"She liked to economize. She was a frugal woman."

"Please answer the question."

"I think the amount was set at sixty dollars a week. But she had the power to alter that at any time."

"Did she alter it?"

"I have no information on that point, young man."

"If she had changed the amount, you would have had to come down to the bank, isn't that correct?"

"Yes."

"And did you?"

"I went to the bank several times, as I remember, and once to her lawyer's when she signed her will."

"What bank and branch did she deal with?" Webley asked, pretending to look at a piece of paper. It was a trick he should have saved for a real trial. Here it didn't mean anything.

"We're talking about the central branch of the Upper Canadian Bank on St Andrew Street."

"Do you know the manager at that branch?"

"Clarence Temperley has been the manager since Egerton Garsington died back in the late 1960s. I have my own accounts at that branch. Naturally, I know Mr Temperley quite well."

"It would have been a help if Mr Temperley could be reached to assist us in this inquest, Mr Ramsden. Can you think of any reason why he has not come forward?"

"Are you asking me to speculate, Mr Webley?"

"You needn't answer that," the coroner directed, giving Jack a dirty look.

"This is the beginning of the holiday season, Mr Webley," Ramsden said. "Many people who have the means flee the inclement weather to warmer climes. And who can blame them?"

I listened to a few more minutes of this, drawing an unpleasant picture of the witness from what he said himself, and then I went out the double back doors for a cigarette break. Of course, since I no longer smoke, it's difficult to figure out what to do during a cigarette break. Chewing on cough candies is something one does in private with the knowledge of consenting adults. It's a private vice and the less said about it, the better.

I was crunching a Halls between my molars when I heard a voice calling me. "Cooperman! Benny Cooperman! What in hell's name are you doing here?" I turned around and found myself staring into the worried little eyes of Stan Mendlesham of Newby, Boyle, Weaver and Mendlesham. They had an office across from St Thomas's Church on Ontario Street. The word on the street was that Mendlesham was a sham Mendlesham, that his name was simply Mendle. But I don't know about that. If he was Jewish, he was even less observant than I was, which was going some. I thought I took the prize in non-attendance and un-belonging.

"Benny! What brings you to coroner's court on a cold, wet day like this?" Stan was a short, round man, with pear-shaped tones to match his figure. He fancied himself an orator, loved to make love to a jury. In fact, his whole approach to law was like courtship. He wooed jurors with winks and nods from the defence table, sent bouquets of lacy words over the crown attorney's head to fall gently into the lap of each juror. He wore gold cuff-links and an expensive watch.

"Just killing an hour, Stan. How about you?" Stan coughed into his fist and avoided my eyes.

"I worked with Thurleigh Ramsden when I got my call to the bar," he said. "That's when Thurleigh made his big bid in politics. I kept his clients happy while he attended rallies and made speeches. I just came to see that he was well represented, that's all. Call it curiosity."

Stan was showing stains under his arms that didn't go with the weather. He was nervous about something.

"Tell me, Stan, who drew up this will they were talking about?"

Mendlesham shrugged. "Search me," he said evasively.

"What are the chances of criminal charges being laid after the inquest, Stan?" It was a naïve question on my part. It was just intended to keep the conversation going. I was surprised by his answer:

"Who the hell tipped you off about this, Benny? What's your game? What the hell do you think you know?" Stan glared at me like I had just corrected his grammar.

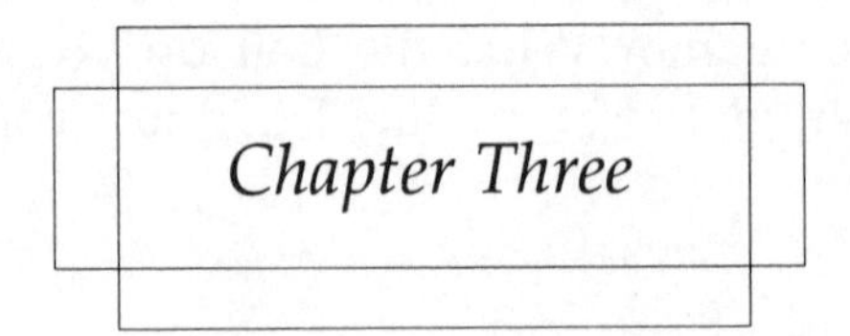

Chapter Three

The weather was still spitting at me when I came out. For some reason it wouldn't just rain; it had to play at being fog. There was a perversity about it that chilled my innards as I crossed the street at the light. I looked up *Oldridge* in the remaining shreds of a telephone book shackled to a pay-phone in the market behind City Hall. There she was:

Oldridge E B 3 Brogan.....960-3829

I tried to place Brogan Street and couldn't. I'd look it up back at the office, I thought, as I continued up James Street. There was a crowd of people outside the seed store on King Street. A pre-Christmas special in tulip bulbs? I didn't investigate.

There were plywood hoardings nailed in front of the glass windows of the hardware store part-way down the next block. After more than one hundred years in business, Foley Bros. had closed its doors. Everybody had been shocked. There had never been a time within living memory when you couldn't buy a bag of three-inch nails or dry paint mix at Foley Bros. On a post next to the hoarding stood a sign I'd never noticed before: Brogan Street. It began just south of the empty hardware store. I worked less than a block away, but I'd never noticed.

To be fair, Brogan Street was more an alley than a street. There were garbage cans, refuse carts and green garbage bags beside the back doors to the stores along St Andrew Street. A deserted loading bay at the back of Foley's had become an aerie for two yellow-and-black cats, who studied my progress through their territory with contained suspicion.

The Oldridge house was the only building that fronted on this back alley. It was a broken-down, two-storey frame house with a tilting front porch and gable roof. I say the porch tilted; the whole building listed, inclined away from the perpendicular. Behind it I could see the lean-to-like summer kitchen with a shed behind that. The rear of the property was marked by a rotting board fence. The house had been painted white, but I doubted that the painter was still among the living. Great gaps in the paint curled back from the doorposts and siding, exposing weathered wood and constant neglect. The boards protested my weight on the porch as I tried the front door. I didn't really expect to find anyone there, but I knocked anyway: a gesture of appeasement to the household gods.

The door was locked, but it gave when I added a slight pressure to the rusty round doorknob. I pushed it open and my expectation of hearing the hinges squeak was satisfied. Inside, the place was a mess. Newspapers in stacks and in plastic bags stood against the walls as though they had been driven there by an internal blast of wind. The kitchen was large enough to accommodate a huge wood stove, which trailed black stove-pipes across the pressed-tin ceiling. Fly-paper strands dangled like spotted corpses from a ceiling lamp and from the stove-pipes themselves. The sink was full of filth and dishes that were covered by a mossy fungus. I didn't look too closely. In the centre of the floor stood a round wooden table with a faded oil-cloth or plastic covering. A spider had spun a web from an empty wine bottle to a plate on the table. On the plate, something moved, then ran along the table and down a leg. I stood back, trying to concentrate on the faded cloth lampshade that was barely attached to a tall floor-lamp from the thirties. Everywhere, the smell was poisonous.

I shouldn't go on describing the mess I encountered, but I became fascinated. "Mess" hardly covers the territory. I was looking at squalor that had the depth of many years behind it. The rats in the kitchen were generations removed from the pioneers who knew a good kip when they found one. The stench in the blocked plumbing was what my father used to call "pre-war," which would have made it at least fifty years old. The bedroom at the back was a woollen mass of moths in bliss. A cloud of dust particles stood in a beam of light coming through the back window, revealing a view of outdoor plumbing just a block and a half away from City Hall. Light fell on a clot of discarded clothes and linen that had been pressed into a kind of felt on the floor near the bed. When something moved in the bed, I took it as a cue to leave bad enough alone. I tried not to run.

Once out in the misty wet, I took a few deep breaths while looking back at the house. Something in me was delighted by the gall of the old lady to pull this off in the middle of Grantham. It takes courage to become an eyesore to all you meet. The house was a wooden sermon on the futility of storing up goods here on earth. Who, in his right mind, could have warned old Liz that she couldn't take it with her?

I rarely take a drink in the afternoon, but after walking through Liz Oldridge's place, I needed one. The Nag's Head was an English pub imitation that had come along some time in the sixties. It did well for a while with the young people, but finally it was left to a few regulars who used to haunt the old Harding House, until they pulled it down. It had a lot of engraved frosted glass on the outside and darts and half-timbering inside. Like all the places in town, they served the same draft beer and all the regular brands. They had tried fancy specialty beer, the imported and the locally made, but the customers only wanted the old stuff, the familiar amber glasses with a few bubbles moving up regularly to the tiny white head on top.

I sat down at a round table near the dark-stained door and ordered a draft, which I downed in a gulp. Without comment, the waiter replaced it. As a non-serious beer drinker, I took my time with this one. It seemed thicker, more tepid, harder to get down, than the first. I looked around me to see who else could spare a few moments for a beer this soon after the beginning of licensed hours. I was curious. Against the wall sat a man whose face I'd seen before. It was a grey, lined face with red hair that had gone dusty instead of white. I guessed he was about ten years older than me, but, on him, it looked more. It took me a minute to remember that his name was Rupe (short for Rupert) McLay. A few of the boys at the registry office used to call him the "Philadelphia lawyer" and grin at one another. I guess they meant that at one time he appeared to be promising. And then he'd broken his promise. Isn't that the way with promise?

There were a string of empties on McLay's table, which the waiter didn't seem in a hurry to replace. He sat patiently, staring into his beer, not trying to locate the waiter in the room. When the waiter took away my next empty, I indicated the empty glasses across the floor. "Oh, him?" he said. "He only gets one trayful and then he's washed up, old Rupe. He likes to sit and stare at them for a while, then he goes down to the library to have a nap. He's got an office around the corner on King, but I guess they don't let him sleep there." I looked around at a few of the other customers, who appeared to be close to that happy state.

There was a fug of warmth and cigarette smoke in the air that both cheered and relaxed me. I didn't blame old Rupe either. Even staring into his last glass, at least he knew where he stood and that was something. Rupe looked like he'd just told himself a joke.

Over behind the bar, a woman with red curls baked into her head was filling glasses from the draft tap for the solitary waiter, dangling a cigarette and squinting over her glasses at the Toronto paper. Wherever you lit up in this pub was the "Smoking Area." A nice arrangement for everybody except a few of us reformed sinners.

"I ain't seen you in here before, Mr Cooperman," the waiter said, looking over my head at the door. "You celebrating the death of a rich relative?"

"Does it take a death to get customers in here?"

"Aw, we got enough business. You stay and see the lunch-hour traffic. We get the overflow from the Mansion House. And the nights! You wouldn't believe." The waiter's flushed and pock-marked face was familiar. I'd seen that blowzy nose on St Andrew Street for years, without ever knowing where it belonged. He should have worn a plaque on his chest that read: "I've been serving drinks to the thirsty and taking no guff since 1952."

"I'll remember that," I said, returning to the here and now.

"But to hear Ev talk, you'd swear we hadn't had a customer for peanuts since Easter." I glanced at the redhead reading her paper behind the bar. She had the concentration of a proofreader.

"Naw," the waiter continued, as though I was giving him an argument, "I've seen pubs of all sorts and this is making a living. What I meant before, Mr Cooperman, is you must be off your trap-line. Never saw you in here, like I said." He placed a third draft in the centre of my collection of beer rings on the Formica table.

"I was doing some exploring in the alley," I said. "Wanted to see where Liz Oldridge lived. I was at the inquest over at the court-house."

"Old Liz?" he said, the grin showing his fillings. "She was a real ringa-dang-doo in her day, was Liz."

"How do you mean?"

"When she was younger, she used to keep a bunch of young boys on her place, looking after it and all. Orphans, some of 'em, and nobody looked too close at what was happening besides spring cleaning."

"That must have been a long time ago. I just saw inside the house."

"Oh, yeah. Police had to put a stop to her. Never got in the papers on account of her father being an alderman and her grandfather a judge. Liz went funny after that, though. Well, I mean, you can see by the look of her house, can't you? 'Funny,' you know what I mean?"

I had settled in my chair to hear more about the late

Liz Oldridge, when an attractive woman in her early forties came into the pub. Without letting her eyes get accustomed to the gloom, she walked directly to Rupe McLay's table, where she hovered, observing him without saying anything. From where I sat, she looked worth Rupe's time. In his place, I would have looked up from the empty glasses. She was wearing expensive clothes, a steel blue suit that hadn't been made on this continent, but the effect was untidy. She had the look of a woman who had thrown herself together in a hurry. Her jacket hung unfastened and the blouse had been buttoned wrong: I could see a glimpse of white and a pucker of flesh through the gap. She was breathing hard. The waiter winked at the woman behind the bar. To me he said: "Antonia Wishart," as though that explained everything.

"Who?"

"Missus money-britches. You know: Harlan Ravenswood's girl. Mrs Orv Wishart."

"Oh!" I said, mainly to stop the bombardment. "*That* Antonia Wishart. Glad to know." The Ravenswoods were the local media family: they owned the *Beacon* and the radio and TV stations.

She stood watching Rupe inspect his rare collection of empty crystal goblets for a few minutes before saying his name gently. His chin came up. There was no smile on his face. Who likes being found out, traced to one's hideaway, photographed in living colour with one's pants down? Not McLay, anyway. Soon they were yelling at one another. Soon there was broken glass on the floor and Antonia Wishart was heading for the door full of sudden resolve and anger, while McLay ordered more beer with a smile that successfully covered his anger and guilt. The waiter brought a single draft and swept up the glass.

I went over to the bar to talk and buy some chips. From the woman behind it I learned some home truths about the idiocy of some women who have it in their minds to save some men from themselves. I also learned that Ev, short for Evelyn, wasn't herself but her absent husband. She was May. She had married Ev after the Renovation. She said Renovation like it was the Renaissance or the Inquisition. She also confided that Bill, the waiter, was depressed because Ev intended to close down the pub in the New Year. I got her talking about Liz Oldridge.

"Liz was a peculiar old 'un, all right," May said. "She drank too much and never in ten years did I see her eat anything. Kogan looked out for her as well as he could. You know Kogan?" I nodded that I did. "She never had any money and Kogan was next to the poorhouse himself. He stood by her, though. I have to give him that."

May could tell me little more about Liz or Kogan or what had happened. "They let her die!" she said, waving her hand in an indictment of us all. When I asked about Ramsden, she could add nothing to what I'd heard at the court-house, except that he was above drinking at the Nag's Head.

At the sound of the name "Ramsden," I thought I saw Rupe McLay's head rise from its stare into nothingness for a moment. I carried my chips back to my beer. Then I got busy with some thoughts of my own. I didn't see McLay get up and carry one of his drafts across the floor to my table. The first I knew of it was feeling the balance of the table top shift. When I looked up it was into that grey, lined face.

"You mind?" he said, trying to bring me into focus.

"Company's always welcome, Mr McLay."

"What's your interest in Liz Oldridge?" He had some difficulty getting the syllables in Liz's name in the right order.

"'Interest' is dressing up idle curiosity," I said. Then I thought, What the hell? "I'm making a few inquiries for a friend of mine. You know Victor Kogan?"

"Kogan? Yes, I know him. A man of hidden deps — depths, of most excellent fancy."

"He thinks Liz was starved to death on purpose."

"He say for what purpose or who did it?"

"Yeah, he says *they* did it. *They* kept her away from her money. *They* got an injunction to keep him away from her. *They* has a lot to answer for. From what I heard this morning at the court-house, *they* seems to be Thurleigh Ramsden."

"Wouldn't argue with that, Mr Cooperman. What the hell's your first name? It's Sam, isn't it?"

"No. That's my big brother. I'm Ben."

"Ben! Or more correctly, Benny! Yes, I've heard about you."

"And I about you. Grantham's a small world. Did you know Liz?"

"Knew her dead brother. He was my age. We were in Korea together. I saw Lizzy from time to time. She was far gone when I saw her last. I didn't know what the infamous *they* was doing to her and, I guess, she was beyond calling for help."

We sat and talked for another twenty minutes. He asked me to call him Rupe at one point. "Can you imagine a mother calling her new baby Rupert?" he asked me, getting a little sentimental. I tried to change the subject, but he had started rambling and I couldn't be sure what he was talking about any more.

"Is the Nag's Head your local pub?" I asked.

"Fixed point. Everything else is variable. Young Devlin is feeling his oats."

"Who?"

"Kenneth Devlin. Of Wilson, Carleton, Meyers and Devlin. Devlin's is the fresh face. Doesn't much like this old face. Ambitious, that's young Devlin. Julian Newby himself speaks highly of him and you know Julian Newby, QC, doesn't scatter praise on barren ground. You'll grow rheumatic before you hear him sound my praises."

"I'm not that set up with the innards of the local legal profession, Mr. McLay — I mean Rupe."

"Your state is the more gracious, I assure you."

Rupe called for another draft of beer from Bill, the waiter, and was denied. I called for one and slid it across the table. This way I was hoping for more useful information, and I would have had it but for two things: Rupe became even more confused in his talk so that I couldn't tell whether he was talking or reciting things he'd memorized in school and I became very sleepy. Beer does that to me. I could see from the faces of Rupe, Bill and May that I was no credit to the Nag's Head during its last winter season.

Chapter Four

I let myself into my parents' town house in the north end of the city. I always carried the key on my chain, it made me feel a little less adrift in the world. Although, what kind of anchor is decorated in burnt orange, I ask you? Ma was sitting in front of the television set, which was roaring away at top volume. She had her head buried in *Barchester Towers.* The continuous news station was being ignored while Ma lost herself in the last century.

"Oh, it's you! I didn't hear you come in, Benny." I leaned over and gave her a hug and kiss, which she returned with Victorian propriety. "It's a good thing I've got a roast in the oven. I must have had a feeling you were coming."

"Ma, I usually come for dinner on Friday nights. Haven't you noticed?"

"Make yourself a cup of tea, I'm nearly finished this chapter."

I went into the kitchen, filled the kettle and plugged it into the socket on the stove. I could feel the heat coming from the oven. The teabags were in the usual tin. Since coming to know Anna Abraham a few years ago, I had started making tea in a pot when I could find one rather than in the cup, which was a family tradition. There was an old photograph of my father's parents on a Lake Ontario beach, probably near Toronto, with a picnic hamper and an old brass samovar sitting in the sand. There was a large teapot set on top. The potless tradition must come from Ma's side of the family. The teapot I finally found was part of a display tea service near the kitchen window. "Leeds Spray" were the words I read on the bottom as I emptied it of keys, bus tickets for seniors, pencil stubs and loose change. I heated it first under the hot tap and then with steaming water from the kettle.

"Will you take a look at the roast, Benny. It's been in the oven two hours. I like to brown it for the last hour."

"Ma, I don't see any potatoes or other vegetables." I went around the entrance of the kitchen to face the chef. "Do you want me to put some potatoes around the roast?"

"Vegetables I've got in the cupboard. There's mixed peas and carrots or corn. It doesn't take two minutes to heat them. And I'm out of potatoes. I know you love my roast potatoes, but I don't have any."

"I could run across the street to the store," I said, trying to be helpful.

"It's not worth the trouble. What more do you want? A good roast and mixed veg? Did you check the roast like I asked?"

"I was just going to." I retreated to the kitchen, took a sip of my tea and opened the oven. The old aluminum roasting pan was covered. I removed the lid with a cloth and discovered the roast submerged under water. I stuck a fork in it and lifted it to the surface. It looked cooked, but not strictly roasted.

"Leave the lid off so it can brown," I heard from the other room.

"Ma, it won't brown under water!"

"Water? What are you talking about?" In a moment she was peering into the roasting pan with me. "That's not water, that's gravy! You reduce it before serving."

"Do you mind if I reduce at least half of it into the sink?"

"Benny! Always joking! Will you get out of my kitchen so I can cook dinner in peace?" I retreated to the couch and the *Beacon,* awaiting the arrival of my father, who got home no earlier than absolutely necessary.

The *Beacon* carried a summary of the morning's testimony in the Lizzy Oldridge inquest. I refreshed my memory reading it and caught up on the witnesses I hadn't heard. The assistant manager of the bank couldn't account for the failure of her boss, Clare Temperley, to appear as a witness. She knew for a fact that he was not planning to be away for the holidays. She read the rubric to the jury about what the arrangements were regarding access to Miss Oldridge's safety deposit box. She said that once the agreements were signed, there was no way of altering the instructions without the further agreement of both parties. She recalled a heart-rending scene in which Kogan and the deceased tried to persuade the manager, Mr Temperley, to breach the rules. She described how this upset the diminutive Mr Temperley, who had to ward off blows from Miss Oldridge's umbrella. In the end, he had threatened to call the police if they didn't leave the building. She admitted that the deceased looked under-nourished and neglected.

A public health nurse testified that she had visited the home of the deceased on several occasions and reported finding the house indescribably filthy, that the deceased had refused to be examined by her and had heaped abusive language on top of the abusive smells emanating from every corner. She could find no sign of a working toilet in the house. I could see the hand of Victor Kogan here at least. The nurse said that she had discontinued her visits because there were no visible signs of sickness to be found.

A building inspector testified that he had visited the house and described the same horrors of dirt and smell that the nurse had seen. He said that he did not deliver his list of items that needed to be fixed in order to bring the dwelling in line with the city's minimum standards because he felt that the shock of it would, in his words, "send the old woman around the bend." Nothing else was done.

I heard my father come in. I looked up and he smiled at me, looking older and wearier than I'd seen him recently. "Were you at the club?" I asked.

"I played a few hands. But those games are getting too rich for my blood. I can't afford the stakes. They're playing over a dollar a line." I split the paper with him and we settled in reading until the call to dinner came.

"I ran out of potatoes," Ma explained as we sat down, "so you'll have to make do with the mixed veg. I can make a salad if anyone wants one."

"Sure," I said and Pa nodded. Ma didn't move.

"Pa, what do you know about Thurleigh Ramsden?"

"Not while I'm eating, Benny. That man! The less you say about him, the better!"

"Why?"

"He reminds me of something you find on the underside of a restaurant table."

"I'd rather eat an unkosher chicken from a supermarket than talk to that man," added my mother. I repeated my question subtly rephrased.

"Thurleigh Ramsden is the worst kind of Gentile," Pa said.

"Jew or Gentile, he's the worst!" Ma corrected. Pa looked at her to see if she had more to say. When she remained silent, he continued:

"He's all gentility and manners wrapped up around a greedy cheapskate. Even the Mallet Club won't let him in. He's what they call lace curtain."

"What does that mean?" I asked. Pa shrugged.

"All I know is that's what they call him on St Andrew Street. He writes letters to the paper complaining that they don't bring back capital punishment. For him they could bring back the lash too, but there I'm only guessing. He thinks we've gone over to the Chinese communists because we have utilities collecting our garbage and selling us electricity. What can I say? If he's your friend, I don't want to meet your enemies. When he ran for mayor, he wrapped himself up in the Union Jack, saying that he was going to send all the foreigners back where they came from. What he didn't notice is that the 'foreigners' — some of them here since before the last war — are the majority nowadays. So, what's the percentage of an appeal like that, except to bring out all the loonies in town?"

"It's too bad he lost that wife of his. That Dora. She was the nicest thing about him."

"She left him?"

"She should have, what with him being the way he is —"

"Silk pants and no underwear, that's Ramsden, if you

ask me," Pa added. I pressed Ma about Mrs Ramsden.

"She was killed in a highway accident a few years ago. Out of town. It was in the paper."

"I heard at the club that Ramsden bought a stereo in Buffalo and didn't declare it at the border. He nearly lost his car over that."

"This is not the sort of evidence that would stand up in court," I said. "It would be called 'highly prejudicial.' And I would tend to agree, in spite of the fact that I love you both dearly."

"Prejudicial, shmedudicial," Pa said. "As long as you're healthy." He gave an old-country shrug. "I'm not asking you to take my word for it. Take his standing in the last election for mayor. He came in after the Independent Marxist-Leninists. And *they* polled lower than the regular Marxist-Leninists. That proves there are a lot of people who think the way I do."

"He moved his own mother out of her house and into a charity ward when she was eighty-seven. That's the kind of man he is."

"Don't give me any ideas," I said.

"You?" Ma said. "You I wouldn't trust with my affairs for a second. You who never remembers to shut a drawer or turn off a light! Would you remember to pay a bill? Would you remember to do the banking? Never in your whole life have I seen you clip a coupon from the paper. Your fate is spelled out in big letters, Benny. Just lucky your father and I have been spared to look after you. Another piece of roast beef, dear?"

After tea was served in the traditional way — the teabag passed from cup to cup, followed by a squirt from the plastic lemon — we gathered around the television set to watch the local news.

"I always like her," Ma said, looking at the face of the evening news, Catherine Bracken. "She's always such a lady the way she rations out the daily calamities. Like she doesn't want us to blame her for them personally. That fellow on the Toronto news, I don't think he gives a damn. But she *cares,* she really *cares.*"

"I think she does a good job," my father said, his old eyes eating her up on the screen.

"Good job?" Ma repeated. "What can be so difficult about it? It's not like she invents the news. She just reads it. Your father's got a crush on her. A cross between Ava Gardner and Liz Taylor. Look at him! He's like a teenager. He could watch her all night."

I looked over at Pa, who hadn't noticed what Ma had said about him. He was watching and listening to the news. Catherine Bracken was wearing a green silk blouse on the screen. Pa watched, I watched and Ma watched. Even *she* couldn't blame us.

Chapter Five

The Mallet Club stood at the head of King Street, where it met Ontario in a "T" intersection. It was in one of the best-preserved older buildings in town, with a severe early-nineteenth-century face and an elegant stone flourish around the central chimney at the top. I'd been inside only once. It was my father's conviction that Jews were unwelcome. When I pointed out to him that I had seen Dr Adelstein going in, he revised his opinion so that now he said that with the exception of Dr Adelstein, no Jews were allowed.

I went in the wide front door and was welcomed by a butler or some sort of doorkeeper. "Mister . . . ?" he said with a rising inflection and a tilt of his head.

"Cooperman. I'm having lunch with Mr Julian Newby," I said. "Is he here yet?"

"Not yet, I'm afraid, Mr Cooperman. Would you care to wait for him in the library or would you like to go into the dining-room? I have your table ready. Mr Newby telephoned to say that he might be delayed by as much as ten minutes."

"I see," I said, trying to give the impression of a man whose sensibilities were easily damaged. "I'll wait in the library."

"This way, sir." I picked the library since that would give me a look at another of the rooms I'd probably never see again. I already knew I was going to spend some time in the dining-room. The butler led the way first to a closet where he put my damp raincoat and hat and then to the predictably dark-panelled library, which stood just to the right of the entrance hall. I'd forgotten to take off my rubbers, so I would be forced to brazen it out if they were noticed. I sat in a big wing chair after selecting at random a fat bound volume of *Punch*.

The wall of books next to me contained hundreds of volumes. The shelves reached from the floor to the high ceiling. The books were all pink bound volumes like the one I was holding open on my lap, dated 1849. I flipped the pages past steel engravings and text. There were full-page cartoons and jokes I would never understand. I looked around me and saw that there were a few quiet figures in other wing chairs like the one I was sitting in. Together we looked like a living cartoon waiting for the right caption.

I was waiting for Julian Newby this Monday noon-hour because he'd telephoned less than two hours earlier, inviting me to discuss a proposition over lunch. It was Friday when I'd run into Stan Mendlesham at the inquest. I was curious about why a man who had never seen fit to call on me before should be doing so after an accidental meeting with a member of his firm. I'm a great believer in coincidence, but this was ridiculous.

I hadn't got very far in *Punch* before Julian Newby's shadow fell across my reading. "Sorry I couldn't get away earlier, Mr Cooperman. Damned sorry. I was in Mr Justice Penner's chambers and he, as usual, wasn't watching his clock."

I got up and we shook hands. Newby had a round face that looked as though he had spent some time in the ring: his nose was slightly flattened and favoured the left side of his face. Besides that, there was a hard mouth and watchful eyes. This rugged effect was spoiled by a mane of white hair, which a blue rinse had suburbanized. He was wearing a dark business suit and carrying a square-cornered briefcase. His grip was temperate; he wasn't trying to prove anything. I followed him into the dining-room, where the waiters smiled at him and he waved at several of the diners under their white table napkins.

The dining-room was crowded but sedate. There would be no lunch-time revelry, no cluster of waiters singing "Happy Birthday." Although I could have guessed this, it was a pleasure to see it in the flesh. I particularly liked the white napery and the gloves on the waiters. Did they suspect that we were suffering from undiagnosed diseases? I accepted an invitation to have an aperitif: I ordered rye and ginger ale, he asked for a dry Martini.

I could feel Newby's eyes on me, sizing me up. I was intimidated into not looking him over until he had finished with me. Meanwhile he was full of forgettable chatter about the club, the weather and the difficulty of finding really first-rate restaurants in town. I was tempted to recommend Diana Sweets, where I usually have a sandwich every day or so, but I kept my mouth shut. If he was feeling awkward, to hell with giving him his out card.

When menus came, Newby recommended the fish. So we both had that. The waiter removed the bones with theatrical aplomb and served the fish along with some under-cooked vegetables which had never done any time in a can. I could see that Newby was having a hard time holding off telling me why he'd called. I made a side-bet with myself that he wouldn't last until dessert. I was wrong, even though I'd let my silences grow to the breaking-point several times. Finally the table was cleared and coffee was served.

"Mr Cooperman," he began, replacing his cup on its saucer without making a sound, "I am told that you are particularly skilled in all branches of surveillance work. Is that so?"

"I used to have a big practice in divorce work. You know as well as I do that the bottom fell out of that a few years ago. At that time, most of —"

"Yes, I understand. Would you be available to do a piece of work for me?"

"Beginning?"

"At once. I thought I'd made myself clear. I'm sorry. Yes, I need someone who would be able to devote a good deal of time to recording the movements of someone."

"Local?"

"Yes. At present. But she may leave town. I would want you to follow her wherever she goes."

"This could run into money." Newby waved his hand grandly the way people do who never have to spend their own.

"I should tell you that I don't keep a lot of fancy equipment on hand. I rent what I need. Saves overhead."

"Are you interested?"

"You know that I don't have a large agency. It's me, myself and I. Some outfits can let you have relays in three shifts. As long as you know that."

"You're the man I'm looking for. You come most highly recommended." He allowed a smile to show a double row of white teeth. I smiled back at him and he held out his hand over the coffee cups. "It's settled then. Stan Mendlesham will be in touch with you about setting up a reporting system and will handle the money end." Newby took a dark notebook from his inside breast pocket and tore out a blue-lined page.

"Right now, I'm more interested in hearing the name of the woman you want followed," I said.

"Woman? Did I say woman?" His eyes opened wide and his Montblanc paused above the sheet of paper.

"Your pronouns gave me a hint. Do you want to let me know any more about her, or do you want that to be part of my task?"

"I like a man with a sense of humour, Mr Cooperman. I wish I had more time to spend with you." As we talked, Newby was writing down details of how I might get hold of Stan Mendlesham at all hours of the day and night. Then he looked up and handed me the paper. "The woman I'm interested in is Catherine Bracken. Have you heard of her?"

"She reads the news at ten on TV? Sure, I know her to see her. Who around town doesn't?"

"Certain interests I represent — you don't mind if I don't go into detail about this? — would like to know where Miss Bracken spends her time when she is not at the television station. Would you be able to discover some of the answers to this by, let's see, next week at this time?"

"I do have contacts at the station. Sure, I think I would be able to sketch in the broad outlines by then." Newby looked pleased and almost grinned across at me. Meanwhile, I was secretly calculating that if my contacts were in good repair, I might know the answers in a couple of hours.

"Naturally, Mr Cooperman," he said looking me in the eye while he carelessly initialled the check, "I would appreciate the utmost discretion on your part. We must protect our clients. You must protect me and I have my own client, who expects nothing less than total confidentiality."

"It's my policy to keep buttoned up, Mr Newby. It's the only way to stay in business."

"Exactly! Good!" he said as he pushed the table away from him and got to his feet. I struggled upright as well as I could with the table pushed into my stomach.

"You're not a member here, I don't suppose, are you Mr Cooperman?" he said, leading the way back to the front hall.

"No, I'm rather lax about keeping my memberships in order. I don't read *Punch* regularly."

"Not published any more. Didn't think I'd seen you around," he said and turned to concentrate on slipping into his toe-hugging rubbers and overcoat. "My son, Gerard, who has just come into the firm, wouldn't consider membership here. Thinks we're too old fashioned I expect. Probably felt the same thing when I was his age."

We shook hands at the front door. Newby seemed to enjoy shaking hands. He said goodbye to me on the sidewalk, assuming that we were walking in opposite directions.

"When I have the information," I said, "I'll leave word with your secretary." Newby frowned and shook his head.

"Best to deal with Mendlesham," he said. "Keep him in the picture." I felt like an idiot. He'd already told me to work through Mendlesham. Ma was right: I'm not to be trusted with serious matters.

Newby turned away from me and began making his way towards St Andrew Street, the direction I was about to go myself. But he'd taken possession of the middle of the sidewalk with such authority that I decided not to challenge him for my share in front of his own club. After all, he'd left me with the remaining three cardinal points of the compass to choose from. I could be big and let Newby have one.

Chapter Six

Robin O'Neil was wearing a shocking-pink turtle-neck and rust-coloured corduroy trousers when he came out into the lobby of CXAN in response to my call from the front desk. There was a time when I had the run of the TV station, when we were rehearsing a play in the downstairs room, but the receptionists who knew me were gone and the redecorated lobby looked strange.

"Benny! So good to see you! What happy wind? Don't you just *hate* this weather?" Robin was one of the two people in town who put on plays. The other, Ned Evans, was his sworn enemy.

"You didn't see our *Who's Afraid of Virginia Woolf?*, Benny. I looked for you to no avail!"

"I was out of town all three nights, Robin. I heard it was very well done."

"A triumph! That's what it was. Nothing less. We had Anna Logue from the *Beacon* to review it and she gave us a *rave*!"

"Robin, I wonder if you can tell me about the shifts you work here at the station. I've got a young cousin interested in the field and I said I'd find out a few things."

"Send him along, dear boy! I'll tell him all I know. Pass on the torch and all that sort of thing."

"She'd be glad to learn the basics from you. I'll tell her to drop around." Robin's face fell at the pronouns.

"Well, *you* can give her the basic gen, Benny. Let her telephone me if she has any questions. One thing, tell her it's no bed of roses. The pay is terrible in the beginning and the hours are killing. I sometimes work around the clock just to keep the station on the air."

"Would things be tamer than that for a news reader?" Robin let his mouth slide into an unpleasant smile.

"Oh, she wants to be on camera, does she? Wants to be the face of the ten o'clock news?"

"She's a regular Catherine Bracken," I said. "How much real reporting would Catherine Bracken get into in a week? Or is it all reading what's been written for her?"

"*I'm* more Catherine Bracken than *she* is. I write most of her stuff."

"So, she just reads what you give her?" Robin let his eyes roll up towards the ceiling.

"Oh, she sometimes gets a bee in her little bonnet. She comes to me with notions she thinks are newsworthy. I tell her to concentrate on pronouncing the Russian names correctly."

"She'd work an eight-hour day?" I asked.

"*Bracken*? Eight hours? Are you *kidding*?" I let my face show that I was ready to be shocked. "She wanders in here in time to do the dinner-time news and she's out of here before we sign off. She's finished by half-past ten. How long does it take to remove her make-up? I ask you?"

"Does she have a journalism degree? Did she ever work for a paper?"

"Look, Benny, I don't want to give your cousin a false idea of the realities around here."

"What do you mean?"

"The way to the top in broadcasting, Benny, doesn't lie through the groves of Academe."

"Are you saying she will need to have influence?"

"I'm saying she's got to have more than looks and brains. She's got to know how to make the most of what she's got."

"Not to put it crudely," I said.

"Hell, Benny, she's *your* cousin! I'm just reading the writing on the wall."

"Who's the main talent scout at CXAN?"

"Try Orv Wishart. Station manager and son-in-law of the owner."

"I thought CXAN was a company?"

"It is and the company is the Ravenswood family, as in the Ravenswood Bridge, Ravenswood Park, Ravenswood Art Gallery and Ravenswood Publishing and Broadcasting Company, the good old RPBC."

The mention of the name Ravenswood — a name that seems to come out of a novel — set my mind going back over the associations it began rattling in my head. Ever since I could read, I'd seen the name printed in bold-face type under the reduced logo of the *Beacon* at the top of the editorial page. When the issues were serious enough, the name Harlan Ravenswood appeared at the bottom of an editorial. Once, on the front page. More recently, the Ravenswood name was kept out of the paper. I used to think it was reverse snobbery: let the parvenus try to get their names into the social notes; those who had arrived kept their doings to themselves. Still, I knew who they were. Old Harlan had been dead now for many years, but I remember seeing his tall white-headed figure crossing

St Andrew Street, waving to friends, like a politician with an election coming up. I'd once stood beside him in a crowd lined up to watch a parade. I can't remember the occasion, except that there were tears in his eyes when he turned away and the crowd began to disperse.

I first saw his widow, Gladys, in this lobby. We'd been rehearsing a play in the basement of the TV building on Oak Hill, and she came in wearing a rose coat that covered her down to the ankles. She was weaving and staggering as she nearly bumped into me at the top of the stairs from the rehearsal hall. In that light, her skin reminded me of an orchid. Her hair was tightly permed under a fur hat.

"What are you doing here, young man?"

"I'm with the group rehearsing downstairs," I said. I hoped that it wouldn't be necessary for me to explain that I had come upstairs with a bursting bladder. I got away as fast as I could, but not before seeing that her eyes were dark and unfocused. She was still there, sitting on the staircase when I came out of the washroom a few minutes later. I told Ned Evans about her, and he had someone drive Gladys home to the big house on Hillcrest Avenue.

"I once saw the old man at a parade," I said to Robin at last.

"They went in for parades, fox hunts and march-pasts when he was alive. They had an in with the Royal Family through their horses and dogs."

"I know a guy who owns one-twenty-fifth of a race horse."

"Nowadays the old woman only cares about the paper and the TV and radio stations. They say she watches Orv like a cat, but she thinks her son-in-law pisses pure lemonade. She wouldn't believe the out-of-town papers when he was arrested for hit-and-run five years ago in Toronto. Not a word in the *Beacon* about it. No, dear boy, Mrs Harlan Ravenswood believes she is living a never-ending romance and the current star is her daughter's husband, Orv Wishart, the son of a bitch!"

"What does the daughter have to say?" I recalled her interest in reclaiming drunks at the Nag's Head.

"Antonia doesn't give a damn. She's been on to Orv from the beginning. I think he tried to sell her bridal train on the way down the nave of St George's. Antonia's got her head screwed on right. I'm not worried about her." Here Robin grabbed me by the arm and turned me so that I was facing the sweeping end of the staircase as it came into the main reception area of the converted old mansion. A heavily built man in shirtsleeves was just coming to the bottom.

"Speak of the devil," Robin said in my ear, in a voice that was heavy with playfulness. "He gets all his exercise on those stairs; never uses the phone."

"Robin," Wishart shouted when he caught sight of us, "what are we feeding CBC radio newsroom at 6:45?" He looked like a confused man trying to come to grips with a sudden accumulation of paper that grew on his desk over the lunch-hour.

"That'll be the Governor Simcoe item that Frank did: you know, a commemoration of the first governor's search for a capital. He went all the way to Detroit."

"What the hell are they going to do with it? It happened two hundred years ago."

"They're very big on history right now, Orv. Maybe it has to do with Christmas?" Orv came up to us and

Robin introduced me. It was probably good for my ego to see that he was only half-focused on me as he gave the small bones in my right hand a massage. In fact, as it soon became apparent, he was looking over my shoulder to where Catherine Bracken stood, pulling off her snowboots. We all turned to see better. Orv immediately set off in her direction. Robin slipped me a wink, before following him. Together they got rid of the woman's camel-hair coat and hung it on a rack. She walked around to the vacant chair of the receptionist and checked her cubby-hole for messages. She let out a loud, rather dramatic sigh as she flipped through the pink slips of paper. Bracken was smaller than I'd imagined from her appearance on the tube. I put her at about five-three or four and just over one hundred pounds. Orv came around to her side of the counter and tried to engage her in conversation. It was plain that she wasn't in the market for any, because in less than ten seconds, she had moved past him and was heading down the long corridor to the back of the building where the television offices were located. Robin and I watched her until Orv's body cut off the view as he followed her. Robin shook his head. "Sometimes, Benny, I think that man knows no fear."

"How do you mean?"

"The old lady could walk in at any time. Or Antonia for that matter." He made a noise with his tongue on the back of his front teeth to express displeasure.

"Has he been giving Bracken a hard time? Is he harassing her?"

"Well, neither of them is talking. But she is reading the news and saying the names wrong night after night. What do you think?"

"That's arguing ass-backwards, Robin. That's only a possible cause of her getting the job. There could be others." Robin's look at me was really aimed at an invisible observer of the scene. It was designed to make me feel unworldly even for Grantham, Ontario.

"Are you suggesting, Benny, that Cath got the job because Larry Hendrick went to the CBC at short notice? Come on!"

"Robin, you sure are giving me a lot of names. Are any of them going to be of any use? That's the question I'm asking myself."

"And what are you answering yourself? You think your cousin has the guts to run and play in this minefield?"

"What cousin? Oh, *that* cousin! Sure, she knows what it's all about."

At that moment, Catherine Bracken came back into the reception area and picked up the *Beacon* from the receptionist's desk. It was four-thirty. If she was working until ten-thirty under the bright lights, I thought she was earning her money. Robin grinned at me as Catherine Bracken quickly ran through the paper, accompanying her noisy page-turning with comments that were not at all flattering to her colleagues at the *Beacon.* I began buttoning up my coat. The last thing I wanted was a well-intentioned introduction from Robin. A word from him and I'd have to come up with the fictional cousin I'd been talking about.

On the way towards the entrance, Robin nodded back over his shoulder at Catherine Bracken. "Not bad in the flesh, is she? Orv sure can pick 'em." I wanted to turn around and confirm what Robin was saying, but I didn't want to make myself conspicuous. I had seen enough of her as she came in and went to work to realize that this was an attractive, well-put-together young woman. I could see that there were aspects to this assignment that I was not going to find hard to swallow at all.

Chapter Seven

Explaining my sudden interest in the queen of the CXAN news room to Anna Abraham was more difficult than I thought it was going to be. I tried to pass it off as just another job, but Anna was quick to see that there was a tiny Orv Wishart concealed in a corner of my heart. I told her over dinner at Lije Swift's place in St David's. I wanted to show Lije that I sometimes ate before two in the morning and in the company of civilized people as well as policemen of my acquaintance. Anna's reaction was to show no curiosity about the client or the job. She was usually ready to join in as my favourite silent partner, but not that night. Was it something about me that had changed or was it something that Catherine Bracken did to other women. I don't know. All I know is that the duck seemed overdone and greasy, the wine sour and the dessert oversweet.

"What's going on up the hill at Secord?" I asked, trying to locate neutral territory. Anna taught a few sections of history at the university.

"Exams, papers to grade. The usual grind," she said. It was an answer, but it lacked the Anna Abraham touch. We sat in silence for a few minutes longer.

"Are you looking forward to the holidays?" She

removed a piece of peach stone and placed it on the side of her plate. By way of answer to my question, she shrugged.

"Come on, Anna! I didn't ask for this job!"

"I don't know what you're talking about."

"You would be talking to me if I'd been asked to track down a painting for your father."

"I've never noticed you salivating when you talk about my father. Daddy has only served to make you interested in the better things of life."

"Some of them. I hope I'm not beyond learning yet. It seems to me that you've played a part in re-educating me, Anna. Don't blame your father for his role."

"Benny, I've always liked you in spite of your rough edges. I even like some of your rough edges. They're what make you you."

"Thanks a lot! I feel like your project of the week."

"Don't purposely misunderstand me. I know that trick; it gets you into a better arguing position."

"Let's order the coffee."

"Let's skip the coffee!"

"If that's what you want. Sure!" I called to Lije, who quickly saw the storm clouds and kept his usually welcome attentions at a distance. The check arrived and I handed over my credit card without a word. I could feel Anna's eyes on me as I tried to figure out the tip. What did I do wrong, I wondered. Why were we fighting when we really love each other?

We drove away from the restaurant in silence. When we reached the turn-off to town, she looked at me and I knew that she wanted me to drive her up the escarpment to her father's house. It was her option. If I guessed wrong, she didn't correct me. Anna's only fault, I thought as I manoeuvred the tight curves up the wooded side of the escarpment, was that she was still tied to her father. That's how I got to know her in the first place. She appeared in my office, like some spoiled brat, accusing me of taking her father for a ride. Just because Jonah Abraham was worth some millions on a good day, she thought I was overcharging him for my services. As a matter of fact, I might have if I'd thought about it. At the time she began hanging on my office door and complaining that I was the latest of a long line of gougers, I hadn't even made up an expense sheet on the man. I thought Anna was playing truant from high school. She looked like she'd just fallen off a motorcycle, wearing old jeans and a black leather jacket. It came as a shock when I learned that she was a lecturer at Secord.

I looked across at her now, bunched up as far away from me as the Olds would allow her to get without opening the door on the passenger side.

The car crawled up to the top of the escarpment. Below us in the dark lay the lake and the lights of Toronto on the far side. Closer, I could see the lights along the length of the canal. Traffic moving over the Skyway, leaping over the dark waters below. The lights stretched along the highway from Niagara to Hamilton.

I drove around the circular drive that led up to the Abrahams' designer house. The lamps on either side of the door were bright, harsh, even as I looked across at Anna.

"Well," I said. She flashed me a look with those salamandrine eyes. I caught it and turned away. I never could take the full blast of her displeasure. I cared for her too much for that. She moved her hand to the door handle. "Hey," I said again and reached over. A moment later we were close and I was taking in her perfume and the smell of her hair and the wool of her coat and her nearness. "I'm sorry," I said.

"You never say that," she whispered. "You usually make me say that." We kissed again and it was a long time before I was aware that there was a figure standing in the open doorway to the house. It was Jonah.

"Your old man's watching," I said. She lifted her head.

"Timing was never his thing. Will I see you tomorrow? Or do you want to carry me away with you and leave only a puff of exhaust in Daddy's face?"

"I'd like nothing better. But I've got to go to work. She gets off at ten-thirty and I've got to be there when she leaves the station."

"Some girls have all the luck."

"And some guys." I kissed her once more while Jonah moved from one foot to the other. Then she hopped out and was swallowed up in that mausoleum of art. As soon as the door closed, I noticed that the engine had stalled.

I parked along Yates Street where I could get a good look both at the door to the TV station and the parking lot behind it. To my left, behind a wall, stood an old brick coach house with a dovecote on top. As a kid, I dreamed of living in this overgrown shed, which wasn't much more than a big double garage. Maybe I liked that it was brick. I don't know.

With the motor and lights turned off, it didn't take long for the car to cool to the outside temperature. This part of Yates Street stood at the crest of the ravine that ran down to the old canal. This side of the ravine was called Oak Park and there were two goldfish ponds down there in the dark as well as a pipe dripping the mineral water that formed the basis for Grantham's long-time fame, years ago, as a spa, a summer watering station for wealthy southern Americans who wished to try the healing sulphurous waters.

My reflections, such as they were, were brought to an abrupt end by the appearance of my quarry on the steps of the TV station. She was alone and walked along the sidewalk wrapped in a man-size camel-hair coat and carrying a leather totebag. I kept my hands off the ignition and waited for the headlights to go on. They did, and shortly twin bright beams stung my unprepared eyes.

I watched and tried to see both the make and colour of the car as well as the plate number. I caught a glimpse of red, noticed a luggage rack on top and missed the rest. I let it get a block ahead of me before I started the engine. Ideally, I would have liked to follow with my lights off, but I didn't want to get pinched by a cop and lose her.

She drove at a steady speed down Yates then took the first convenient route to Church Street. I caught up to her at the stoplight in front of Robertson School, where I'd gone to complete my primary education. One of the oldest buildings in town, it had once been called the Grantham Academy. That was when it was first built in 1829. It was a pre-Victorian classical building with two gables, a tower and alternating round and pointed pediments over the windows. There had been talk of pulling the old building down, or modernizing it, but the city fathers in their wisdom decided to preserve it as it was for the enlightenment of generations to come. She was two blocks ahead of me when I came out of my reverie. I tried to catch up, but she'd turned north up Court Street. It took me a minute of panic and a pint of adrenalin before I found her rounding the corner to Welland

Avenue. I managed to suppress my thoughts about the old junction yard of the electric railway system that used to occupy the south side of Welland Avenue. I was rather proud of myself. I had also recorded her licence number and had the year and make of her car. I may have been easily distracted, but at least I was in an occupation where it didn't amount to a disability. She went north on Geneva, passed Balfour, Maple, Dacotah, Ottawa, Russell Avenue and Junkin. She turned right on St Patrick and then right again into the driveway of a small house. I kept driving and came to a stop half a block beyond my target.

Walking in the shadows across the street, I arrived just as she had given up ringing the bell at number fifty-two. I took cover behind a privet hedge and watched while she slowly returned to her car and backed into the street again. As soon as she was gone, I ran back to the Olds, which was still warm enough to remind me that mine was an outside job fifty percent of the time. Traffic was light so it was no trick to find her again. She made a left back to Welland Avenue, then, through a series of turns, she was going down into the valley of the old canal off Queenston Road. This was a long, lonesome stretch; I allowed a lot of space between us as we followed the path of the old canal up towards Papertown. She parked in front of a low bungalow opposite the yard of a paper-mill on Oakdale Road. It was a stucco house with a veranda running across the front and around the right side. She let herself in with a key and turned the lights on. From where I'd parked after doing a U-turn I could see her moving around in the front room. There wasn't much chance of being spotted as long as she kept the lights on.

I didn't get to stay as long as I wanted to, because a car, travelling slowly with the lights off, bumped into the back of my parked Olds. I shot out of the seat and into the road.

"What the hell are you doing? Don't say it's driving!" I shouted.

"What are you up to? Why are you parked here? What are you fucking doing here?" It was a big black man, with heavy shoulders that might have meant that he pumped iron regularly. His face was angry and I was sorry to be messing with him so far from a police call box.

"I was deciding whether to take a chance and empty my ashtray when nobody was looking. Now you come along and spoil it."

"Don't joke with me, asshole. You'll end up picking my fist out of your face!" I wanted to call "time" and get the hell out of there. The last thing I needed was a run-in with this hulk.

He came towards me and I knew there was going to be a fight. I was totally untrained and unprepared. But what was there to do? I blew out my chest and brought up my hands, keeping them flat and straight, like I held a black belt in karate or something. I came on faster than I thought I was moving and he took a step back. I shortened the distance again and brought up my right with what sounded like a kid's idea of a Ninja's cry of kill-kill-kill! He backed away, moving around the back of his Accord.

Just then, a light appeared on the veranda and Catherine Bracken came out the storm door and stood under the lamp. "Is that you, McStu?" She came to the edge of the porch steps so that the light was now behind her. McStu, if it was McStu, was looking at her.

"Get back inside, Cath! I can handle this!"

"McStu, you get in here! I don't want your blood on my street."

I watched while McStu lowered his guard and walked towards her without looking back at my relieved face. He stopped for half a second at the bottom of the steps, then they both went in. I made a note of the address and the Accord's licence number and went back to my car. Through the car window, I watched the lights, first on the porch and then in the front room, disappear. I turned on my motor. Home seemed to be the only shot left on the table. So I whispered the word to the Olds and it took me there.

Chapter Eight

A little checking around in the morning brought me the news that Willard McKenzie Stewart owned the Accord with the noted registration number and also was the owner of the house on St Patrick Street. Very interesting news to ponder while enjoying a cup of coffee at Diana Sweets at ten-thirty on Tuesday morning.

Cath Bracken drives from work to visit McStu at his house. Meanwhile, McStu is out in his car driving to see Catherine Bracken at her house in Papertown. What meaning could I read into these facts? They know one another well. That went without much thinking. They could practically read one another's minds, or they tried to. They didn't make detailed arrangements, kept things casual. His place, her place, it was all the same to them.

On his way out of the Di, Bill Palmer of the *Beacon* stopped at my table. He was a middle-sized, shaggy man, who looked as though he kept all of his wardrobe in a tangle for the cat to make a nest in on the floor of his single room. He was wearing an overnight beard. I indicated the empty space in the booth and he slid into it. I didn't say anything and won points for it. I waved to the waitress who brought a fresh cup of coffee and set it down quietly in front of Bill. He placed a paper napkin under the cup, not to sop up spillage but to deaden the noise of moving crockery. The waitress gave me a refill, part of the Di's bottomless coffee policy. Up the street, at the Venus Art Club, they had a topless policy. What was the language coming to?

"That feels better," Bill said, replacing his cup and lighting a Player's. "It always takes three cups. Funny, eh?" I nodded, just to keep the racket down. He noticed and added, "I'm okay now. I've climbed over the hump. I'm restored to the human race. How are you, human?"

"Middlin'," I said, for no good reason.

"Barney and I got in a poker game last night and we ended up driving to Buffalo for cigarettes for some stupid reason. And me with a column to finish." We let a few dozen angels fly by.

"What do you know about the people who do the news over at the TV station?" I asked. He tilted his head, thankful I wasn't probing his misspent evening any further.

"There are about six of them. Most double as readers on camera, but they swat their own stuff together. Orv Wishart is the senior man. Remember, he used to do the weather? Now he just keeps the house in order. I don't know how they do anything; they don't have room to move in their shop. If they were in a union, the union would grieve on grounds of subnormal working conditions. Frank Hawkins is a bit of a pain: always whining. The sports guy, Larry Singh, knows his stuff. I like Cath. She's got a good head on her shoulders. Nice head, nice shoulders."

"I agree. What's her story?"

"You're too late, Benny. McKenzie Stewart got there first."

"Who the hell is he?"

"I thought you read detective stories?"

"I do. What's that got to do with it?"

"Stewart's the creator of Dudley Dickens. You know, the sleuth who is supposed to live in Hamilton. Dud's a black, ex-steel company security guard. Stewart's written half a dozen books: *Dudley Earnest* is the best known. Haven't you read him? He's like a Canadian Walter Mosley. Or aren't you an Easy Rawlins fan either?"

"Sure, I like his stuff, but Stewart's new to me. I'm always discovering new people and old ones I should have read years ago. When I get through the last part of *War and Peace,* I'm going to blitz all the mysteries I've been neglecting."

"Start with *Blood on the Floor*. That's a good one."

"I will, I will. What else does he do?" Doing my research in the Di has always been the best part of my job. And usually my informants bought their own coffee.

"He teaches up at Secord. Finds time to write magazine articles in *Harper's* and *The Atlantic*. He used to review crime novels in *The Toronto Star,* but he gave it up."

"Making too many enemies, I bet."

"Could be. I don't think he's rich by any means, but he's not on the dole either. Maybe he's got the Canada Council and all the other arts councils funding his activities. Who knows?"

"Since when have mysteries counted as fundable art, Bill? Next you'll be telling me they give grants to pet barbers."

"Listen, Benny, I know a reformed bank robber who hasn't hit a steel box since he discovered the Canada Council and the word processor."

"Bill, I've lived too long. I'm out of my time. What's happening to the world?"

"Read my column in tomorrow's paper. Tell you all about it. If I live to finish it, Benny. Thanks for the company. Here, let me get your coffee," he said scooping up my check. "See you later."

There was a cold wind blowing up St Andrew Street when I came out of the Di. I let it decide my next move. By turning my back to it, I let myself be blown along towards the corner at Queen Street. Once in the lee of the bank, I was able to make decisions again for myself. I went into the bookstore across the street from the *Beacon.*

"Benny! It's a long time since I've seen you!" It was Susan Torres, who ran the place. It was her reminders of my long absences that kept me away, I think. She always made me feel guilty I wasn't reading four or five books a week.

"I got a message that you had the book I ordered," I said, using this gambit as a club to beat her back. She reached under the counter and opened a bag with my name on it, after blowing the dust off rather theatrically. It was a feminist book I'd heard Anna talking about; so I'd ordered it. Susan looked at me suspiciously, as though my sudden interest contaminated the whole movement. She rang up the sale and I handed her my plastic.

"Do you have any of McKenzie Stewart's crime novels?" I asked as an afterthought.

"Are you kidding? McStu is never out of stock in this store. He's a dear, even if he does rearrange the shelves near his books when he comes in. We're going to have a big signing for him when his next one comes out."

"When's that?"

"Here's your personal invitation," she said, handing me an orange piece of paper with a date that was less than two weeks away. "We'd hoped to have the book sooner, but I guess the printers were held up."

"What have you got of his that I would like?"

"Let's see, let's see, let's see." She was sucking or chewing on the temple of her half-moon glasses, which hung around her neck on a black cord. After a moment, she pulled two paperbacks from the shelf. "He's really very naughty, you know. I straightened these shelves on Saturday. Now look at them! All of his covers are showing and only the spines of his competitors' books. Poor Kit Small and Heather Sigworth. And they have such nice covers too!" As a sample she showed me a cover with a picture of a woman in a nightgown dangling by the neck from a curtain rope. "Benny, I think you might like these." I looked at the titles: *Dead Letter,* which had a bloody hand peeking out of an envelope, and *Dudley Earnest,* which showed a pair of scissors sticking out of a mass of blonde hair tied up in a ribbon. I picked up *Blood on the Floor* as well. "I think you'll love these, Benny. If you do, I've got more."

"You sound like you know him quite well. What's he like?"

"Oh, he's a real charmer, Benny. Not that he tries to be. He's as little aware of his effect on one as a good dinner. When he tries to turn on the charm, it's really quite funny. He's shy too: he'd never dream of asking to have his books put in the window, but it gives him great pleasure to see them there. I think you'd like him.

You've probably seen him around town."

"He doesn't sit at the counter in Diana Sweets, does he? Scribbling?"

"No. That's Malcolm Binny. He's another story."

"I call him the Mad Scribbler."

"Bit of an understatement, if you ask me," she muttered, smiling, with her glasses dangling from the corner of her mouth. "No, McStu looks like a school teacher: tweeds and corduroys, you know. He never wears a winter coat, but has a long woollen scarf that he can't be separated from."

"Is he the guy I've seen with Catherine Bracken?" I tried this on just to see if it would fit.

"She's really quite bright, you know. Not just another pretty face. I think they're well suited. I hear that McStu's a wonderful cook. That wife of his was never at home long enough to cook a meal. But that's talking out of school."

Armed with my introduction to the work of McKenzie Stewart, I wandered towards my office by way of the farmers' market. What it was about a few dusty baskets of beets and apples, a few links of smoked sausages and blocks of Cheddar cheese, I'll never know, but they gave me a feeling that the ozone layer isn't as cracked as it's reputed to be, that the earth still has a corner or two where the sod can't be traced back to the Love Canal. Maybe I'm living in a fool's paradise, but that's the feeling the market gives me.

On my way up James Street, I picked up a coffee-to-go at the Crystal, and carried it upstairs to the familiar sound of the running toilet mingled with that of my telephone. Naturally, the phone stopped ringing as I was in the act of lifting the receiver. Save me from triflers.

I opened *Dead Letter* and the rest of the morning vanished into the streets of Stewart's crime-ridden city, where the streets weren't so much mean as they were ill-tempered. There wasn't a body behind every garbage can, but he did enjoy having Dud Dickens hit over the head regularly. I wondered whether the beautiful police reporter was Cath Bracken in a clever disguise. The fact that she kept her clothes on throughout the novel while dozens of others were losing theirs supported my theory. Dud Dickens was okay: no Sam Spade, but no slouch either. He made a few deductions that could have brought a smile to the face of Sherlock Holmes. The ending caught me completely off guard. I turned the pages back to see if the crucial clue was where it was supposed to be. It was, but deftly placed where it would not scream out at the reader. It didn't scream out at me at least. I put the book down with a feeling that I knew something of the life in the underworld of Hamilton, Ontario. And I felt that I knew the writer and his girl-friend better too. It helps to get inside the head of a client or even a near client. I now knew that the girl-friend loved fast cars and had no family and that the writer counted his money and had trouble with his drinking. Now, you couldn't really call that taking the morning off, could you? I left the question dangling, like Susan Torres's glasses, while I opened the second of his books.

Chapter Nine

Feeling guilty about taking off time to read a novel, I went downstairs and bought a paper. The *Beacon* always brings me down to earth. The first thing I saw was that the inquest into the death of Lizzy Oldridge had concluded. Those things are usually over in a day and forgotten in two, but Lizzy's was different. There had been two days of testimony and the verdict was announced after the weekend. Barney Reynolds had written it up, although I don't remember seeing him in the courtroom while I was there. Barney was the true pro. He could make me believe he was there listening to every word, even when he wasn't. He had an eye for salient details. He knew how to arrest the attention of a TV-distracted reader. Some of his conclusions packed a wallop. It came as a surprise to me that Lizzy had more than eighty thousand dollars in term deposits in her safety deposit box at the Upper Canadian Bank. That made a fair contrast with the less than ten dollars in her savings account. Another stunner was the fact that Liz had left her estate to the Guild of the Venerable Bede, the outfit that had been founded by Thurleigh Ramsden, who also just happened to be the sole executor of her will. The fact that didn't surprise me was that it was unlikely that any criminal charges would be laid following the jury's verdict that the woman died of emaciation, dehydration and malnutrition primarily induced by her despondency over losing control over her financial affairs. There was no mention in the actual verdict of Thurleigh Ramsden. I looked through the two columns and couldn't find words that directly linked Ramsden to the cause of death. Was I wrong to think he should be? Maybe coroner's courts aren't empowered to be that subtle. Anyway, that wasn't any of my business, was it? I had a job, and if I was on it, I wouldn't be sitting around on my butt speculating about something that concerned only Kogan, of all people. Kogan, who made my life a misery of running water and unemptied waste baskets.

The other item in the paper concerned Clarence Temperley:

> Niagara Regional Police are increasing their efforts to contact the manager of the Upper Canadian Bank. Clarence Temperley, 49, of Lisgar Street, failed to appear as a witness in the just-concluded inquest into the death of Elizabeth Oldridge, 78, of Brogan Street. "While he hasn't been missing long enough to be considered a 'missing person,' " Detective-Sergeant Chris Savas told the *Beacon*, "his absence at this time is causing some anxiety and we are looking into it." Temperley has been manager of the bank since 1969.

The article went on to describe his wife and family of three boys who were joined by neighbours in searching the course of the Eleven Mile Creek above its junction with the Old Canal.

When it was getting on towards one-thirty, I went around the back of the office to see if the Olds was up to a run back to Papertown. It was and when we got there, McStu's car was still parked outside Cath Bracken's house. In daylight, I could see that the place had the scale of a cottage from the last century. It reminded me of a picture I'd seen in the library of the house in St Helena, where Napoleon spent his last days. It was compact, without the horizontal spread of suburban bungalows of the 1950s. There were no large picture windows to help me in my research. There were no lights or any signs of movement through the two windows facing the veranda.

I pushed in the car lighter while I waited and sucked on a Halls cough drop. I did this a few times as though I really thought I was going to like cough drops better than cigarettes.

After about forty-five minutes, I turned the key in the ignition and pulled away from the curb. What had I accomplished? I wondered as I pointed the Olds back to town. What does surveillance ever accomplish? It looks good in a report, but there is rarely much that tells you about the characters you are following. In the old days when I used to do a lot of divorce work, you weren't interested in character as such, just the movements: from home of subject to the Black Duck Motel and back again. It was crude but it told enough for a judge to make up his mind.

When I parked behind the office and came up the alley breathing heavily, Kogan was waiting for me at the top of the stairs. I walked past him and unlocked the office door. He followed me in.

"So, Mr Cooperman, what have you found out?"

"I don't usually report whenever a client drops in, Kogan. Besides, didn't you tell me that you weren't interested in my services?"

"I only meant I can't afford to pay you. I didn't say I didn't need your help," he protested. Kogan grinned. Even he could see the funny side, and he was straight enough to let me see that he recognized hypocrisy as well as the next man.

"How far does that argument get you at the liquor store?"

"There's a branch where I get credit."

"Credit! I don't believe you. Booze is strictly cash and carry."

"Except when I deal with Norton. Norton's an old school friend. It's a question of the old school tie. That's what private schools are all about. It's a brotherhood, really." I'd heard that Kogan had attended Cranmer College on the other side of the canal, but from the look of him now, you wouldn't believe it. Even in a blazer and flannels, he didn't have the look of a Cranmer old boy.

"Kogan, you have a way with everybody. How come you haven't figured me out yet?"

"I don't know what you mean, Mr Cooperman. What you're doing on the Lizzy Oldridge case —"

"You got a name for it already. Good. Keep going."

"— is for her, not for me. You would have liked her. She had a swell voice."

"Great! Too bad she didn't think enough of it to play up to some of the people who tried to help her."

"She had an independent streak."

"You're telling me!" I walked around and sat behind my desk. "Kogan," I said, "I don't know any more about your friend than you can see in the paper. Thurleigh Ramsden doesn't come off as a hero, but he won't land in jail. He's covered his tracks too well. The question that's bothering me, Kogan, is why did Ramsden do this to Lizzy Oldridge? Why did she trust him with her money and her life and why did he take her on?"

"They both belong to the Bede Bunch."

"The what?"

"The Guild of the Venerable Bede. It's a place for people to go who want to listen to patriotic speeches and then have an old-fashioned 'Knees up, Mother Brown.' "

"Sorry, Kogan. I don't follow."

"It's mostly old dears like Lizzy, you know; getting on and remembering the old country through rose-coloured glasses. They sing the old songs, salute the flag and toast the Queen on her birthday."

"What's wrong with that?"

"Well, if you ask me, the old country never did all that much for them and half of them have forgotten what it was like over there. They give themselves airs, talk about the UK as though a bottle of milk never went sour on a window-sill. Some of them are harmless, but there are a few like Ramsden, who think this country's going soft because it did away with the noose and lash. They need their heads examined."

"Apart from that, Kogan, it doesn't sound like they eat their young. This is still a free country. You can join the Flat Earth Society if you want to." Kogan gave me a look. He wasn't convinced. "Apart from wringing its hands at the creeping disintegration of society, Kogan, what else does the Guild of the Venerable Bede do?"

"Sponsor scholarships for poor bluebloods."

"Is it a wealthy organization?"

"Lizzy could have told you. You better ask Mr Ramsden. He's the executive officer."

"Have you any idea why Ramsden singled Lizzy out, Kogan? There were other old-timers. Was Lizzy richer than the others?"

"None of 'em is rich. Lizzy had her own place, that's all. She had a few dollars put by, like you heard at the inquest. And the house is worth something, being downtown and all."

"I still don't —"

"The thing about Lizzy is that she did everything her own way. She never listened to advice; she never would have taken it. She had her own ways for everything."

"I had a look at that house of hers."

"Yeah, you wouldn't see that in *House Beautiful*."

"Who holds the mortgage on it? Do you know?"

"Oh, there's no mortgage. Lizzy didn't hold with mortgages. She paid that off years ago."

"So Ramsden, as executor, passes on her house to the Bede Bunch."

"Yeah, that's about the size of it."

"But he's part of the executive, isn't he? Wouldn't he have some say in what happens to the property?"

"Place like that needs a lot of upkeep. Could become the international headquarters of the Bede Bunch."

Kogan went on talking, but I tuned him out. Slowly I was becoming aware that there was an unusual situation developing on Brogan Street. For the first time within living memory a big, established business, Foley Bros., closes down. At the other end of the street, a pub that has been doing a fair business over the years prepares to close down in the New Year. In between, the Oldridge property has passed into the hands of a hang-'em, flog-

'em outfit that has resisted every innovation since the invention of the wheel. I didn't know borscht about real-estate values in Grantham, but I had a good nose and it told me to find out more about this nearly forgotten strip of land behind St Andrew Street. Something was going on. I knew that much.

". . . so I spent a couple of hours fixing it."

"What? Fixing what, Kogan?"

"The back fence. At Lizzy's place. She wouldn't have me working underfoot in the house, so I propped up the fence for her. Least I could do."

"Kogan, I sure would appreciate your spending some time with the plumbing in the little room down the hall. If you listen closely, you can hear it singing to us. Please, Kogan! It's driving away my business. I'm on my knees, Kogan!" Kogan retreated, embarrassed at my unmanly show of emotion. Whether he got anywhere near the toilet, I don't know. But I hoped.

Chapter Ten

I made a few phonecalls. In each case, at the last minute I chickened out of saying what was on my mind. There was something wrong. Mind you, I'm not badmouthing my contacts: they've done the firm some service. I won't say a word against them. But, in each case I decided that I would be starting a rumour trail that would lead back to me. So, I dropped around to Scarp Enterprises just before lunch and caught Martha Tracy coming out the big glass door.

"Benny! As I live and breathe! I thought you were away for the winter already. I was expecting a card from Miami Beach. Something to brighten up these gloomy days."

"Are you busy for lunch?"

"Now I am. Where shall we go? I've only got about forty-five minutes. Benny," she said smiling, "you're looking well, you little devil! Have you sold your soul for a good complexion? Is that your secret?"

We walked up to the end of James Street and then west on St Andrew. We found a place for two in the centre area of the Di, where a stained-maple partition separated us from a couple of teenagers and their Cokes. I ordered my usual, accepting Martha's banter of abuse after she gave her own order to the waitress. While we waited for our sandwiches, I told her about the last six months of my life and heard about her difficulties with a tree that is dying at the corner of her lawn on Monck Street.

"I had Dr Bett, next door, put cement into the hole, but it didn't do any good."

"You got a specialist?"

"Dr Bett is a doctor of music at Cranmer College," she explained. "He's only an amateur gardener, but I'm impressed by anyone who has a load of manure delivered every autumn. It has a serious look about it. And I've seen him weeding his lawn for hours at a time. He doesn't know the meaning of 'quittin' time.' The only lawn to beat Dr Bett's is Mr Hill's, the vicar at the English church on Lisgar Street."

"Martha . . ."

"Here it comes!" She leaned forward and looked pleased.

"What?"

"Benny, I knew you didn't just happen to run into me. You've got another problem. I know it. Don't lie to me."

"It's not a problem. And I was thinking about you anyway."

"Oh, sure. You and a million others. Okay, Cooperman, let's have it."

"Martha," I began, swallowing the last of the first half of my chopped-egg sandwich, "I have to find out whether somebody is putting together a series of properties behind St Andrew Street."

"Hmmmm. You came to the right place, Cooperman. I'm up on all the information. I should have held you up for a fancy lunch in that seafood restaurant near the market. But I've only got another twenty minutes and I hate to rush a lobster."

"I'm all ears, Martha."

"When aren't you? I wonder if people can see the wheels going around inside me as easily as I see them going around inside others?"

"You're fey, Martha. It's the little people's way of thanking you for not disturbing their crock of gold."

Martha took a long sip of her coffee and then settled back against the much-initialled panel behind her. "When Foley Bros. went out of business, Benny, a lot of people started thinking about the properties on Brogan Street. You had Foley's on one side and the backs of other places across the street. And there's the Nag's Head at the corner and an old cottage belonging to that —"

"Lizzy Oldridge."

"That's right! Well, when we noticed the pattern here at Scarp Enterprises, we soon discovered that Foley's had sold to Steve Morella and the Nag's Head was in the process of being acquired by... guess who? Steve Morella. Morella was in there before anyone knew the properties were for sale. I heard that about a year ago he found out that Foley's was only ordering stock up to August. That's what tipped him off."

"Who is this Morella? I thought I knew everybody in town."

"Remember the 'Stop Me and Buy' truck that used to sell French fries at the corner of Queen and St Andrew?"

"Sure. But that's going back a long way."

"While you've been walking with your head in the clouds, Benny. Steve Morella traded in his truck for a restaurant across from the Lincoln Theatre."

"I think I remember that. Sure." It was the same sunny face over the frying vats. I could see it clearly. "So, what are you telling me, Martha?"

"Benny, Steve Morella has expanded and expanded since those days. You've heard of Frenchie's Fries, I presume? Well, Frenchie is Steve. He must bank at least a quarter of a million every week — what with the US and trans-Canada sales."

"And it all started with nickels and dimes and a 'Stop Me and Buy' truck?"

"Makes you think, doesn't it?" We both thought about it for about ten seconds. Then Martha added: "Benny, not only has Steve assembled a food chain that ranks with McDonald's and Wendy's, but he's into real estate and even film production. He's got a finger in a lot of pies and they all come up 'finger-lickin' good.' "

"My memory of Morella is of a big, wide face under a blond military haircut. Is that Steve Morella?"

"That's him. He comes from the north of Italy. Not all Italians are Mediterranean types, Benny, just as all Italian cooking isn't done with tomato sauce."

"Martha, if that's an invitation to dinner, I accept." She gave me a dirty look. To change the subject back again, I asked: "Where does he do his business?"

"In the Venezia Block. He owns it. You know, the building that replaced the old post office on Queen?"

" 'Venezia.' He comes from Venice, right?"

"Right neighbourhood, wrong street. Ever hear of Friuli? He knows a lot about fine Italian wines."

"And he's assembling a group of properties around Brogan Street. Why?"

"He calls it the 'Backstreet Revival.' That's his way of saying that he's going to revitalize the space between

Queen and James. He's going to build new stores along the north side and try to force the St Andrew Street property owners to fix up the backs of their places, add rear entrances to their stores and so on. The centre of the project is an office tower that will go up as high as the city will let him build. It'll be the highest building on the peninsula, higher than Brock's Monument. We're talking big bucks, Benny."

"Is Morella in this all by himself?"

"Steve doesn't work any other way. His is a private company. That way there's no annual general meeting, no chairman of the board, no public access. That's the way he wants it."

"What's he like?"

"Steve? He likes to pretend that all this hasn't happened to him. That he's still unspoiled by his money. It's true in a way, but, come on, get real, he's loaded. He can buy and sell half the town. He's always been a loner, but since Sue Ellen left him, he's become a hermit crab."

"Sue Ellen?"

"It was a messy divorce, Benny. Few years ago. That's when Claudia, their daughter, moved out. Put herself through law school. Bright kid, but she has a thing about fathers. Who's to blame her, after what Steve tried to do to Sue Ellen and then what Sue Ellen did to Steve."

"Are you writing a soap opera, Martha, or are you playing games with me?"

"Word of honour, Benny. I wouldn't kid you. Sue Ellen took a very fat half of Steve's assets when she left town. He's still as bitter as a February frost about it. Claudia's coming home helped, but not much. He goes away in the winters when he can. He likes buying vineyards in

France and Italy. That's his way of easing the pain. Ha! But I think he's still around. Myrna Yates said she had lunch with him a couple of days ago. What's this all about, Benny?"

"Oh, it's just some work I've been doing to bribe the caretaker at my office to fix the toilet. His old girl-friend owned the property that lies between Foley's and The Nag's Head."

"Whoever inherits that property will be able to make a very good deal with Steve Morella. He'll practically give whoever it is a blank cheque. The Oldridge place is the lynchpin in the whole 'Backstreet Revival.' And you say Liz Oldridge was your caretaker's girl-friend?"

"You know Kogan? Liz and Kogan were like cake and custard."

"More like old tea leaves and carrot peelings from what I hear."

"Scandal's red tongue has been wagging, Martha. Kogan did his best to save her, but he couldn't get around Ramsden's stranglehold on her safety deposit box. And there's not going to be a criminal prosecution."

"Aw, Benny, you know the law as well as I do. Coroners can't go around pointing the guilty finger any more than I can tell you where Scarp Enterprises is going to start buying its next batch of peach orchards for a commercial development. It ain't done, you little rascal, and you know it. One thing I'll tell you for no extra charge: watch out for Thurleigh Ramsden. He's a street fighter and a dirty one!"

"You're a gold-mine, Martha. Why don't you come into partnership with me?"

"On the principle that two can starve as easily as one? No thanks. Myrna Yates doesn't pay me enough, God knows, but it comes regular. I'll take regular over enough any day."

"Well, if you ever think of moonlighting . . ."

"Sure, sure."

"Martha, how would I go about meeting Steve Morella?"

"He still spends an hour a week in his flagship store."

"Across from the Lincoln?"

"Uh-huh. Mondays between two and three. He thinks it keeps him in touch with his roots. Go figure."

"I'll remind him of the time my brother, Sam, and I tried to get him to divide ten cents' worth of French fries into two paper cones."

"You had a nickel each, right?"

"Yeah. We presented our proposition to him, he thought a moment, then said he wouldn't be able to do it. A second later, he brightened and said that he would be able to give us a toothpick each, which was just as good. He had a fine head for business even back in those days."

"You remind him of that story and he'll throw you out! He doesn't like jokes, Benny. He's a sunny sort of fellow, but not given to jokes. Jokes confuse him, make him uneasy, pull the rug out. He doesn't like that."

"Okay, I'll keep my mouth shut. More coffee?"

"I have to be getting back. But you stay, Benny. You don't have to sit through a board meeting for the next three hours. Myrna won't let me smoke. Life is one living hell!"

Chapter Eleven

The Kingsway Hall was a second-floor walk-up auditorium that I thought had disappeared years ago because of fire regulations. I came up one of a double set of stairs that led the way from the entrance on Ontario Street. The steps groaned as I climbed them and the hundreds of empty chairs watched as I crossed the floor. There were exit doors at the back, one marked with a cracked red glass, and two fire extinguishers on opposite sides of the wide room. A small stage formed the focus of attention at the front with a huge Union Jack pinned to the backcloth and an upright piano to the left. It was deeply out of tune. Each note found an echo an octave above and below it as I struck a key. The keyboard cover had been fitted with a hasp and padlock which had been broken off, leaving the dark mahogany around the lock scarred. I could see them trying to keep people away from illicit playing on the instrument. Perhaps they should invest in some kind of meter to regulate and record all users. Maybe there might be extra time for excellence or time off for discords.

On the piano I found a song sheet that contained "Rule, Britannia," "The White Cliffs of Dover," "Over There," "There's a Long, Long Trail Awinding," "Let the

Rest of the World Go By," "The Maple Leaf Forever" and a few more ditties from the past. The meeting was scheduled to begin at seven o'clock. It was just half an hour short of that now. I always liked to be able to spy out the land ahead of time when I could, just to get the feel of the place. I still had time to get a fast bite to eat. As I lifted my head above the piano, I saw a figure standing in one of the two archways at the top of the stairs to my left. It had been moving when I saw it, but, on catching sight of me, it stopped and then ran back down the stairs. What I could see of the face told me two things: he hadn't expected to run into me and he didn't want to be seen lurking about the meeting rooms of the Guild of the Venerable Bede.

On my way down the same stairs, I wondered why Orv Wishart — for it couldn't have been anyone else — wanted to spy out the site of the meeting. Was he doing his own private investigation when he could have hired me? He could have hired Howard Dover too. We all have to make a living.

Still chewing on this, I found a place on St Andrew Street with a huge anchor in front of it. It had belonged to one of the schooners that used to be pulled through the canal that still ran behind the stores on this side of the street. The man behind the counter made a very tidy chopped-egg sandwich for me to go with the vanilla milkshake. Outside, I could see the entrance to the Kingsway Hall. When the lights came on, it looked like a theatre from the 1940s, with tiny bulbs outlining the triangular pediment over the entrance. I decided to let things get moving without me. I didn't want to create a distraction.

I sipped slowly on my straw until it protested noisily.

Again I was craving a Player's, but I accepted a cough candy instead. I'd been off the weed now for several years, but I had not been able to substitute a cough candy habit for the old habit. It wouldn't take. I paid my bill and crossed the street again. Three elderly women with blue rinses were talking in front of the entrance. I held back until they'd preceded me into the hall.

A quarter full, the hall looked emptier than when I'd been there half an hour earlier. The three old women who had come in ahead of me had lost themselves in a group of a dozen or so others, some wearing hats. Against the back wall, a clutch of elderly men, one in a wine-coloured cardigan with darned elbows, gossiped among themselves like teenagers as they watched the women take chairs near the front. A light had been turned on so that now the flag on the stage was brightly illuminated. A portrait of Her Majesty the Queen had been set on an easel near the piano. A portly woman in a blue lace dress with a blue underslip was rummaging through music she'd taken from an old-fashioned music roll. I took a seat at the back not far away from the old men with their sparse hair and lusty eyes.

Thurleigh Ramsden came into the room wearing a carnation in his buttonhole and waving to the assembly. He blew kisses, especially at the front rows, and shook hands with the pianist, rather as though he meant to give a *lieder* recital. Instead, he asked us all to rise and he led us in singing the British national anthem. His steady baritone carried above the fluty voices of the women. The sound filled the room, bouncing off the patterned tin ceiling, lifting the hearts of the assembly. "God Save the Queen" was followed by "The Maple Leaf Forever," an anthem I'd not heard in over a decade.

The group seemed to know half a dozen verses. I began to feel like I was in church where it's blasphemy to skip verses to get to the end faster. Again, Ramsden's voice carried above all the others. I joined in for the first verse with what I remembered, but listened in to a vaguely recollected account of what happened at Queenston Heights and Lundy's Lane. For a moment, I thought they sang that here our fathers "bravely fought and no one died"' but I think I got that wrong. It must have been "and nobly died."

When the singing was over, we took our seats again and listened to Ramsden's welcoming speech. He spoke in a firm, ingratiating voice that testified to his ease in these surroundings. It didn't take him long to get to the inquest. That was what the audience was waiting for; he didn't disappoint us:

"They have tried to crucify me, my friends. They have tried to nail me to the cross of their evil natures. They have dragged the name of me and my family through the mire of their spite, and dishonoured the memory of our friend, that dear lady, whose cheerful face we all miss in this company here tonight." He looked around the room to see how his words were sinking in. It was easy to see that he felt on home ground; he knew these people and he played on them like Rostropovich on his cello. He went on to suggest that the causes of his problems were all inspired by the local media baroness, Gladys Ravenswood, through the *Beacon* and her TV and radio stations. "With her harping on me every day for weeks this has been a scandalous political witch-hunt! The Ravenswood woman is in the hands of the communists and pinko fellow-travellers who are a continuing menace to the British way of life we brought with us from the old country. Elizabeth Oldridge, our dear departed friend, understood this. She refused to have the *Beacon* inside her house, and, as you know, she couldn't abide the degraded nonsense that passed for news reporting on the radio and television stations controlled by the Ravenswood interests. She told me herself that that woman was the very incarnation of the Evil One. I don't know about that, but I'm not the only one who has referred to these last few days as a witch-hunt.

"We all loved Liz Oldridge. She was our dear friend. Now that she has been taken from us, we must remember what lengths the Reds will go to to brand me a villain, to pillory me and my family. Between you and me, I want you to know that I'm not going to take this lying down. I'm in a fighting mood and I have briefed my legal counsellors to proceed on any breaches in the law that have occurred. We can't let these people get away with flouting the God-given rights of true born Englishmen!" Here the audience broke into spontaneous applause, which brought an ingenuous grin to Ramsden's bland face. His prominent front teeth fairly glittered with pride. It was easy to see why the old ladies liked him. He was Liberace wrapped in a Union Jack.

I looked around and now cursed my position at the rear. The old boys to my right were enjoying the show; the women leaned forward in their plywood chairs. When Ramsden talked about a recent visit to England and described the royal regalia in the Tower of London, there was hardly a breath drawn in the hall. And when he mentioned that he had actually stood by the graves of the faithful canine companions of the Queen, an ant's step might have been heard. "I stopped there, with my head bared for a few moments and thought about Susan and Sugar and Heather, the favourite corgis, and how they knew nothing of Her Majesty's exalted station, her untold wealth and power, how they loved her simply and sincerely in their fashion. I thought how privileged we are, at this distance, to know that she is informed, that she cares and that she applauds our meeting here in this fellowship of the Guild of the Venerable Bede." He went on and on. I tried to follow the drift of it, but his thoughts weren't all that clear. It was as though he was dieselling on on the power of the sound of the words alone. He was a proud turkey-cock, tidy, except for his shoes, which still showed signs of standing close to the graves of the departed royal corgis.

When he finished talking, he introduced Maureen McAlpine to lead the singsong. He shook her hand again, as the woman in the blue lace dress turned to see the faces. She brought down her plump hands on the keyboard with a great thumping chord and we were off to the races with "There's a Long, Long Trail Awinding." I joined in and the words I didn't know, I faked.

Later, when the white styrofoam cups had been collected and the empty platter of cookies had been passed back to the makeshift buffet on the stage, I moved closer to hear Ramsden in conversation with his supporters.

"Well, Ingrid dear, you ring me at my office about that. I'll get the details from you and call the mayor. This has got to be stopped!"

"It goes on all night long! Well, at least until after eleven."

"It's shocking. Leave it with me and I'll see to it."

Another woman took Ramsden by the hand and said something I failed to catch. "Thank you, Vi!" he said. "I'll tell you, it has been harder than anything I've known. You can't fight fair with people like that. But I can't make myself stoop to their level, Vi, I can't."

"You always were a straight shooter, Mr Ramsden. That's what Walter, my dear Walter, used to say."

"A dear, well-loved man, Vi. Well, he's God's soldier now, as the bard says, isn't he?"

"You said a mouthful when you said that," Vi admitted and Ramsden patted her liver-spotted hand and arm. I moved in closer still.

"Mr Ramsden?" I said, trying to get his attention. But a heavy woman with her hair moulded into a cascade of tight unnatural curls got his attention first. I watched Ramsden listen, nod agreement and let his eyes wander over the woman's ample bust.

"Mildred, that's just not so!" he said. "The papers have got things wrong from the beginning. I'm too old to believe they're going to change their tune now. If you ask me, I think someone should retire Mrs Ravenswood to a home. There's no end to the parade of her malice, dear. None!"

"Mr Ramsden?" I tried again.

"Yes?" He looked at me with suspicion. There were no other men asking questions. Even around the coffee urn, the men had stood in a group that the women ignored. "Are you one of us?" he asked. "Are you one of the happy few?"

"I was tempted by the power of the music which I heard from downstairs." I was sure my lie wouldn't be challenged. He didn't look like he had kept an eye on the comings and goings very carefully.

"Yes, we love the old songs. And this is a haven where they may still be heard. You must give us the pleasure of your company at our Christmas meeting next week. Maureen will undo herself with all of the beloved old carols. Did I get your name?" I liked his command of the language.

"Cooperman. Ben Cooperman." Ramsden's face fell as though I'd said Herod or Pontius Pilate. Of course, I may be sensitive.

"Yes, Mr Cooperman. I've heard something about you, haven't I?"

"I can't think what, Mr Ramsden. I haven't been to a meeting of the guild before."

"Someone pointed you out to me at the court-house. Look here, I won't be harassed in this way! I suggest you finish your oatmeal cookie and leave as quickly as possible."

"Chocolate chip," I corrected. Ramsden's eyebrows went up as though I'd flung hot coffee in his face. He took me by the arm and began pulling me down the aisle.

"Hey! Let go!"

"I want you out of here!"

"This is an open meeting! Nobody stopped me coming in!"

"The meeting's over. This is now a private party and you are not invited! Most assuredly *not* invited!" Ramsden had me at the top of the stairs and I was getting mad. I kept crunching tiny clods of dried mud that came from Ramsden's shoes, giving me the feeling that the floor was on his side as I nearly tripped. The open mouths around me looked like fish in a tank. I felt I had to make a stand, or I would be pushed down the stairs. I tried to get a hold on the handrail. I could feel it bend as my weight hit it. I found my footing and leaned back in Ramsden's direction.

"Just a minute!" I protested. Ramsden went over backwards above me as I turned into him. Maybe he didn't expect even a feeble counter-attack. Anyway, he was down on the floor with all the women suddenly groaning, like I'd hit him or something. Immediately, he began pulling himself away from me, sliding in the dust and in his own clods of earth, away from the lethal terror of my famous right hand, which, incidentally, I was holding out to him to help him to his feet.

"You get away from me!" he said. "Get out! You're not wanted here!" By now he was supported by the stack of chairs he had pulled himself up to.

"This is ridiculous!" I said. "Get up yourself if you don't want help."

"I don't need help from you or your kind!" he said.

"And what kind would that be?" I prompted. I didn't know whether he was being racist or whether he thought I was one of the Ravenswood myrmidons. Like a surprised beaver concluding a yawn, Ramsden's jaw, which had been hanging slack, snapped back into place.

"Get a doctor, Maureen! I think my back is gone!"

"Oh dear!" said Maureen and the thought was echoed by the group in various ways.

"I can't feel my feet! Maureen, get a doctor!" Maureen disappeared in a blue smear down the other stairs. "I'll have the law on you, Cooperman! You can't bully freeborn Englishmen and get away with it!"

Ramsden groaned and rolled around in the dirt at the foot of the stacked chairs. "You newcomers think you can run everything! We'll teach you a lesson, won't we friends?" His appeal to the guild members was less than overwhelming. Shock was written on most of the faces, but, at the same time, they pushed themselves forward so as not to miss a moment of the show.

Suddenly Maureen was back at the top of the stairs. She was alone. But her eyes were as big as platters. "There's a man out there in the street without any clothes on!" For a moment no one moved. Then, in a rush, everybody moved past Ramsden and me and down the stairs to see this marvel. Ramsden had to hitch himself out of the way in order not to be trampled. He was on his hands and knees before the room was half empty and fully upright by the time the room was cleared. As I looked him over, he sneered at me, like a heavy in a Chaplin two-reeler. I looked him up and down as though I was witnessing a miracle.

"Hallelujah!" I said, bursting out laughing. "Hallelujah! The Lord be praised!"

"Go to hell, you dirty bastard!" he said, spitting out the venom. I turned to see what was going on downstairs in the street.

Chapter Twelve

Except for Ramsden, I was the last down the steps and out into the street. I don't know what I expected to see. I don't even recall whether any picture formed in my mind as I came out to see what was going on. Now, when I think back, I can't see how I could have failed to guess what I would find.

Coming from the warm hall and the activity at the top of the stairs, I found the night air sharp against my face, a cold reminder of winters past and the winter that was just beginning. As soon as my eyes adjusted to the dark, I could see him: Kogan, in the middle of Ontario Street, naked as a jay-bird and carrying a placard that read: "Ramsden Killed Lizzy Oldridge." The Bede Bunch was gathered on both sides of the street, taking in Kogan from every angle. There were still no signs of the Niagara Regional Police, but I thought I could hear a siren in the distance. Kogan was drunk, of course, but not drunk enough to miss the effect he was having on the blue-rinsed women on the sidewalk. Even the old gentleman in the wine-coloured cardigan looked shocked.

Kogan did a sort of pirouette on a manhole cover and shared his smile with all of us. His face altered, however, when he saw Thurleigh Ramsden come out into the street. "There he is!" he shouted, pointing at Ramsden framed under the lighted pediment of the doorway. "Look at the bastard!" The crowd turned to stare at Ramsden, who was now red above the collar. The noise of the siren was growing louder. Kogan didn't seem to hear it, or, if he did, he didn't care. I thought that I'd better try to get him out of there.

While the crowd was still surrounding Kogan, perhaps even protecting him from being seen from a few points of the compass, I took off my coat and went over to him in the middle of the street. "Here!" I said. "Put this on!" I threw the coat over his shoulders and tried to get at least one button through a buttonhole. I'd never thought of Kogan as a big man, but I never thought he was so little either. My coat was dragging on the pavement as I pulled one of the armless sleeves towards the far sidewalk.

Even Kogan realized that the time for action had arrived. The arrival of the police was announced in flashing red and yellow lights. Kogan grabbed at a plastic shopping bag with a shirt-tail hanging out and dropped his placard. I pushed him into the convenience store across the street from the Kingsway Hall and hurried him down the middle aisle. When I turned around, two policemen had just come to the entrance, their breath making white patches on the glass door as they opened it. Just then, Kogan pulled away from me and ran in the direction of the cops.

"Kogan!" I shouted, but he ignored me. What he was doing was a flash of genius in a hunted man. He opened up all of the vents in the coffee-bean receptacles. A Niagara of coffee beans from half a dozen openings began bombarding the floor. Into this the two cops blundered. As I rounded the end of the aisle, with Kogan right behind me, the two lawmen were skating and falling into one another. We heard, rather than saw, them fall, as we went out the side door into the alley that runs behind St Andrew Street to William. At the head of the alley, I could see the lights of the cruisers throwing tall moving shadows against the walls of the buildings.

Once I had started Kogan running, he stopped being a problem. He had dropped his protest at the earliest opportunity and entered into the problem of escape with the concentration of a chess master. Soon we had come to the back door of the *Beacon,* which was a dark corner. We sheltered between two parked delivery trucks and waited for our panting breath to give us away to the cops who came through the alley behind us. There were two of them. One poked a flashlight beam over the truck that stood between us, but he quickly lost interest. For some reason, I wasn't ready to put a hand over Kogan's mouth. I thought that his moment in the sun was over and that he had given up his one-man protest. If I had been right, I wouldn't have spent the next hour and a half in the corridor at the Niagara Regional Police Headquarters on Church Street.

What I'm saying is that Kogan shouted an obscenity in the direction of the investigating officers and the rest of our evening plans were settled for us. I'm glad I hadn't made an arrangement to meet anyone. I just hoped that Ramsden himself wouldn't put in an appearance at the station. That's all we needed.

At least I was able to get some black coffee into Kogan before he was taken in for questioning. He was still wearing only my overcoat, but by now he had invested an arm in each sleeve. I watched the way the cops walking up and down the hall either looked him over or overlooked him, as Miss Lauder, my old history teacher, used to say.

I had just thanked my stars that there was no one of my acquaintance working this shift when I caught a glimpse of Pete Staziak going into his office down the corridor. Staziak and I go back a long way, to high school in fact. I knew that he was working in the homicide area, so I didn't worry too much about seeing him officially that night. But, of course, he had to stop by to kibitz.

"Why, hello, Benny! Long time no see!" We shook hands. Pete was trying to keep a straight face. "Are you mixing in another murder, Benny? Anything I can do?"

"Pete, go blow it out the flue! I've got all I can handle with Kogan playing Lady Godiva. Don't *you* start."

"Kogan? You don't say. What has the citizen of the year been up to tonight?"

"You tell me, Pete. I haven't seen the sheet on him. The only thing the investigating officers got —"

"Those worthy young men, Martin Ayre and Leslie Green. So young, so impressionable at that age, don't you think?"

"Okay, Pete, have your fun. Has Ramsden come down to make a complaint? If he does, he'll only collect more bad notices. The *Beacon* doesn't like him."

"Ramsden hasn't turned up yet, as far as I've heard. But there are three blue-haired biddies from the Bede Bunch talking their heads off to Bedrosian downstairs."

"Some people have all the luck."

"Didn't Bedrosian pinch you once for B and E, Benny?"

"That was years ago and you know it!"

"I don't know about the people you're hanging

around with, Benny. Isn't protecting Kogan gutter traffic even for you?"

"Go to hell, Pete! Climb off my shoulders and cut the rope! It's time to either book me or let me go home to bed. I'm getting tired of all this. All I need is for Chris to walk in and add a little gingerbread of his own. You guys!"

"Chris is on a heavy murder, Benny. The sort of thing you used to be interested in in the old days."

"Okay! Okay!" I shouted. "I confess! I confess!" Doorways opened up all along the corridor and heads looked out. Pete turned pink and retreated behind his own shut door. Nobody appeared to take a statement, but after about five minutes Pete came back with some drinkable coffee.

Chapter Thirteen

The heavy murder that was occupying the attention of Chris Savas that Tuesday night turned out to be that of Clarence Temperley, whose dead body was found in an open grave in Victoria Lawn Cemetery. According to the *Beacon,* which printed the story for the first time on Wednesday, Detective-Sergeant Savas said that they were treating the death of the bank manager as a homicide. Pete Staziak told me that the post-mortem finding of two bullet holes in Temperley's heart led them to this view.

The paper said that the body had been found on Tuesday morning under some loose earth when the grounds crew were arranging the lowering mechanism for a funeral scheduled for that afternoon. James Balham, who was in charge of the grounds crew, said that it was only by chance that the body was discovered under the freshly excavated clay. The investigation is continuing, the paper stated at the end of the article.

The word on the street about Temperley was mixed. He was a likeable little fellow; he was a tight-fisted son of a bitch. The nicest, most endearing fact I learned was that he and his wife were veteran bird-watchers, who took a few weeks every year to spy on the mating habits of their feathered friends. I recognized the face on the front page of the *Beacon*. I'd seen it sitting behind his desk at the bank and also in the Di at lunch-time, often eating alone. Of course, everyone expressed his shock and disbelief that Temperley, who had no known enemies — apart from those whose loans he had refused to approve — should have been so cruelly murdered in the autumn flowering of his life.

While I found this diverting to read, and enjoyed Pete's gloss on the newspaper account, I couldn't see how I could turn it into rent money. I'd been talking to Pete on the phone about the fate of my dear friend Kogan, the well-known buff-artist. Naturally, Pete took this as another opportunity to kid me about the company I was keeping, but in the end he had to admit that as far as he knew, Kogan had been turned loose some time Tuesday night.

"So they didn't book him?" I asked.

"Doesn't look that way, Benny, but what do you expect a humble cop from Homicide to know of these weighty matters. Hasn't he turned up at your office?"

"His not turning up doesn't mean anything. You can never find Kogan when you want him."

"Let's hope he finds some clothes soon. It's going to be a long, hard winter."

During the middle of the week, I kept myself busy with the case I was working on. I had to collect data for Julian Newby, or he would find another PI to do his legwork. Wednesday and Thursday, I followed Catherine Bracken from her job at CXAN to either her house in Papertown or to McStu's house on St Patrick Street. McStu spent a few hours a day up at Secord University, while Bracken did shopping in the malls along the

Lakeshore Road, which was a little off the beaten path for her. When I checked it out, I found that she used to live in the North End, near the lake.

Although it was good to be in work, Bracken wasn't the most exciting character I ever followed. Her movements were regular and predictable. As far as I could see, she was an outstanding citizen. She checked out her library books and returned them on time. She recycled her newspapers and plastic and metal containers. She bought miles of dental floss every time she went into a drugstore. She bought books, liked peppermints, didn't buy products that were harmful to the ozone layer. If I wasn't already predisposed to admire the woman, I would have been won over by her routine.

McStu and I avoided further confrontations. He didn't spot me parked outside either of the houses where he left his hat. And I have to confess that after reading all of his books, I sort of liked the guy. Mind you, he was no Dashiell Hammett or Raymond Chandler. He didn't come near Ross Macdonald either. But, he was a good read, if you know what I mean. He played fair with the reader and his hero, Dud Dickens, wasn't the smart-ass private eye who is always ordering wines I can't pronounce or picking out the murderer by the pipe mixture he's been using. Except for the beatings he took from the thugs, Dud Dickens was my kind of private eye. I could identify with him and envy him his coach house across from the old Hamilton Jail on Barton Street.

When I wasn't out in my car, I was in the library doing some homework on as many of the names I'd recently heard as I could. I read all I could find about Thurleigh Ramsden. He had, according to one recent article about him, been elected alderman in 1985 and had been returned two years later. After that, in 1990, came an unsuccessful bid at the mayor's chain of linked gold S's. His late wife, Dora, had been born a Rudloe near Welland, Ontario. Ramsden himself had been born in Toronto's east end. So much for all his talk about "free-born Englishmen."

While Ramsden was on my mind, I put in a call to his office from a pay-phone across from the library's snack concession. He didn't keep a secretary, so I left a message on his tape. I said I wanted to see him about business relating to the late Elizabeth Oldridge. I thought I might say something about the unpleasantness of our last meeting, but decided that I'd better wait until I was in the same room with him. I get intimidated by answering machines; they make me turn the simplest of messages into a scrambled mess. I left my office number and waited for him to try ignoring me to death.

A guilty thought kept pulling at my pantleg, like an insistent poodle: what was I doing to earn Newby's money lately? The nightly drive to Papertown after the evening news wasn't getting me anywhere. Maybe I'd better get in touch with Stan Mendlesham and talk things over with him. I invested a quarter in this notion and got an invitation to meet Stan for coffee. When he asked me to suggest somewhere, I could only think of one place. It's not that big a town, after all.

He was sitting in one of the booths in the middle of the Di. "I got no time for lunch, Benny; just coffee and a roll. Then I gotta meet Mr Newby at the office for a lunch meeting."

"Too early for my lunch too," I lied. I was thinking that his firm only bought one lunch per customer as I settled down opposite him, looking up at the clock above the swinging double doors to the kitchen.

"What have you got to report?" He was resting both of his pudgy hands on the table top. There were dark stains under his arms. Newby keeps his juniors on the run, it seemed. There was a lot of glitter about Stan: gold chains, expensive watch and three big rings.

"I don't know exactly what I've got, to be frank with you, Stan. I've been following the subject and I know one or two things about her, but I don't know what's important or not, since I've not been let into that part of the bargain. I know she's living in an on-and-off way with McKenzie Stewart. But that can hardly be news to anybody. I know where she does her shopping and gets her hair fixed. You want to know about that, Stan?"

"You better give me your full report."

"Interim, you mean, or are you telling me I'm finished?"

"Sure: interim. Whatever you've got. I've no instructions to cut you loose."

As succinctly as possible, but without leaving out anything significant, I went over Cath Bracken's daily grind. He made a few jottings on an envelope and nodded to show that he was still plugged in. I ended up telling him that there was some indication that Cath was getting some unwelcome harassment from her boss at CXAN, Orv Wishart. I told him that I was going to look into that and he didn't tell me not to.

Mendlesham puzzled me. He didn't seem interested in anything I'd found out about McStu. In fact he seemed cool on the girl-friend as well. Maybe it was just a job to him: his not to reason why; just carry the news home to Newby and send me off to gather more of the same. Were they looking for a break in the pattern? Did they expect both of them to book flights south or to France or something? I was still in the dark about that when Stan reluctantly took the check up to the cashier at the front of the restaurant.

"Any additional instructions?" I asked, hoping for some clue about the direction all of this was coming from. But there weren't.

"Just keep up the good work and give me a call in a couple of days, okay? Eventually, Mr Newby will want to see all of this in writing, Benny."

"What's it like working for a man like Newby, Stan?"

"What do you mean? Julian's the best there is, Benny. We're the busiest firm in town. Julian's very well organized. He's got a team of specialists working for him. He also helps bring along the next generation. He's got his son on the payroll and Steve Morella's girl. He keeps us on our toes. That means we all work like hell when we're working, but he makes sure we all get time to enjoy the better things of life too. He's got his three antique Morgans he likes to putter with and I've got my golf. This is a high-class outfit, Benny. Not like the shop your cousin Melvyn runs. Not by a long shot."

"I'll remember that. You ever need any titles searched, Stan, you come to me. I still do a little of that on the side, when I'm not too busy."

"Sure, Benny. Sure. You take care now." And he was off down St Andrew Street, rocking from side to side like a plump pigeon.

I had learned nothing from Mendlesham about what I was supposed to be looking for. Did they think that Cath Bracken was secretly flying to New York overnight to do the morning news on NBC? Was she suspected of—? And then it came to me. Of course! It had to be McStu's gadabout wife who was raising the fuss! Who else would give a damn about what Cath Bracken was doing in her spare time?

Further thought about this was stifled by the sweet smell of a Player's coming over my shoulder. It was Bill Palmer just coming into the Di. He looked shaggy and in need of a shower under his ancient raincoat, but his cigarette smelled like heaven itself. I came closer as he caught his breath. I greeted him with the stale formula that passes for a friendly hello, and he dragged me back to a booth not far from where I'd been sitting.

"Oh, Benny! It's been like the old days around here!"

"What do you mean?"

"Takes me back to my time with the *Star.* They've pulled out all the stops on this murder. We haven't had a week like this since Red Hill went over the falls in a barrel."

"What makes this so special?"

"Temperley? Hell, he was a prince of a financial institution, a cardinal of the counting house, a . . ." He ground to a stop. "I'm all written out. You finish it." When the coffee came, he didn't so much drink it as absorb it directly. A wink and it was gone.

"I've read all about it. Great stuff, but you do look done in, Bill. Have you been working double shifts?"

"I've been up to my knees in that Victoria Lawn gumbo, Benny. And it's cold out there! Those yellow plastic ribbons the cops put around the scene of the crime don't keep the cold out. This is my second pair of boots I've dragged through the muck. Ruined my dress shoes the first night. Damn it all!"

"Are there any leads? Do they have a clue who did it?"

"If they have, they're wary of spilling it to the media.

I can't get Chris Savas to answer his phone. And him owing me from last Monday's poker game!"

"Was Temperley dead when he went into the grave or was he killed in the cemetery, Bill? Did the coroner say anything about lividity?"

"Hell, he wouldn't tell me anything. He just grinned at me with those phoney new teeth of his."

"Bill, remember when you were telling me about McKenzie Stewart the other day?" Bill nodded suspiciously. "Well, do you remember telling me whether he was married or not?"

"McStu's an estranged man, Benny. His happy home is no more."

"So, a divorce is in the wind?"

"That's what I hear. But hell, Benny, I don't hear all that often from that quarter. They could both be back together again for all I know. But remember to be careful of that wife of his. She can be a dangerous woman."

"Good! That's just what I wanted to hear." I got up and found my way out into the weather again.

I sympathized with Bill and the working press. At least he was working on a big story. My talents were totally absorbed in another direction. Mendlesham couldn't have been clearer: nothing fancy is wanted from Mrs Cooperman's younger son, just the facts, please. If McStu's wife wanted to share in the riches to be had from writing crime fiction, that was her business. My job was to furnish the information. That was what I was good at, after all. That's what I did in the divorce trade. Why did I now start feeling like a hired gun, a mercenary? I used to be proud of what I did. Suddenly I felt like a heel. Maybe I was getting senile, taking on a bad case of that disease I can never remember the name of.

I stopped at the sight of my office door and turned around. I was not in the mood to be serenaded by the sound of running water — not after spending so much time in the library. I didn't want to run into Kogan again. He'd probably want a progress report too. Just like Mendlesham. When I stopped chewing my lower lip and noticed where my feet were taking me, I found that I was heading in the direction of the TV station. I was just passing the park with the cenotaph in it. There were a few bruised wreaths leaning against the white stone, spilling faded ribbon on the steps, left over from November eleventh. Across the street stood another monument, the one to the builder of the canal that still ran along behind St Andrew Street. Today the canal was a horrible example of what unchecked pollution can produce; back then it was a symbol of trade, commerce and progress. The smile on William Hamilton Merritt's face was fixed in the past.

The receptionist at CXAN didn't quiz me about my business with Orv Wishart. It was enough that I wanted to see him. She said, "Top of the stairs and to your right," so I did that. The door was standing open.

The room had probably been a bedroom in the original mansion, which went back to the 1860s, when it was built as the home of the man who built the canal. Now the radio station occupied the ground floor of the building and the TV studios were set up in an extension added to the back in the 1950s. All the changes had failed to erase the charm and beauty of this high-ceilinged, white, old house. Take the long, curving staircase I'd just climbed, for example. You could still see ghostly figures from the last century in dark suits and long dresses sweeping up to the ballroom. I'm sure the original house had a ballroom. It was that sort of place.

Wishart was rapidly coming around his big desk and I stood in the entrance.

"Mr Cooperman!" he said. I was always flattered when somebody remembered my name after a casual introduction. We'd shaken hands less than a week ago when I'd been pumping Robin O'Neil about Cath Bracken's routine. Of course, I wasn't giving Wishart credit for remembering who saw him briefly in the Kingsway Hall last Tuesday. Once again I had my finger bones rattled, and the rest of me was directed to one of the comfortable-looking chairs that gazed up at the big judge's chair behind his desk. "Since I met you, Mr Cooperman, I've been hearing your name around town. Funny the way that happens, isn't it?"

Orv Wishart was well built, heavy, athletic-looking. His jacket was well cut, but the necktie had been loosened and pulled to one side, like this was the middle of a dog-day heatwave in August and the air-conditioner was on the blink. His face was large and round. The beard looked like an afterthought and not a good one. Like his other hair, it was brown and curly. From his appearance I could see he looked after himself. Besides a simple digital wrist watch and wedding ring, he wasn't showing any jewellery. "What's on your mind, Mr Cooperman? Or is this a social call?"

"I wish it was, Mr Wishart, but I'm afraid it's simply business. Strictly business." Wishart relaxed back into his chair, let it tilt towards the window, through which I could see the bronze form of William Hamilton Merritt holding out his hand to the pigeons in his little park across the street. "As you may know," I went on, trying for routine blandness, "a private investigator is often asked to make credit checks on people. It's just routine; nothing to get excited about. As a matter of fact, I usually do them by phone. A couple of the banks send a little of this work my way and it makes a comfortable filler between assignments."

"I see. How did I rate a personal visit?"

"Frankly, I was curious to see you again. You're a powerful man in this community, Mr Wishart. But, if you like, I could go through the Credit Bureau and the Department of Transport."

"You've been asked to check on somebody who works here, is that right?"

"That's it. Strictly confidential, of course. But I don't have to tell you that. It must happen all the time in your position."

"It can be a headache. These young announcers are here today and gone tomorrow. If I don't help them get a credit rating, they won't ever put down roots." He took out a pack of cigarettes and then put it back into his top drawer without taking one. Another reformed character in the making. "Who is it this time?"

I reached into my inside breast pocket and brought out my electric bill. I pretended to read a name scribbled on the back. "Catherine Bracken," I said without expression. Orv's chair ratcheted him a notch or two in my direction, but his face didn't change.

"She's been here well over a year. She's steady, dependable, honest, trustworthy —"

"— reliable, friendly, resourceful, talented. I get the picture. Unfortunately, I have to give them all that spelled out in detail. It takes longer, I know, but it's the insurance companies. They want all the *i*'s dotted and the *t*'s crossed, if you know what I mean. Do you have her employment file handy? It'd help if you could refer to it. Notice, I'm not asking to see it myself."

"Only take a minute," he said, getting up and leaving the room. For a horrible moment, I thought that when he returned it would be with Cath Bracken herself. I didn't have a plan of action to cover that. I'd have to brazen it out.

The woodwork in the office was white, the walls were a light blue with stripes like you see in shirting material. The effect was blue and restful. There was plenty of light coming in through the window and the big brass light on Orv's desk was turned off. Wishart silently came back into the room.

"Here it is, Mr Cooperman."

"Ben, please. Call me Ben. Let's get the personal statistics first." Wishart returned to his chair which welcomed him back with a resounding poooof! of pleasure. "Is 'Catherine Bracken' a stage name?"

"Not according to this. Born 12 January 1965, in Toronto's Wellington Memorial Hospital." I made a note. He went on giving me details of education and past employment. If I'd wanted baptismal records, vaccination, or high-school marks, he was all for passing the information along.

"Now we come to the hard part," I said. "I don't know why they have to know this, but they want to. What is her marital status?"

"Unmarried."

"Okay. 'Unmarried.' Does she have what they used to call a 'common-law' relationship with anyone?"

"Hey! What is this, Ben? What kind of bank wants that kind of information?"

"Just one of the routine questions they gave me. If you

don't know, I'll leave it blank. Look," I said, smiling, "like I said, if there's a problem, I can go through the usual channels. It all comes out the same."

Orv thought a moment, then spread his hands on the desk. I read this as an invitation to continue. "Does she own her house or is she renting?"

"Renting, as far as I know, Ben." Orv was noticeably tiring of this interrogation. I was going to have to cut it short.

"Next of kin?" I asked.

"None. She's an orphan. No relatives at all."

"I *see,*" I said, making a note. Orv looked worried, as though he had just given her a less than passing grade. I began putting my notes away in my pocket. "Well," I said, "that just about covers it. I don't think she'll have any trouble. I shouldn't think so anyway."

"Do you know if this is for a loan or a mortgage?"

"Sorry. They don't tell me these things. Any more than they tell a bird dog the recipe for roast duck, eh?"

Orv laughed and got up. I extended my wounded hand to him again and he added insult to injury, but with less vehemence. I got up and allowed him to show me the way to the stairs.

"I'm glad you could help me out like this, Mr Wishart," I said, getting a start on the stairs.

" 'Orv,' please, Ben." He hit the steps just behind me. I felt a little awkward being a step or two ahead of him. They were *his* stairs, after all. At the bottom of the staircase, the receptionist was not at her desk. If fact, she was busy trying to hold up the fainting form of an old woman in a black coat with a silver fox collar.

"Mother!" Orv called, before he had quite reached the bottom step. "What a nice surprise to see you here." He moved around the woman and took some of the weight and responsibility from the receptionist. I recognized the redoubtable Mrs Gladys Ravenswood. From the look of her, she was on a tear of some kind.

"Orville, I think that you are about to preach to me and I won't have it. I don't need a reason for coming into my own office."

"But, Mother, I said how nice it was to see you."

"Yes, but I know what you meant. You want me to sit like Patience at home, and I'll not have it." She didn't look up. "Jenny's just helping me. I felt faint for a moment, but I'm quite recovered." She was exaggerating her recovery from where I stood.

"But what brings you downtown?" Orv asked, trying to soften the question.

"Does there have to be a reason, Orville? I don't like the line you're taking with me. I'm not an invalid and I'm not mentally incompetent. Don't crowd me, please."

"But, Mother. I worry about you."

"Don't 'But, Mother!' me, Orville. I'm not ready for Webster and Powell yet, you know." Webster and Powell were a firm of undertakers with an establishment on Ontario Street within easy reach of most of the big churches.

"At least come and sit down," Orv said as he began to lead his mother-in-law away from the counter. He got her halfway to a chair in the waiting area, when she began to fall again. I caught an elbow on the other side of her along with a whiff of what her problem was, and helped Orv settle her into a chrome-rimmed black leather chair. When she lifted her head, she was looking at me. I couldn't tell whether it was brandy or rye on her breath, but there was a lot of it.

"Thank you, young man. What have you done with Orville and Jenny?"

"I'm right here, Mother," said Orville through thin lips. "Would you like me to bring the car around?"

"And why would I want that? I just arrived." She began to struggle with the arms of the chair. She was trying to get up.

"Mother, is there something I can help you with?"

"I have to urinate, Orville. I doubt if you would be of much use where I'm going. Come along, Jenny!" she called and, almost unassisted, walked until the receptionist caught her under one arm. Together they disappeared into the ladies'. For a moment, Orv and I watched the closed white door with the skirted silhouette on it.

"She's getting on," he said, as much to himself as to me. There lingered behind her the perfume of strong drink. Neither of us commented on it.

"Apart from the Ravenswoods, Orv, do you have a lot of relatives around town?" I was trying hard to fill the silence and not doing a very good job of it.

"I have a brother in Oxford, Mississippi, and a few cousins on the North Shore, above Boston."

"I didn't know you were an American."

"I'm not. I'm one hundred percent Canadian. I say 'eh?' and everything."

"Sorry. What I meant was —"

"Don't let it bother you, Benny. I was one of those draft-dodgers you used to read about. Only, I put down roots. You want to see my papers?"

"Orv, who put you on trial? I was just asking." Was he nervous about me, I wondered, or was it the old woman. Maybe he was thinking, as I was, about our near meeting at Kingsway Hall a few days ago. The presence of Gladys Ravenswood, even behind a door, made it difficult to talk about. It was one of those mysteries that would have to be solved another day.

Chapter Fourteen

Once again I was at my post when Catherine Bracken came off duty after reading the evening news. She came carrying a large totebag, which she had been dragging around with her since I picked up her trail in Papertown just before noon. She'd led me the same merry chase she always did from the Wool Shoppe to the butcher, from the library to the *Beacon,* from lunch at the seafood restaurant Martha Tracy was talking about to her parking spot next to the CXAN mobile TV van. This was the point I usually had my dinner, so I'd gone to the Di for a snack and to reread a few chapters of a book by Bracken's literary friend, McStu. It sustained me through four courses. I'd only meant to eat two, but I got immersed, caught up, and I knew Catherine Bracken wasn't going anyplace as long as my watch was ticking properly. I'd phoned my mother to tell her that I was working and wouldn't be there for my regular Friday dinner. I explained about all the work Julian Newby could throw in my direction. She sounded doubtful.

Bracken got into her car and started it up. I let her creep out of the lot and pull ahead. Yates Street is always quiet, so I let her get a few car-lengths ahead of me. I kept a healthy distance between us for a long block, even though I had a good idea where she was going. In the next block she pulled ahead. I could live with that. I could even let her get out of sight and pick her up again on Welland Avenue. But when I came out on Ontario Street, she was nowhere in sight. Maybe I wasn't committed to the idea that what Bracken did with her free time was any business of Julian Newby or his client. But that kind of thinking is bad for business. Once I start getting soft-headed ideas, it's time to hang up my skates.

I was mentally trying to balance Bracken against Newby, while waiting for the light to change, when I heard a car horn honking at my back. I got mad and made a rude gesture without even turning around. The honking continued and the light was still as red as ever. If the driver wanted to make a left turn at this intersection he was going to have to wait until I made mine. There was plenty of room to turn right. Turning right on a red light is one of the four freedoms that Ontario pioneers had fought for. The horn kept honking.

I got out of the Olds and walked back to the honker. "What the hell is this all about?" I asked as the driver rolled down the window.

"Suppose you tell me!" an angry Catherine Bracken shouted.

"Now wait a minute!" I blustered. "You're doing the honking. And if you noticed the light just changed."

"To hell with the light, you know why I'm leaning on my horn. Why are you following me? You've been behind me for weeks!"

"What are you smoking, lady? Give me a break. If you've got head problems, see a shrink. But get off my case!" I was trying to sound both stupid and outraged.

"Deny! Deny! Deny! Sure, I know the policy. Don't ask me to buy it, though!"

"Look there's a car behind you and he's going to start honking himself. Goodbye!" I turned around and got back behind my wheel, trying to remember if I'd given anything away. How could she have seen me behind her? I'm a good shadow. Nobody's ever seen me. What was going on?

I started the motor again. (The car had stalled.) And soon I was headed north on Ontario Street. She was right behind me. I took three right-hand turns around Montecello Park. She was still in my rear-view mirror. I pulled over near the corner of Lake and Ontario. We got out of our cars at the same time. There were globes of mist glowing around the light standards in the park. There was a bite to the night air.

"Okay, what's this all about?" I thought that I'd try the aggressive, aggrieved approach.

"Don't play dumb. My eyes are twenty-twenty and I keep my rear-view mirror clean. You owe me an explanation!" She was wrapped up in her camel-hair coat, which made her look taller than I knew she was. Her long hair was swinging freely as she shouted; her face had taken colour. I backed off a little.

"I still don't know what you're talking about. All I know is that first you started honking at me, then you followed me around three right-hand turns. You know how often that occurs in nature?" She suppressed a more friendly expression and went on with her questions.

"Who sent you? Who are you working for? Did Orv hire you? I have to know!"

"Look, lady, you've got me mixed up with a bad movie."

"Not a chance. I'm still in my right mind. I'm not paranoid. I haven't started talking to the birdies yet!"

"What's that supposed to mean?" I asked.

"And I'm still this side of Alzheimer's," she shouted, running on, not listening.

"A man'd have to be out of his mind to follow you." Then I pretended to do a double-take. "Hey! Aren't you the woman who reads the news on CXAN? I thought I'd seen you. Just wait till I tell the wife that I saw you!" I laid on the celebrity recognition bit to try to change the subject. She looked like she was buying it and backed towards her car.

"If I see you again within a car-length of me, I'm going to the cops! I'm not kidding. This is what they call harassment. And harassment is something I know all about!" she said, opening up her door. In a moment she realized that she had spoiled her exit by opening the front passenger door. She slammed it angrily and walked around her BMW. I let her see my grin as she drove off with a screech of tires.

I killed the expression as soon as she was out of sight. As I started to the right door of the Olds, I pondered a few things. First of all, I had to admit that I was getting sloppy in my technique. When McStu drove up behind me that first night, I had called it a case of bad luck. It could have happened to Dick Tracy and to Sam Spade. But this, tonight, this was faulty technique. There was no way around it. I was going to have to be careful: all of the people I shadow aren't under five feet three.

Then there was the other thing: she thought that Orv Wishart had set me on her tail. She complained of harassment. Was this the general harassment that a good-looking TV anchor has to wade through or did she mean

Wishart specifically? What was it that Robin O'Neil had said? He'd hinted that Catherine Bracken might owe her job to Orv and may be having to play games with him in order to keep it. It was certain that there was no "part" in the local media world that ranked quite as high as the job Bracken had landed and kept. Robin had hinted that she kept it in spite of bad performance. I can't remember seeing any spectacularly bad performances. Sure, she goofed on a word once in a while, but they all do. No, I was sure that she could have held the job on her own. She didn't need Wishart's influence any more, even if she had once upon a time. The question was, did she know that?

I was driving over the high-level bridge in the direction of the station. I had no business there, but I thought that the ride might help clear my head. And I knew that this was one direction in which Bracken was unlikely to drive.

"Did she know that?" I said out loud. In the time I'd been following her, she hadn't once driven to Wishart's house. Nor had she met him anywhere. She had a full life with McStu. That was certain. She didn't need a second string. Lucky McStu! Poor Wishart. How could he be taking this change in his plans? He wouldn't be happy about it, but there was little he could do. She was doing a good job; he couldn't fire her, even if he had a long-stemmed replacement for Bracken warming up in the wings. Someone who was more obliging than Cath Bracken. Maybe he did.

I bought a few packs of cough drops at Binder's Drug Store, where I used to get cigarettes and the best milk-shakes in town. I would have stayed to have one at the greenish marble counter, but I felt that I hadn't been earning my money this evening. I had to find out more about Orv Wishart's hold on Bracken. I found a parking spot on St Andrew Street and went up the stairs. Naturally, the toilet was calling out to the empty hall and locked offices. It was like the Siren in the story of Ulysses, only she didn't have a good location for picking up homesick sailors and the only rock around was the stained porcelain of the toilet itself.

I looked up the notes I'd made on Wishart. From all accounts, he was a frisky devil, an opportunist of the first water, and one who was no longer as young as he used to be.

My research was interrupted by the telephone. Thinking it must be Anna, I answered it: "Cooperman."

"Benny, is that you?"

"Ma! You never call me at the office. Is something wrong?"

"That's a matter of opinion. The clerk here thinks I'm a crook. I'm collecting quite a crowd. Will you come and get me out of here?"

"Where are you? I'll be right there."

"You know the new twenty-four-hour supermarket on Lakeshore Road, Benny? The one with the posts so you can't wheel the buggies out?"

"I'll find it. Tell them I'm on my way. Try to stay calm!"

"Calm? I'm like an English cucumber. I'm vibrating with control. Only I haven't got any money. So, Benny, for once come right over."

"I told you I'm . . ." I heard the click and spoke the rest of the sentence to the wall across from me. Grabbing my coat, I snapped off the light on the run. In a minute I was making a left turn and beginning to find my way to Ma's side. It was Benny to the rescue. Even I could see it. What

I couldn't figure out was how she got herself into such a scrape at such an hour. The very idea of Ma shopping at all gave me a shot of anxiety. She who shops by phone, if at all, what was she doing cruising Lakeshore Road at midnight?

The place was well lighted. But that made it almost invisible in that neighbourhood, where every gas station and fast-food outlet is lit up like a Mardi Gras until all hours. But, I was able to locate the place with a gigantic "24" spinning above the nests of shopping carts. I abandoned the car illegally near the door and raced inside to see what was the matter.

"What kept you?" Ma was in good form. The manager, three clerks and a crowd of onlookers surrounded her heaping shopping cart near the "express" check-out shoot.

"Ma, tell me exactly what happened. Take a deep breath and stay calm."

"Calm! I told you on the phone I'm calm. The manager, talk about calm to the manager!" I looked at the manager and tried to catch his attention, but he was busy with one of the clerks, rehashing the argument that had failed to work on my mother. He seemed genuinely puzzled about where he had gone wrong.

Ma was wearing black stretch pants with a top that combined six or seven different samples of handicraft weaving. To top it off, she was wearing a gold medallion on a chain that made her look as though she could invoke invisible powers.

"Please, Ma, tell me what's happened."

"It's a simple story, but he, that manager, he won't believe me."

"From the beginning. Please!"

"It's your father's fault. He said he was going to bring home the groceries, but he got into a game — you know your father and his games!"

"Yes."

"Well, I told him I'd go out for them myself when he came home and I got him to give me the money. You know I never carry the stuff."

"Yes."

"And I meant to bring it with me, but I left my purse in the hall by the door."

"How did you get here?"

"I was going to take a cab, but I saw Shirley from next door. She dropped me here. She was going to pick up her Karen who's been babysitting over on Lake Street."

"Never mind Karen. So, Shirley gave you a lift?"

"If she hadn't I would have discovered that I'd forgotten my purse when I went to pay the taxi! Then I could have gone home for it. If Shirley hadn't done me such a big favour, I wouldn't be standing here!"

"So, it's all her fault for being a good neighbour?"

"I didn't say that! Shirley's a wonderful person. You don't know half the things that girl has done for me. She's a saint. Still, if I'd taken the cab . . ." She shrugged and left the thought unexpressed. I turned to the manager and he identified himself as though there might be a rival claimant.

"How much does my mother owe you?" I asked, and he looked at me as though I was missing the point. I hoped he couldn't guess that I was carrying less than twenty dollars in my wallet.

"Are you Mrs Cooperman's son?" I acknowledged that I was. "Well, Mr Cooperman, your mother has no right to expect to get credit when she isn't carrying any identification!"

"My mother forgot her purse! I'm sure she told you that."

"Oh, she said *something*..."

"Which you chose not to believe? Do you have many elderly customers? Do you know anything about the aging process, Mr...?"

"Carmichael. Lester Carmichael. Ah, no, I can't say I do."

"For your information, Mr Carmichael, elderly people have pride and dignity just like ordinary people. In fact they *are* ordinary people. They try to remain independent for as long as they can. And with some compassion and common courtesy they do very well. Occasionally, of course, they run into a manager like you!"

"Really, Mr..."

"Did my mother say that she would get the money?"

"She said *something* about..."

"And again you chose not to believe her! I see. The world is full of people like you, Mr Carmichael, people who won't give our senior citizens a chance to make it on their own. Have you made out the cash-register receipt?"

"Hawkins has it, haven't you, Robert?"

"Right here, Mr Carmichael," said an acne-spotted young man.

"Have you any serious objections to my driving my mother home and returning with the money?"

"Well, it's highly unusual..."

"Then, suppose you keep the groceries and I take my mother home or to the Emergency Department at the General to have her blood pressure checked?"

"Now, look here, Mr Cooperman, I . . ." Carmichael went on talking, but I didn't hear a word of what he said. This was because at that moment I caught sight of Catherine Bracken standing with a shopping cart, watching the proceedings. She was quietly amused by the battle of the check-out counter. I swallowed hard as our eyes met briefly. I had lost steam when I turned back to Carmichael.

"What did you say?"

"Please, Mr Cooperman! Take your mother and the groceries with you. Drop the money off in the morning or when it is convenient. Please accept my apologies for this whole misunderstanding."

"That's easy to say now!" I said, turning away from the manager's pale face. "Shall we go?" I asked Ma.

"Your father will be wondering what's happened to me, son," she said in a faltering voice. I averted my eyes. "You know how your father worries."

A clerk loaded half of the plastic bags of groceries into the trunk of the car. A second clerk, Robert, carried others and put them on the back seat. With great dignity and carrying a plastic bag of oranges, Ma walked regally to the open car door.

Chapter Fifteen

Except for a skeleton staff left at the supermarket, we all ended up at Ma's place: Mr Carmichael, Robert and another clerk whose name I didn't get, a fellow customer named Bill and Catherine Bracken. How did that happen? Don't ask. Ma and I'd been ready to leave, I was walking around to the driver's side of the car, when Ma yelled, "Stop!" I looked around and saw that Ma's bag of oranges had split. Oranges were rolling all over the Tarmac. People from the supermarket, who had been watching our progress under the mercury lights, came running to help. While we were racing after oranges, a clerk appeared with a forgotten shopping bag. Carmichael picked up his apology where he had broken it off. Cath Bracken was watching it all standing beside an island of shopping carts. Then I heard my mother inviting everybody back to her house for a drink. I couldn't believe it! She shouted the address and waved at the crowd as she got into the car.

While we were driving, of course, Ma had her chance to get to me.

"Thank you for coming, Benny," she said. At least she'd dropped "son," which she hadn't called me since the day I recited my Bar Mitzvah portion without distinction.

"Quite all right," I said.

"Eh?" she said. "Stop whispering!"

"It's your hearing going, is it?"

"There's a lot about the aging process you know nothing about, Benny. All we old-timers want is a little dignity and courtesy."

"Knock it off, Ma, or I'll let you walk."

"Benny, this is your mother you're talking to!"

I had just piled the groceries on the kitchen counter when the supermarket arrived with more bags. Ma poured Carmichael a drink of rye and tried to overcome the two clerks' reluctance to drink under the gaze of their boss. Robert was coughing after a swallow of VO, when Catherine Bracken came in the door with an armful of oranges and frozen vegetables.

"Put them down anywhere, dear," Ma said. "We're drinking rye and water." Bracken put her burden in the refrigerator and caught my father coming up from the TV room to see what was going on in his kitchen at nearly one in the morning.

"I'm Cath Bracken, Mr Cooperman. How do you do?"

Pa blinked and grinned and took her arm to lead her into the tangerine-coloured living-room. Ma looked up just in time to hand Cath a drink. "This is for the heroine who saved my oranges!" Cath took a sip, while Ma poured a drink for my father. "If the bag had ripped here in the living-room," she said, pointing at the broadloom, "We might not find them all for weeks."

I took a chair across from Cath Bracken, waiting to see if I was going to be offered a drink. Ma was sometimes funny about drinking with either of her sons. Cold sober, she knew we wouldn't try to upstage her; after a drink, there was no telling. Bracken had taken off her coat and was wearing the green silk blouse I'd admired a few nights ago on the small screen. She was listening to something Carmichael was saying, but her attention was on Ma, who was telling Robert what to do to clear up his complexion. Ma believed that an active sex life was a boon to the whole system and to the complexion in particular. Robert was listening like he'd never heard the word "sex" spoken above a whisper before. Cath was grinning.

I got up and found the heel of the bottle of rye in the kitchen. "What the hell," I thought, "I might as well join them." I poured a shot and added some ginger ale from the fridge. I had just taken a gulp when Cath Bracken walked into the room. "My name is Cath Bracken," she said with a warm smile. "Shall we start all over again?" I took her hand, which was cool from her glass, and held it for a moment while I tried to figure out what I could salvage from this shipwreck.

"I'm glad to get a second chance," I said. "Thanks for helping out."

"You didn't need any help. I was very impressed. Your mother tells me you're a private detective."

"Investigator. She doesn't listen. What else do you want to know?"

"Who set you on me, naturally. But that can wait."

"Miss Bracken —"

"Cath. People I like call me Cath. And you're . . . ?"

"Benny. I prefer Ben, just Ben, but everybody calls me Benny." We clicked glasses and drank in silence for a moment. "You know I can't tell you who I'm working for. That's rule one. Break that and I'll be condemned to searching titles for my cousin Melvyn from now on. I'd prefer not to, although my parents can't see the life of a private investigator as something to boast about."

"She boasted to me about it. Right after she told me about your brother, Sam."

"Yeah. Sam's the big success."

"I think she likes you."

"She can't remember I'm here."

"It's just her way. Trust me. I know a thing or two about women."

"You seem to handle both sexes well," I said.

"Ah, that's right. That was you who had a blow-out with McStu, wasn't it? He sounded ferocious. But he wouldn't have hurt you. He couldn't. He doesn't see well enough without his glasses to do any damage."

Carmichael came into the kitchen and got some ice from the freezer. We both watched him being aware that he was interrupting something. When he had gone, Cath asked if I'd rather not talk shop and I nodded. "I'd just as soon talk about the rich and famous, but I don't think I can."

"Yeah, you're right. Until I can fit you into a context, I'd just be rattling on."

"No focus. That's right. To tell you the truth, I'd like to find out why I was hired in the first place," I said. Cath raised an interested eyebrow. "McStu is married, right? Is his wife giving him a hard time?"

"*Moira?* Moira wouldn't sic you on me. She's happy with the way things are. She's got McStu's money, such as it is, and I've got McStu."

"People change. Could she be looking for a bigger piece?"

"What's bigger than all? Look, Benny, she's a healthy, childless woman in her mid-thirties. She's smart and has a degree in business management. She's sitting pretty. I admit she put on a show of being a cast-off little church mouse, but that was just for the settlement. Since the divorce was final in September, she has been spending a lot of time in Mexico between consulting jobs. My heart cracks wide open for her. It would be different if McStu was loaded, but he isn't. He lives on advances from one book to the next. Just because he appears on television whenever they need a black commentator, everybody thinks he's independently wealthy. He needs that teaching job at Secord. It's the only steady thing he's got."

"And you," I offered. She grinned, tilting her head to show that she was no prize package. From where I was standing, I could have argued that. She was little, but there's nothing wrong with little when it looks like Catherine Bracken.

"I may have this all wrong," she said. "Maybe Moira is on the warpath again. He got wonderful reviews in the *New York Times* for his last book and a mention in *The New Yorker.* That sort of thing means a lot to Moira. Still, she has no further claim on him. He's all mine. When we tie the knot, I mean. She used to be an Olympic fencer. Those people have to be damned dedicated. So, watch out if she comes looking for you."

"I'll keep my back to the wall," I said. "So, if Moira is happy, who isn't? Who would think enough about your comings and goings to put an old divorce investigator on your case?" Cath rolled her eyes to the ceiling, but she didn't say anything. "You thought earlier that it might be Orv Wishart. Why would you think that? If you want to tell me, that is."

"Orv thinks he was the making of me. I was the

diamond and Grantham was the rough. Orv was the talent scout. He came on like an eager boy scout, but it wasn't badges he was collecting. You don't want to hear this, do you? He gave me my start. I owe him everything, but I'm through saying thanks."

"There are laws about that kind of thing, you know?"

"Oh, yeah, tell me about it. Hell, Benny, I don't want to send him to jail, I just want him not to be there whenever I turn around. How can I say this? He has an abnormal appetite for everything about me. He knows my shoe size, where I buy my clothes, what books I read, everything!"

"So, you think he could be interested in having you followed?"

"But he already knows about McStu. What more are you going to be able to tell him?"

"If not Orv, then who?"

"I don't know. I get a lot of funny letters from fans. Maybe one of them. It's happened before. You know, people seen regularly on television."

"Orv's marriage is shaky, I hear."

"Sort of wavering. But Orv will never seriously get on the wrong side of Antonia. She's got his future in both hands. He lives for that TV station and he can't keep it if Antonia cuts him off."

"A delicate balancing act. How does he manage it?"

"The Ravenswoods are an old patrician family. Antonia will put up with a lot as long as it stays out of the press. As long as Orv keeps his extra-curricular activities under wraps, and turns up for her parties and remembers opening nights at the Shaw Festival, she's a reasonably contented woman."

"Could it be the old lady checking up?"

"Gladys Ravenswood? Ben, what are you giving me? Don't *you* know who you're working for?"

"I'm working for an agent of the person who wants the information. I don't know who this agent represents."

"I see. Someone like a lawyer."

"Like a lawyer. That's right. Back to Gladys."

"Gladys is a spoiled, elderly alcoholic. She's trying to hold her family business together. She's trying to keep her family, if not together, out of the papers and off the air. Since media is her business, she's batting a thousand. She can be as bitchy as they come and she can be as nice as pie. But you have to watch her. She knows the power game and has friends in all the right places."

"Is Wishart a shoo-in to take all of this over when she retires?"

"That's not a word I'd use in her hearing, Ben. Retirement isn't part of her plan. As for Orv, she keeps him guessing. He never knows where he stands with her unless he's being attacked from outside. Then she'll go to bat for him. She doesn't like what he's done to Antonia. But if you asked her about it, she'd look you in the eye and ask you what you meant. Canny. That's the word for Gladys."

"Well, I give up! I can't figure this out. Don't get me wrong. Of all the people I've had under surveillance over the years, you have been a choice subject. But why?"

"Your glass is empty." She leaned over with the bottle and gave me the last of its contents. I added ginger ale from the fridge and again we touched glasses.

"Are you doing any stories on your own for the station?" I asked.

"Do them all the time. That old maid Robin O'Neil tries to keep me reading his copy. Most of the time that's fine, but once in a while a story comes along and I think it needs to be covered."

"Like what? I mean in the last week or so."

"I did the firemen's gift box for the poor kids. But that was an old idea they do every three or four years. There was an old-fashioned barn raising."

"Can't be that."

"I was doing some interviews with people who knew that old woman who starved to death on Brogan Street."

"Bingo! That's it!"

"But the story's still in pieces. It hasn't been edited. It's all over the place, really. Nobody's even seen it."

"Nevertheless. The people you talked to know you have been working on it. Who did you talk to?"

"Rupe McLay, the head of Community Services, the bank manager and a couple of others."

"You talked to Temperley? You know what's happened to him?"

"Yes, for just a few minutes. But I couldn't get hold of some of the people I wanted."

"Thurleigh Ramsden didn't return your calls?"

"Oh, he returned them, all right, but he wouldn't say a word about Miss Oldridge. Said he was too busy."

"I'm sure. I nearly got into a fight with him a few days ago trying to get some information."

"Maybe you got him to change his tune, though."

"What do you mean?"

"He called me at the station this afternoon. He says he'll be glad to see me tomorrow morning at 8:30. He's had a complete change of heart."

"So, at 8:30 you and a TV crew are going to tape him in his house?"

"No. He just wants to talk to me first. I'll take a tape recorder in case he changes his mind. He could say plenty if he would. I'm a little nervous seeing him on his own. He's a terrible man from what I've heard, but a story is a story."

"I hope you get more than he told the inquest. He was as vague as a fifth carbon copy when I was there."

"Benny, what's your interest in Ramsden and the Oldridge case?"

"Just a favour I'm doing for a friend. It's not a job, really. I . . ." At this point Ma came into the room and saw us standing together talking away with some intensity.

"I see you're getting on well!" she said, coming through into the middle of the room. She had leaned slightly on the door jamb as she came in. "I think your father has a bottle of rye in here that he's been hiding on me." She began to rummage about the cupboards until she found the brother of the VO we'd just finished. When I opened it for her and poured a drink into her glass, I noticed that she was giving Cath a thorough examination. She did everything but ask her to say "ah." Women can get away with looking at one another. If a man tries it, he's ticked off for being rude.

"You do the news on television, don't you?" She was using the serious voice she used for serious conversations. I had a premonition about where it was leading. Cath answered and Ma assessed it while forming her next question. "Benny's friend Anna Abraham, up at Secord University, does some TV work. She comments on American politics. Maybe you know her? She's the daughter of Jonah Abraham."

"I may have met her. I honestly don't remember."

What Ma couldn't do to me by forgetting her purse and having a fight in public at a supermarket, what oranges rolling all over the parking lot couldn't accomplish, she finally managed with this gratuitous information about Anna. I was angry now, maybe even a little guilty, not wanting to be caught out so soon in getting to know Cath Bracken. Did Ma think I was putting the moves on Cath right in Ma's own kitchen? And was I? I wasn't sure of anything except that Ma was suddenly too much mother for me. She had played the innocent once too often.

"How do you come to know my Benny?" she asked with ironclad naïvety.

"Oh, we just keep running into each other," Cath said. "You know what it's like in a small town." I could see by her eyes that Ma wasn't buying any of this. As her dreams of being welcomed into the mansion of Jonah Abraham as the mother of the groom were threatened, I wondered whether she was going to tell how I wet my bed until I was six and how I still brux my teeth while sleeping.

"We met through business, Ma. Cath and I were just trying to figure out how that came about. We've covered the ground and we can't find a reason."

Ma looked from me to Cath and back again. "It's so hard to find a reason?" She took a sip of her drink and shook her head. "Maybe it's like in Sherlock Holmes," she said. "If you can't find a reason, that's the reason."

"How do you mean?"

"Well, remember the story about the Red-Headed League?"

"Refresh my memory."

"Look it up. I've got guests. I'm like Liz Taylor getting the guests, in . . . what was the name of that movie?" She got up and returned to the living-room.

Cath was looking at her watch when I looked at her. When Ma gets the guests, they stay got. Cath was the first of the merry crowd to say goodnight. Pa walked her to her BMW, leaving a room full of supermarket personnel standing between me and bruxing the rest of the night away.

Chapter Sixteen

I found a copy of *The Adventures of Sherlock Holmes* on the shelf near my bed. It was an old copy with the name Robert A. B. Otto in it written in ink that was turning brown. "The Red-Headed League" began on page 29. I read it all the way through, still not understanding the point Ma had been making. Then, of course, it hit me all at once and with a terrific, almost physical, blow. Of course! I had been hired by Julian Newby to follow Cath Bracken not because he was interested in the movements of Miss Bracken, but because he was interested in *my* movements! He was indifferent to where Cath Bracken went — or at least, it wasn't of great importance. What he cared about was keeping me off the scent I had apparently been sniffing when I ran into Stan Mendlesham at the new courthouse. Newby wanted to keep me away from Lizzy Oldridge, her estate and her involvement with Thurleigh Ramsden.

Conan Doyle's Jabez Wilson got four pounds a week for writing out the *Encyclopaedia Britannica;* I was earning more money, but I was at least as stupid as Doyle's red-headed pawnbroker. I should have seen through it. I should have been reminded of my promise to Kogan every time I climbed the stairs to my office, serenaded by Kogan's unique water music.

To be fair to myself, I hadn't neglected Kogan's business entirely. I had seen Lizzy's house on Brogan Street, found out that Steve Morella was putting together a gold-mine of real estate just behind St Andrew Street, and had nearly been pinched when I went to hear how Ramsden operated within the Bede Bunch. Kogan may not have had a full and just pound of flesh from me, but he had had a few good ounces. Then I remembered the ribbing I'd got from Pete Staziak. It was a pound, damn it!

As I turned out the light, I thought that Ma, in a manner of speaking, had recalled me to duty. I had to hand it to her for that. But, clever woman that she is, at the same time, she was getting me away from Cath Bracken. She knew that I would recognize that I'd been paddling about in red-herring-infested waters when I should have been paying attention to Anna Abraham, in her eyes the catch of the century. Ma loved doing a good turn almost as much as she enjoyed mischief. Putting me back on what she thought was my true course was a good deed, getting me away from Cath brought out her warped sense of my destiny.

Maybe Cath's interviews would be interesting to hear; they might shed some light on what's been going on, but the most important thing for me in the next few days was to try to find out what was vulnerable about the Morella property deals. There had to have been an unsavoury side to them or Newby wouldn't have gone to such lengths to sidetrack me. All I had to do was figure out where the smelly bits were hidden.

Newby was a crafty fellow to throw Cath at me. I

should be more suspicious when the senior partner in any firm takes me to lunch. I guess Newby thought he could read me the way Ma can read a teacup. Clever Newby. Poor Cooperman.

Well, the truth is I didn't sleep much that night. There was too much going on in my head. It was like a battle scene in a movie running backwards. The booze didn't help either. I tried reading one of my McStu books, but he kept grinning at me out of the pages with that gap between his front teeth looking like it was leading the way into the Channel Tunnel. I heaved the book across the room and punched the pillow. When that didn't work, I took a shower. Eventually, towards dawn, I slipped into a cross-grained sleep that was laced with bad dreams and bad thoughts. I was glad when the clock-radio came on at eight o'clock and set me up for a brand new day. New day. New problems. New disappointments.

After a shave and instant coffee, I went out to the Di for a cup of the real stuff. On St Andrew Street there were Christmas shoppers and Christmas carols on tapes. The big day was only a week away, and I had not even made out a shopping list. Outside, the sky was the colour of gun metal; inside, the management had turned on the lights. "Frosty the Snowman," coming through a loud speaker, was making thought difficult.

I was trying to figure out how to get back on the main highway of the investigation, since, unfortunately, Cath Bracken had been turned into a detour. Where were the ramps to help me drive back into the action? Ramsden, of course! I could try to find him in a better mood. Maybe the finding of his friend Temperley would make him more agreeable. All I wanted was a short chat with him.

I paid my bill, bought a Toronto paper, read the headlines and the story about Temperley's murder, scalped from yesterday's *Beacon,* and found my way back to the office. I nearly fell over when I saw Kogan sweeping the stairs. He looked at me as though I'd discovered him cavorting in a pink tutu.

"Morning, Kogan! You're up early," I said as I passed him and headed for my door. "And on Saturday too!"

"There's going to be a big storm," he said. "Blizzard!" I'd missed seeing it in the paper, but I wouldn't have been surprised if Kogan's source wasn't a newspaper.

"Where did you disappear to the other night?" he asked. "They wouldn't let me go until it was getting light out."

"So, they didn't book you into the Venus Art Club?"

"Nope. You knew that? Right?"

"If they had a clean case, you wouldn't be sweeping the steps, Kogan. I'm guessing that the cops had trouble getting a witness to come forward. Happens all the time. Nudity, cases like that. Nobody wants to get his name associated. You understand?"

"I hear you and Thurleigh had a fight up in the hall!" Kogan was grinning as though he could picture the main event.

"Who told you?"

"Oh, I've got my contacts same as you. I hear it was a real dust-up."

"In that crowd, I must have looked like Muhammad Ali in his prime."

"I'll bet Ramsden was in good form. I figure him for a dirty fighter, Mr Cooperman."

"We collected quite a crowd, Kogan. Then you turned up. We couldn't compete with your act." Then I had a thought. "Kogan, have you ever run into the Ravenswood family? Do you know Orv Wishart?" To an outsider this might seem a silly question to ask a former panhandler, but in Grantham stranger things have been known to happen. For instance, I knew that Kogan and a well-known local police magistrate used to play football at Cranmer College years ago. Nowadays Kogan, who has not been above dining on cat food, has spent evenings in the company of this esteemed member of the judiciary drinking everything from fine wines to aftershave, if my sources have it right. So, I wasn't surprised when he told me that he and Gladys Ravenswood (née Kyrle) used to attend Mrs Rankin's dancing class and that Orv Wishart was the maker of prize-winning trout flies. I couldn't see how I could use this information, but I filed it away in my head just in case.

There were a couple of things for me to do once I had opened my office door. The first was to contact Julian Newby and tell him that I was no longer able to keep Cath Bracken under surveillance. I always hated turning off the money-tap, but I try to stay as honest as I can without starving to death. The other thing was to see what I could find out from Ramsden. I put in a call to Newby's office and was startled to get a live secretary instead of an answering machine. She explained that the office is always open until noon on Saturdays. I detected no trace of bitterness in her voice. I love these fine old firms. I asked her to have Mr Newby call me when he came in on Monday. I was sure that at least the senior partner in the firm kept bankers' hours. She assured me that the message would be relayed to Newby.

The other call I placed was a second attempt to raise Ramsden. I left a message next to my last message on his machine, and leaned back in my chair the way Orv Wishart had. The wonderful thing about the telephone is that it gives you the feeling that you have been working when only your Peter Pointer has. It wasn't even ten o'clock yet, but I already felt like an efficient executive who had made a few smooth moves. Next to pegging stones into the Old Canal, it was my favourite early-morning pastime.

That's when the phone rang. It was that hard-working secretary at Newby's office. Would I kindly come by to see Mr Newby in an hour? I said I would and hung up. I was surprised that Newby wanted to see me today. I thought it would keep until Monday. And what about Mendlesham? I thought Newby wanted me to work through him.

I killed the better part of the hour drinking coffee at the Crystal. I couldn't quite bring myself to return to the Di, where the seat was still warm from my last visit. Luckily, I was carrying a copy of one of McKenzie Stewart's novels with me and the time went quickly.

It was just about fifty-five minutes later that I drove the Olds into Newby's parking lot along the side of the house on Ontario Street that served as one of the oldest law offices in town. I was congratulating myself on being early, when I saw Newby himself, driving a dark Lincoln, leaving the same lot. Where can a Lincoln take you in five minutes that's so important, I wanted to know. I wanted to know badly enough to back out of the parking lot myself and follow the big car.

After my experience with Cath Bracken, I kept at least two cars sitting between me and Newby. I wasn't going to get caught again. Too much of my income depended on having the confidence of the legal community. A man like Julian Newby could kill my reputation in less than a minute. All he had to say was that I couldn't follow a suspect without showing myself.

Newby drove down Ontario Street to Welland Avenue, where he made a right turn. He had the green light. It was harder for me to make the same turn after the light had changed, but I managed to insinuate the nose of the Olds into the traffic in time to see the Lincoln make a northern turn onto York Street. Now there were no cars between us, so I pulled to a stop. Newby continued three or four blocks and parked the Lincoln. I moved the Olds up the street slowly until I came up behind a parked car about five or six houses below Newby. I got out just a moment after I saw him leave his car. He wasn't referring to a scrap of paper with an address written on it, so it was clear that he knew where he was going. Through the windows of a parked car, I watched him walk back in my direction. He went up to the front door of a house on the corner of Lowell Avenue and used the knocker. When he didn't get an answer, he tried again. Again, no response. He backed away from the door, then stood on the edge of the porch for a moment, jiggling the keys in his pocket with his right hand, no doubt debating with himself about what to do next. Then he pulled out a clutch of keys from his pocket and examined them. He selected one and returned to the door.

In a second, the door was open and Newby had disappeared inside. I left the cover of the parked car and began crossing the street to where a thick maple would offer me similar protection and a better view. I had only reached the centre of York Street when Newby came running out of the house. He was coughing and dry-retching. He held on to the white balustrade and heaved.

I forgot about the maple tree. Newby needed help. Something was wrong. Surveillance work suddenly dwindled to a cheap charade. I ran up the steps to help.

"Are you all right?" I asked in spite of the evidence to the contrary. He looked around to see where the voice was coming from.

"You?" he said, opening his eyes in a question.

"I saw you," I said lamely. "Is there anything I can do?"

"Inside!" he said, pointing to the front door with its brass Medusa's face on the knocker. "Inside! It's . . . it's Ramsden!" By now Newby had his handkerchief out and had started pulling himself back together. I took this as a cue to go inside.

Inside the front door, I found myself in a hallway decorated with the sort of prints you see on placemats in the windows of china stores. There was the *Cutty Sark* and several other big clipper ships under sail. Facing a dark green door, I saw the first of a long line of military prints, engravings of soldiers wearing the uniforms and regalia of the last century or the one before that. I opened the door and entered what would have been the living-room in the old house except that Ramsden had claimed it for himself. There were flags on the wall, a group of framed letters, as well as pictures of various crowned heads. A glass case showed off a red and yellow drum and dark bugle. Above it was a globe with a great deal of pink on it. Behind the desk stood a flagstand. Here were the red maple leaf flag of Canada and the older ensign flag that it replaced. I recognized the flag of Ontario hanging limply from a pointed flagstaff. There was also a space reserved for a Union Jack, the flag of the United Kingdom, but it was not to be found in its proper receptacle. Instead, it was sticking through the torso of

Thurleigh Ramsden, who lay stretched across the floor of the den. The flagstaff had been shoved or pushed right through Ramsden so that his mortal remains were transfixed on the pole with the flag pulled part of the way through the wound.

I wanted to grab onto something. For the moment, I didn't give a damn about leaving fingerprints for others to find. I felt my knees about to play traitor and I soon found myself sitting on the floor not far away from the open, staring eyes of the corpse. With the blood looking black and the dead look in the wide eyes, I didn't have to move in closer to try to find a pulse. Ramsden was very dead and had been so for some little time.

When the whirling stopped, I was aware that Newby had come into the room behind me and was calling the police on a telephone he was carrying. I couldn't hear the words, but I managed to get up and tried to pull myself together for the series of police officers who were going to fill up the next few hours of my day. Newby was shaking his head from side to side in a vague, hopeless way. He moved his briefcase closer to him and sat down in a Queen Anne chair not, apparently, giving a damn about fingerprints either. Together and without speaking another word, we sat and listened for the sound of the sirens coming north to find us. Instead, we heard the honking of horns as a wedding procession made its noisy way along Lake Street.

Chapter Seventeen

There was no lunch being served at Niagara Regional Police that afternoon. Or at least I wasn't offered any. From time to time either Chris Savas or Pete Staziak would disappear from their offices, leaving me in charge of the other. I suspected they were making trips to the cafeteria downstairs. I even thought I detected crumbs at the corner of Pete's mouth on his return from such a trip. I didn't have my copy of the Geneva Convention handy, but I'm sure there must be a section on this type of harassment.

By the time I got to the level of my old friends Savas and Staziak, I had told my story at least three times. It was recorded in three notebooks and I had made a statement as soon as I was brought downtown. I stuck to the events of the day as much as I could. There was no sense dragging in irrelevancies like the fight Ramsden and I had had at the top of the stairs at the Kingsway Hall on Ontario Street the other night. That would only confuse matters.

I lost sight of Julian Newby early on in the questioning. He was being questioned by an inspector wearing kid gloves, I suspected. The chief wouldn't send him through the works with a trainee seconded from traffic. He would also make sure Newby got lunch.

"Okay, Benny, let's get serious on this thing," Pete said, tapping my statement with his ballpoint pen. "Once again, why were you tailing Newby?"

"I had an appointment to see him and saw him driving out of his parking lot. I wanted to see where he was off to."

"What did you want to see him about?"

"It says that in my statement, Pete."

"Humour me." Pete lit a cigarette and offered me one. I shook my head. Pete knew I'd quit smoking. It was his way of getting at me, keeping the pressure on.

"I was going to give him a progress report on a job I was doing for him."

"The statement says you were going to beg off the case. Why?"

"Because it wasn't going anywhere. I found out all I was going to find out on the first couple of days. I wasn't earning my money."

"Come on! What was the real reason? Give me something I can swallow."

"Okay. The subject that I was following blew my cover. I was no good after that. I don't have an office full of operatives to put in my place, Pete."

"That sounds more like the Cooperman we all know and admire. I don't suppose you'll tell me who this is?" We exchanged grins. Queen's Gambit Declined. "Okay, okay! Continue!"

"Pete, for crying out loud! I already told you! I followed Newby. Newby went into Ramsden's house —"

"He had a key?"

"No, he walked through the wall! Yes, he had a key!" I said, wishing I'd accepted the cigarette. I could have mashed it between my fingers and let the tobacco fall on the floor. "He wasn't in there more than a few seconds, then he comes out, all shook up after finding the body. I went in, did a little serious gagging and then Newby called you on his handy pocket telephone. I could see that Ramsden had been dead for some time."

"Now you're an expert on 'time of death' too. Maybe you'd like to take over the Temperley investigation as well. I wouldn't want to miss hearing your theories about that!"

"I figure the deaths are linked, Pete."

"Let's get back to this script, Benny. I'll pass on your thoughts about Temperley to Chris. How long was Newby in the house ahead of you?" Pete mashed his cigarette into a half-empty styrofoam cup, like he was reading my mind.

"Pete, you can't try to pin this one on Newby. I told you he wasn't in there long enough."

"Just answer the question!"

"Ramsden was colder than a smoked turkey when I got to him. He wasn't going to get any deader. You've got a preliminary medical report, haven't you? He'd been dead for a couple of hours at least."

"He was in there with Ramsden alone, Benny. He could have gone through his desk, removed documents. Who knows? How long was he out of your sight?" Pete had neatly rescued a stupid question and remodelled it so that it looked more interesting. I thought about it.

"You'd have to measure it in seconds, Pete. He wasn't gone a full minute."

"But he could have gone through Ramsden's papers if he knew where to look?"

"How the hell should I know? He didn't have a file folder stuffed down his shirt, if that's what you want me to say. He didn't dispose of anything while he was with me. I didn't smell burned paper, and he wasn't out of my sight until your people separated us for questioning. Check his pockets. Check his briefcase."

It was at this point that Chris Savas returned to the room. I'd met Chris about ten years ago. He was a hard man, but a good cop. He demonstrated both of these characteristics as soon as the door was closed.

"Where does it say in here . . ." he was waving a copy of the statement I'd just signed, "that you and the deceased exchanged angry words followed by blows in the Kingsway Hall last Tuesday night?"

"Was it last Tuesday? I've got such a lousy sense of time."

"Tell me, Benny. I want to hear it all." He perched his butt on the edge of Pete's dull grey metal desk and crossed his big arms. He was still wearing a short-sleeved shirt. I wondered whether he'd be as slow changing out of his winter wear in the spring. "Benny, what happened up there?"

I went through the whole thing, beginning with the run-in with Ramsden on the evening in question and ending with Pete Staziak's elbows in my ribs at police headquarters after Kogan's nude demonstration. I wanted to get in the part about Pete, because it told Savas that Pete already knew about all this and I hadn't been being stingy with the facts. I didn't tell him about Kogan's getting me to look in on the inquest or my suspicions about Lizzy Oldridge's property.

"So where does the bad blood between you and Ramsden come from?" Savas wanted to know. He pulled on his earlobe and readjusted his purchase on the corner of the desk.

"He took a dislike to my surname when I told it to him. He made an oblique reference to 'me and my kind.' " Savas and Staziak exchanged a look.

"That's at least consistent with what we know about him," Savas said. This was his way of saying he was sorry on behalf of Niagara Regional Police for what had occurred. Chris never gives information away without a reason. This was partly because of his police training and partly because he comes from a long line of taciturn Cypriot farmers, who know when to talk and when to listen. "And then what?"

"He tried to throw me downstairs. When I turned around, he fell over backwards and started yelling that he couldn't move his legs. But he got up fast enough when everybody ran down to see Kogan's buff."

"You didn't throw a punch?"

"No. Neither did he. You think I killed him, Chris, because he tried to eject me, or because I didn't like his racist suggestions?" Just to bug him, I held my wrists together waiting for him to reach for his handcuffs.

Our meeting went on for a few more minutes. Pete and Chris wanted to know all I knew about Ramsden and I demonstrated that I wasn't a good source for anything they didn't know about already. When they finally let me go, I headed directly to the seafood place in the market and ordered a trout the way my father likes it, cooked in butter and served without adornment. The place was full of shoppers meeting for lunch. Overheard talk was about shopping; packages stacked on the banquettes furnished more proof of the season. This wasn't the usual late-lunching business crowd of the weekdays, the people without two-o'clock appointments. There were no prospectuses on the tables. By the time I paid my check, the place had nearly emptied. Already the waiters were spreading the coloured tablecloths for the dinner trade.

When I got back to my office, I checked with my service. There were three calls: Stan Mendlesham from Newby's office, Detective-Sergeant Chris Savas and, to my surprise, Orv Wishart. I called Mendlesham first. It must have been a home number he left, because the voice of a three- or four-year-old answered and asked what I wanted and why. I was in mid-reply, when the phone was wrenched away from the child.

"Is that you, Benny?" I told him it was. He went on to tell me that Newby had taken to his bed and wouldn't be able to see me for a day or two.

"Then I'll deal with you, Stan. That's the way it was set up in the first place."

"Julian now wants to handle you himself, Benny. You've hit the big time!" Stan laughed, then spoke to the youngster with his hand over the phone for a moment. "Great kid!" he said back to me again. "He can do jigsaw puzzles with two hundred pieces and he's just turned four! Can you beat it?"

"Terrific!" I said. "When's he joining the firm?"

"He has to get through school yet, Benny, but I'm telling you . . ."

Stan went on about his son for some minutes. The important part of the message was to give Newby a day to recover. I wanted to ask Stan about how Newby had keys to Ramsden's house, but I kept my mouth shut. Maybe I could smoke that information out of Pete Staziak.

Next I phoned Chris, but he was out, so I left word that I wasn't ignoring him. Then I tried Wishart.

"Oh, hello there!" he said when I'd identified myself.

He made small talk for a minute — something about the challenge and responsibility of the media — and then he said he'd like to see me. I let him suggest a place and time. When he'd hung up, I wrote "The Snug, Beaumont Hotel, 6:00 p.m." in my book. I was wondering what it could all be about. I thought of the figure I'd seen lurking under the archway in the Kingsway Hall. My speculations were interrupted by the telephone. This was getting to sound like a busy office.

"Cooperman?" It was Savas.

"You got him, Chris. What can I do for you? You hiring outside consultants?"

"You can tell me what your voice is doing on Ramsden's answering machine for a start. Why the hell do you starve us for information, Benny? You ration it, you forget to mention it, and I'm supposed to roll over and wag my tail! What the hell was going on between you? What business is Liz Oldridge to you?"

"Just business, Chris. I was looking into her death, that's all."

"The inquest didn't name any names, Benny. Ramsden walked away from that."

"And we all know how far he got: three days. That's a pile short of a home run."

"Benny, I'm only going to say this once: I don't want you fucking up my investigation! You hear me? Ramsden's mine and I don't want to see you anywhere near him. You still listening?"

"I hear, Chris. But when have I ever —?"

"Don't even ask! First I find out that you two were scuffling at the Bede Bunch meeting, then I discover you're trying to get back in his good books. I know you can give me a good reason, but I want to hear it without any creative flourishes, if you know what I mean?"

"Chris, it's like asking a reporter for his sources. I've got to think about it. I've got a client-investigator relationship to preserve. I'm not trying to make waves, Chris, I just want to get to shore."

"Two days, Benny! I'll give you two days to get your shit in order, then I want you to give me the facts. That's forty-eight hours from now and then we talk! You got that? Because if I don't have a murderer in the cells downstairs by then, I'm coming calling on you!" I could hear him sucking on his teeth over the phone. It was serious sucking. I could tell.

"Easy, Chris! Take it easy! I want to find out who did it as much as you do. If I knew anything that was in my power to pass on to you, I would. But I don't and I can't."

"I've lost my sense of humour where you're concerned, Benny. I don't want any sheep-dip from you when we talk. You hear? Be seeing you in two days!" He hung up loudly, hoping, no doubt, that my ear was still close to the receiver.

I replaced the phone slowly, thinking of the unworthy object I was sticking my neck out for. Kogan hadn't even formally retained me to do anything. I was acting on my own, spurred on by a passive-aggressive layabout who capered under the moon in the buff. I needed my head examined.

I could also see that Kogan had a good motive for killing Ramsden. Hadn't Ramsden just caused the death of Liz Oldridge? What could be clearer than that? Who was closest to Liz in her last days? Kogan. Who would resent her death most? Kogan. Who cared enough to demonstrate in the nude? Kogan. Both Ramsden and Temperley had played a part in Liz's death. Both had kept her away from her money. Who would at the very least shed no tears at their demise? Kogan. I could see Savas coming around to this view if a better prospect didn't materialize. Without money to hire a good lawyer, I could see Kogan's future plans put into the hands of the Minister of Corrections indefinitely.

So, what was I doing? I was trying to stop it. And in order to do this with a mind unclouded by feelings other than those that are right and fitting to exist between a PI and his client, I opened the bottom drawer of my desk and removed an assortment of coat-hangers I'd accumulated there. With them in hand, I went into the bathroom and began fixing the running toilet myself.

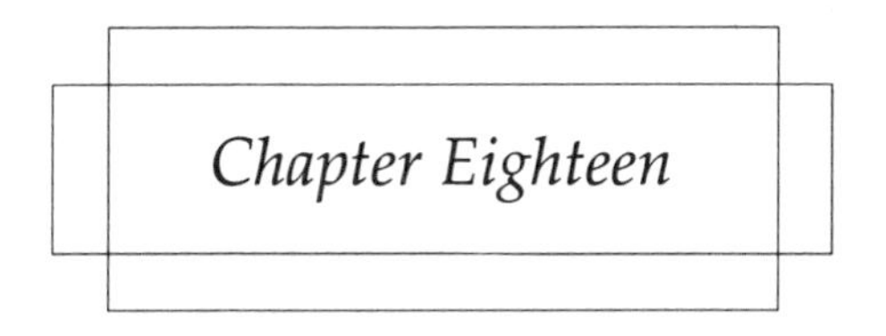

Chapter Eighteen

The Snug in the rear of the Beaumont Hotel was a small-town imitation of an Irish pub. The décor tried its best to make you believe that you were sitting in a hideaway long after closing time. This impression was not sustained by all the local faces in the room. They were all people I went to school with — well, some of them were. They were too Canadian, too caught up in the here and now to help the image The Snug was trying to create. On my way to my seat I heard phrases like ". . . What's the bottom line on that?" and ". . . I didn't want to take delivery of the goddamned pork bellies, I wanted to unload them!"

I was about five minutes early for my appointment. That was easy for me since the hotel was just a short hike up St Andrew Street from the office. I returned the greetings of a few familiar faces, who made no attempt to join me, nor did they invite me to join them. It was that kind of place. It was an intimate extension of everybody's office. The rules were "keep to yourself and mind your own business." Orv Wishart must have come in the back way. I'd been watching the front door.

"Hello, there, Benny," he said. "Sorry I'm a few minutes late. There's always a string of people waiting for me when I'm trying to get away. I should try using the fire escape."

"How is your mother-in-law, Mrs Ravenswood?"

Wishart looked solemn. I couldn't tell whether my question had been taken as an impertinence or whether he was sincerely worried about the old lady. "She's at home. I've got a nurse staying with her for a few days. She hasn't been all that well, you know." I didn't know, but I now knew how her drinking was to be treated. I'd been given the official line. How like a news director: everything had its pigeon-hole.

I sat back and watched the waiter avoiding eye contact with his customers on this side of the room. When he could ignore us no longer, he came to the table, where Wishart ordered Campari and Perrier and I a rye and ginger. I couldn't make Wishart look me in the eye. His hands were actively making patterns on the arm of his chair. He continued to make small talk until the drinks came, then he downed half of his pink concoction that looked like cream soda in one gulp. Finally, the moment arrived. He ran his fingers through his hair and leaned close to the table.

"You remember the other night?" he asked, his eyes still dancing all over the room, like a glitter dome that had lost all but two of its mirrors. I nodded agreement but said nothing. "I saw you there behind the piano," he continued. "I guess you wondered why I was there?"

"Sure. I didn't think you were one of the regulars."

"Ha! That bunch? Catch me!" He took the rest of his drink in one swallow. This time the waiter replaced it before I even looked up. "What would it cost me for you to forget you saw me, Ben?"

"Are you talking seriously? I want to get this straight."

"What's it going to cost?"

"You know that Ramsden's dead? That I was there when Newby found him?"

"Just tell me what you want."

"I'm not a bribe-taking man, Orv."

"Then you haven't told the police that you saw me?"

"I see all sorts of people; I just answered their questions. If they ask me if I saw Orv Wishart lurking around the Kingsway Hall last Tuesday, I'd have to tell them the truth."

"And I can't name a price that would make you forget?"

"It doesn't work that way. I've been told to stay out of the way of the cops in general and away from this investigation in particular. So I'm not volunteering information I'm not asked for."

"You don't think I killed him, do you?"

"It entered my mind. I don't know what I think. Nobody's hired me to think about it. You weren't his only enemy."

"That's for goddamned sure!" I'd guessed right and tried not to let it show on my face. "Maybe you'll come and work for me, Ben?"

"Not likely, Orv. Not after your introductory offer. I'd never be able to keep my right and left hands straight in my head if I did. I try to keep things simple. Why did you want to see Ramsden? Why didn't you leave a message on his machine like the rest of us?" Again I was guessing. Maybe there are some lurkers in the shadows who leave messages on tape, but I was betting that Wishart wasn't one of them.

"It was business. Just business," he said.

"I see. Look, Mr Wishart, I appreciate your friendly

offer, but I can't make it work that way. Okay? If you want to talk, that's another matter; I still have most of my drink in front of me. If you don't want to talk, that's okay too."

"Ben, Ramsden collected things, things belonging to other people, things they would just as soon forget about. Thurleigh kept on reminding them that he still had these things handy, hidden in a safe place. He had something that rightly belongs to me. That night, I wanted to see him about getting it back."

"What are we talking about? A photograph? Letters? What?"

"Why should I trust you?"

"Damn it, Orv, I'm just trying to get a picture of the size and shape of what Ramsden had! It's smaller than a doghouse but bigger than a stamp. Right?" He moved his chin around like he was chewing on a bad almond. It looked like impatience. I could see that he didn't like my questions. Maybe he didn't like being interrupted. It didn't happen that way at the station. On the matter of trust, I gave him my set speech.

"Look, Orv, what you're telling me tonight is private. It's between you and me; it's privileged information. I wouldn't tell anybody what you've told me. But, you started off by offering to buy my silence. That doesn't sit so well. Nobody likes being dragged through a murder investigation. I can appreciate that. If Ramsden was a blackmailer, then he probably had more fish than you. That means the cops aren't going to go after you exclusively."

"If they find his hiding place."

"I wouldn't short-change the cops — even the local cops — on shaking down a house. There aren't all that many places you can hide a doghouse, or even a stamp, when it comes right down to it."

"A letter," Orv said. "We're talking about a letter."

"Does it contain a threat? Is your name on it?"

"No, no, no. It's nothing like that. It's a letter from someone I used to know. This person, in his lifetime, committed an indiscretion. The letter acknowledges this and sets up a trust fund to deal with the consequences." He was talking in generalities, but I was getting good at seeing through them. I put a mystified look on my face and urged him to continue.

"It's not my secret, Ben, or I'd tell you. The letter was written by a very dear friend and mentor. I just can't tell you any more."

"But this letter affects the life of someone else, isn't that so? Someone who probably knows nothing about this?"

"And bloody well isn't going to! Ever! If she . . . Never mind. I've said too much already."

"Why do you want this letter back?"

"So I can burn it or tear it up. Just so I know it's gone."

"And you'd risk a lot to get it. Why? You said it doesn't touch you." Orv wet his lips with his tongue and then wiped his mouth with his knuckles. He stared at them for a moment before answering.

"There's somebody who shouldn't find out about this. It would kill her. If the police find it, they'll go right to her. That's what's eating me up. I couldn't get him to part with it when he was alive and now he's dead I can't get to it."

"You don't like the feeling."

"That's right. I guess I get my own way most of the time." I'm glad he said it. I was surprised that he had that much insight.

"Why did Ramsden turn to blackmail? He was a practising lawyer, wasn't he?"

"He never recovered from that political career of his. Cost him the earth. Especially that run for mayor. That left him in debt. And his legal practice had been badly neglected while he was at City Hall as an alderman."

"I guess things became worse when he lost his wife."

"Yeah. But even when Dora was alive, his affairs were in bad shape. And, you're right, since her death in '89, things have slipped. But you wouldn't know it to look at him. Always the cock of the walk, Burlington Bertie from Bow."

"What does that leave us to talk about?" I asked. "I'm still working on that credit report about that woman on your payroll, what's-her-name?"

"Cath Bracken? Oh!" For a moment he had a cornered look in his eyes. Then he smiled and looked into his empty glass. "Was that really a credit report?"

"It was a job. I get to do things like that now and then. You didn't tell me anything I couldn't have got elsewhere. Saved me some time, that's all." I put my glass down on the placemat. Orv watched me, leaning back in his seat. He'd failed in his mission to buy my silence, but he'd been reasonably assured that I wasn't about to shoot my mouth off. In exchange I'd found out a few things. One of them turned Orv into a reasonable suspect in Ramsden's murder.

We both got up, shook hands and found our way to the front door. I was running into a lot of handshakers these days. The last I saw of Orv Wishart that night was of his large back disappearing into the neon-lit gloom surrounding the hotel.

Near the door of The Snug, I saw two heads close

together. They belonged to Rupe McLay and Antonia Wishart. Neither appeared to notice that Antonia's husband had just left the room. I thought that if I was ever involved with the wife of a member of this community, I would arrange it better than this. In the meantime, the couple sat, huddled over glasses of imported beer and letting the rest of the world go by.

Chapter Nineteen

Anna met me outside my office as we'd arranged. She was driving her own car, so I moved into the passenger seat and buckled up. She leaned over towards me and we kissed. I couldn't help thinking of what a sight we must have looked: two figures restrained by seat belts, kissing with some difficulty.

"What kind of week have you been having?" she asked, putting the car in gear.

"Ramsden's been murdered."

"Yes, I heard that on the radio. How are you involved?"

"I was tailing the guy who found the body."

"Did he do it?"

"No, it had to have happened hours before we got there. You're looking particularly nice this evening."

"Is that a compliment or are you trying to change the subject?"

"Both. Where are we going?" She looked in my direction and frowned.

"You've forgotten! The Christmas party, Benny! The History Department's Christmas party!"

"Damn it. I remember your telling me about it. Should I go home and change?"

"You look terrific. We're only hungry academics. If it's hot, we eat it; if it burns, we drink it; if it's footnoted, we read it."

"Where is it?" I was already on the defensive, beginning to feel warm and ready to squirm.

"Oh, you know Chuck Marley. Immigration History. You've been to his place at least once before."

"Sure. What's his wife's name?"

"Sheila. The kids are —"

"Don't overload my circuits. Wait until we get to the door."

We drove out of town by the Queenston Road and then on to Niagara-on-the-Lake, a town I hadn't seen since last summer when we went to see something that wasn't by George Bernard Shaw at the Shaw Festival. Marley owned one of those sandblasted brick houses that dated from the early 1800s. The place had been restored to within an inch of its life. I got the feeling that the place was so authentic that the original owner would have felt uncomfortable.

We were greeted at the door by Marley, who was an oversized guy with long arms, both of which he used to give Anna a big Christmas hug. He then went on telling me what a gem I had in Anna, as though I was a collector and she an uncut diamond. It made me feel as though I made it my business to slight Anna every chance I got. By her expression, Anna wasn't enjoying Chuck either. This ended when Anna gave him a dig in the ribs with her elbow. Sheila, his wife, came along the hall collecting coats and waving a plastic sprig of mistletoe. The light above us was festooned with plenty of the real thing as Chuck pointed out as he went back to Anna for an encore in front of his wife.

Parties have always been a chore for me. For every conversation you get interested in, there are ten that don't go anywhere. I sometimes think that the coats on the bed are having a better time that I am. It's bad enough when you know the people; here with the university crowd, I felt like taking cover behind three straight Scotches. But I'm a coward. Besides, then I would have missed the fact that McKenzie Stewart was standing at the punch-bowl, filling two cut-glass cups with a cut-glass ladle. He carried the punch over to where a woman was sitting. It was not Cath, but an elderly authority on the American Civil War, as I later discovered.

When he saw me, a smile that was meant for his date died on his face. We made no other contact until much later in the evening, when I found him holding forth on Canadian politics while leaning on the refrigerator door, stopping up the access and passage to more beer. Later still, after the punch-bowl had been emptied for the last time, I heard the name "Ramsden" mentioned. I tuned out the voice of the young man telling me all about his summers in Provence and concentrated on the voices behind me.

"He was something of a military historian, wasn't he?" asked the second voice.

"He had no real credentials as far as I know, but he was an enthusiastic amateur of the Second World War. He was the man to talk to if you wanted to find out what outfit was where. He kept track of regimental movements, details of units, that sort of thing. He didn't care much for overall strategy. Not much interested in high command politics. But he knew a thing or two about ribbons, arms, medals, men mentioned in dispatches."

"I hear he was a colossal snob, Bob. Is that right?"

"That's a bit exaggerated, I think. He was quite proud of the museum he set up for the regiment. I think he liked being the official historian of the Royal Grantham Rifles. You know he was a monarchist with extreme views."

"Extremely unctuous, I heard," said the other.

"That must have been for the joke. But he wasn't 'nice,' whatever that's come to mean."

"Founded the Bede Bunch, didn't he?"

"Yes." Here they both laughed and then changed the subject, which was just as well, because Anna had arrived to try to interest me in Christmas cake.

I could see out the twelve-pane windows that it had started to snow. This was no simple frosting, a rap on the knuckles, a warning of serious snow to come. This was the Great Canadian Winter itself, sending heavy cotton-balls of snow to the ground and covering the cars parked in the driveways and along the street. Christmas lights in the houses opposite glinted through the downfall. Distorted golden fanlights coloured the snow-covered front yards.

Some time later, returning from the bathroom — the toilet seat, by the way, was quilted; the restoration of this house was relentless — I had my third and last meeting that evening with McStu. He was sitting on a staircase leading up to a third floor. He looked up at me and pulled at my pant cuff. "Sit," he said, like a hunter to his retriever. I sat.

"You're McKenzie Steward, right?"

"Cooperman, you know goddamned well who I am. Don't play games with me. Not when I'm pissed, anyway. That's when my mind's super-acute. Where'd you learn karate?"

"From a ninja in Kyoto who was reputedly one hundred and six."

"Goddamned liar! You've never been further away from here than Las Vegas. I looked you up."

"I went to Miami a few times. You don't want to miss that."

"Your fakery saved you a broken nose the other night."

"So I hear. I'm glad I saw that ninja movie."

"You been talking to Cath." He was smiling at the name and I didn't blame him. "She told me. I know about you and your mother and your father. Anna now. I've know Anna for years, you lucky bastard. You don't want to screw that up."

"What's left to talk about?"

"Why were you after Cath?" he asked simply.

"That's my job. One of the things I do. A client hired me and Cath — she asked me to call her that — caught me in the act. Nothing for my résumé in what happened. Either I was careless or somebody told Cath to watch out for me. Maybe you know about that? Where is she tonight by the way? She's not working."

"Some detective!" he laughed. I didn't see the funny side. I'd goofed again. "If she's been snatched the kidnapper took her skis too." He didn't look worried.

A woman reached the top of the main stairs and went into the bathroom. McStu didn't resume his questioning until the lock clicked. "You know who your client is but you don't know who he's fronting for. That right?"

"It's more complicated than that. He may not be interested in Cath at all; he may be trying to keep my nose away from something else. But, supposing my client and his have an interest in Cath, I can't guess what it might be. You may know something there too."

"You were at this for a week?"

"About. It's been like the divorce work I used to do. I noted where she went and who she met, when I could find out. Apart from you, her life isn't full of secrets. I was wondering, Mr Stewart, whether your wife might not be behind this."

McStu told me to call him that and I gave him full play with my given name in return. He pondered my question and worked on his drink, which he was balancing on a tweedy knee. "Moira's been my ex-wife since September. I believe she's happily enjoying her share of my wealth, which isn't much. Shee-it, all I've got left is my ability to make more books. She isn't dining high on my residuals, because there hasn't been a big movie sale."

"You knew Cath while you were still married, isn't that right?'

"Yeah, a long time. Can't pretend I've been a regular senior sixer where Moira's concerned. The biographer will say: 'He was a man of his time in many ways...' Shee-it!"

"Could she have sicced me on Cath, McStu?"

"She put up with a lot from me over the years: all sorts of abuse. Maybe the physical kind was the easiest to take. She saw through black moods, dry spells, moodiness, drinking bouts, depression. What the hell can I say? She deserved the settlement she got."

"How did you two meet?"

"Moira was a champion fencer at university. I was a pair of padded shoulders on the line of scrimmage. Now she wears the shoulders."

"I meant Cath."

"Up at Secord. I was giving a short course on crime fiction. She was in the class."

"Uh-huh."

"No! Nothing like that! I wasn't ever alone with her. She struck me as bright, a good student. That's all! I didn't see her again until she began to work at CXAN."

"When was that? She's been there for over a year."

"It was soon after she started. My publisher arranged a promotion appearance on TV; Cath was the assigned interviewer. I guess you could say the interview is still going on. We met out of town for most of the year. Toronto, mostly, but there was Buffalo and Niagara Falls." He shook his head slowly. "It's not an episode I'm proud of. But it happened."

"I'm not your father confessor, McStu. Things like that happen all the time. People in white hats, people in black hats. Doesn't necessarily make you into a bad guy."

"I suppose it will all be kosher when we make it legal in the spring. Naturally, it won't ever be okay with some. But it will at least stop some of the hounding that's been going on."

"There's a lot of that?"

"Sure. Midnight phone calls, anonymous letters on lined paper, words written in spray paint on my car. We've both had our fill. Even Orv Wishart over at the TV station has had a few surprises in his mail. But, I'll say this for him, he's stuck by Cath. He's never let on that a minority of her public didn't approve of her private life."

"You're talking about racism? I just want to get this clear."

"Sure. Nobody gives a damn about two grown-ups sharing pillows when they're the same colour."

"How do you know about Wishart?"

"He told me and made me promise not to tell Cath."

"For a man of his reputation, he hasn't done badly by

Cath. Why doesn't she like him?"

"Usual reasons. He crowds her, appears to be taking advantage of the employer/employee relationship."

"Has he tried to force himself on her?"

"That's the impression I got. She didn't go into details, but I don't think she'd lie about a thing like that." I didn't quite believe this. I don't know why, but there was a tin note in it somewhere.

This conversation on the steps was interrupted by Anna who was looking for me. She wanted to show me the snow from the window of the front bedroom. With the pile of coats loading the bed like pelts in a Hudson's Bay outpost and catching the light from the window, we looked out onto the snow. I now realized how long I'd been talking to McStu. The snow was burying the cars, covering them so that they looked like they'd been dipped in white chocolate. Heavy flakes were still coming down and there was no sign of a let-up.

"We'll be snowed in in the morning," I said.

Anna put an arm around me and said: "Who cares? I've got a tray of lasagna in your fridge. We can survive for days."

"We have to get there first." She gave me a kiss for my clear-sightedness and we began excavating for our coats.

A few minutes later, I remember feeling the cold snow on my face and kissing Anna again and making an angel in the snow, while Anna laughed herself silly before bottling me up in her car for a slippery ride back to town.

Much, much later, I saw the snow blocking the lower portion of my own windows. I'd crept out of bed. The moon was shining on the street. For a moment, I thought it was getting light out, but it was just the moon. Cars outside were buried, trees were shrouded in white.

Nothing was stirring. I smiled to myself when I remembered where the words had come from. As I turned back to the bed, I thanked whatever powers there be in the world and beyond it for the bump under the covers on the left side of the bed. Then I got back in and tried to close my eyes, eyes that kept flashing back to the events of the morning, and surrender myself to another couple of hours of uninterrupted sleep.

Chapter Twenty

Somewhere there was an aroma of coffee and a feeling of moving about. Instead of opening my eyes, I settled back into sleep again. The smell of coffee and the comforting feeling of bustle around me gave me a sensation of security and peace. It was an illusion, of course, and was exploded by the sudden awakening of the telephone.

"Cooperman," I said, trying to sound alert. I looked around and saw that all signs of Anna had fled. I sat up.

"Savas. You awake?"

"Barely. What's up?"

"I think I'm going to have to bring your buddy Kogan into this Ramsden thing. I know you'd want to know."

"Kogan! Geez, you must be hard up, Chris! Can't it wait till Monday?" I flipped my legs out of bed and wiggled for slippers. Savas didn't say anything. "Kogan had a motive, Chris. I'll give you that, but I'd check out opportunity before booking him. Would Ramsden have let Kogan into his house, let alone invite him into his den?"

"I know all that. I don't like much of it either, but he's the best I've got. It would be different if we knew who was the last person to have seen him alive. But we don't know that, do we?"

I thought of Cath Bracken's early morning appointment to see Ramsden and swallowed hard. "Are you at your office?"

"No, I'm in a pool in Acapulco drinking rum toddies! Where the hell do you think I am on a working day?" Weekend duty was always a sore point with Chris.

"I'm coming over. Give me twenty minutes and tell the desk to let me through."

I skipped the shower and finished the coffee in the carafe before launching myself into the weather. From the apartment, the snow looked like a prize-winning photograph. From the bottom step, it was nothing but a mess. My galoshes were full of cobwebs. My winter hat could not be found. Still, I threw myself out into it and tried to aim towards Church Street. No one had shovelled his share of the snow from the sidewalk. There was enough of it to make walking hard and even dangerous. I took a spin and a tumble before I'd gone more than a few hundred metres. A gang of hungry starlings had a good laugh at my expense as I picked myself up and moved on through the uncharted landscape. It took more than three times the usual time to cover the distance. I arrived out of breath and ready for a long sit.

The pile of galoshes, rubbers and outer boots somehow humanized the normally sterile entrance to Niagara Regional Police Headquarters. It appeared to be peopled by men and women subject to the same natural laws as the rest of us. It was a beginning. I asked for Detective-Sergeant Savas and an East Indian cadet came out to collect me and usher me through the corridors to Homicide. Savas was sitting in his chair with his head buried in paperwork when I came in. There was a puddle of water on the linoleum under the coatrack. From somewhere I thought I got a nostalgic whiff of wet wool drying over a radiator, but there was nothing visible.

"Well, that didn't take long!" Savas said, getting up and heading out the door, as though he was going to take off on a lunch break. But he was back in less than a minute with a styrofoam cup of coffee and a few packets of cream and sugar. He cleared a place for me to use as a camp-site and I settled in. While I was prying off the lid, I could hear him sliding noisily into gear.

"I don't like this Kogan thing any more than you do, Benny." I took a sip from the cup and said nothing. Savas was too good a cop to get himself caught in a stupid error. All I had to do was to make sure I didn't get his back up. "Ramsden was at the very least guilty of negligence in the case of Kogan's girl-friend. Did you know Ramsden swore out an injunction against Kogan coming on the property. Bet your pal didn't tell you that!" The coffee tasted burnt. The cream and sugar didn't help. Chris kept dieselling on. "I can get witnesses to come forward to testify to the defamatory things Kogan was shouting outside the Bede Bunch's meeting. Threats, profanity, libels, slanders, the whole bit. Benny, are you listening?"

"First of all there were no libels, because there was no publication, Chris. Let's stick to the facts. As for the rest of it, I thought they couldn't get anyone to come forward. Why wasn't Kogan booked for these things at the time? It seems like a tasty morsel to hand over to the crown, doesn't it? Before there was a murder involved, your gang just went through the motions. 'Boys will be boys, eh? No harm done. Move along now.' And what about Temperley? Whoever killed Temperley had to have a car."

"One thing at a time. Forget Temperley."

"I still don't see Kogan in this."

"Who else is there?"

"That's better. Half the town hated Ramsden for one thing or another. He was that kind of guy. The liberals hated him because he wanted capital punishment to come back. The minorities hated him because his vision of this country had no place in it for them. The Tories hated him because he gave them a bad name. If there are Reds around, they hated him because he was always blaming them for everything wrong with the country from the weather to the post office."

"Rein in, Benny! Shut up a minute. You're opening up the whole city! I don't need to weigh suspects by the ton. All I need is one that looks as good as Kogan does right now. That's all I want."

"What about the whole blackmail thing?"

"What whole blackmail thing? You talking in tongues, Benny?"

"Ramsden, to my knowledge, kept things — papers, photographs, letters — that would prove embarrassing to several people in this town. He made money off these things and collected it regularly. Didn't you find any of that stuff over at his place? This shouldn't come as a surprise to you at this stage of your investigation, Chris." That was a bad move. I shouldn't have come that close to crediting him with professional sloppiness. That made him mad, and mad wasn't going to help Kogan.

"Now stop right there! What the hell are you talking about?"

"I have a client who says Ramsden was blackmailing him — has been for more than ten years," I lied. Anything to save Kogan. "Hell, my client has a better motive for killing Ramsden than Kogan, Chris!"

"Of course, you're not prepared to tell me who that is, are you?"

"We've been here before on that one, Chris. I can't stay in business if I turn snitch. We both know that. But my point is that if I happen to have stumbled across one extortion victim, there must have been others. You know as well as I do that blackmailers don't outlive rally drivers."

"You think he has a lot of incriminating stuff over on York Street?" This was Chris's way of telling me that his gang hadn't found anything. And why should they? Ramsden wasn't the killer, he was the victim. Why should they toss his place?

"He's got it hidden somewhere. That's as good a place to start looking as any. You still have keys to the house?"

"Now hold on!" Sometimes Chris can see right through me. "I'm not taking you with me! This is police work and last time I looked, you were still freelance."

"Best of luck, Chris. How will you recognize the good stuff when you find it? It doesn't all come boxed and labelled. If you haven't got it already, it means that Ramsden's done a good job of hiding it. Might take you all year. If you can afford to throw away an offer to assist your investigation, I've misjudged how close you are to wrapping this thing up."

Chris pulled at his ear, the way he always did. Sometimes he sucked on his teeth. Pete Staziak lets his mouth gape like a pistachio in its shell. Everybody thinks differently. I'm not sure what I do when an idea is playing around in my head. I hope I still don't pick my nose the way I used to when I was in kindergarten and got told off by Miss Alton about it. It wouldn't be an asset to my practice.

"Okay, Benny. Put on your hat. We're going on a searching party that better not turn out to be a wild-goose chase."

I didn't think I'd ever see the inside of Thurleigh Ramsden's house again. Even with the body removed from the rug, it did not send out waves of welcome to Chris and me as we came across the threshold and into the narrow hall.

I forget what I said about the place the first time around; there were more serious things to talk about. This time I got a feel for the place and through it for the man who'd lived here. It was a small house: the usual rooms downstairs and three bedrooms on the second floor. Two of these had been closed, the beds dismantled and the drawers in the bureaux emptied. The drawers were lined with the same kind of wallpaper my landlady had recently applied to the walls of the stairwell leading to my apartment. I'd have to have a word with her about that.

The downstairs was off balance, because, as I've already said, Ramsden had been using the front room as an office. He had opened up the double doors leading to the dining-room and had relocated most of the soft sofas and chairs there to be close to the television set and an old stereo phonograph. I would have been surprised if Ramsden had converted to CD. The kitchen was small, yellow and untidy. More than the other rooms, the kitchen proclaimed Ramsden's widowhood. He dined alone, at a simple wooden table.

From the pictures, flags, plaques on the wall, I got the impression that Ramsden thought this was a much bigger and grander house. The addition of imitation wood panelling in the study, the large desk all testified to the fact that Ramsden was something of a self-deceiver. The belongings looked like they had been chosen for a bigger house. Perhaps they came from one.

"Well, Benny, this is your show. Where do you want to start?" Chris was in a good mood. He knew that if I found some new evidence, he would profit by it. If I failed to turn up anything new, he was still the winner because he would be able to make a few jokes at my expense. Either way, he was looking good. And, I was forgetting, he still had Kogan.

I knelt down and began pulling back the rug near the desk. Chris squatted noisily, with a knee sending out a crack like a rifle shot. He began rolling the rug back too. First we did the part behind the desk and then the larger part in front. I was looking for loose pieces of hardwood that might be hiding a cache of papers. Unfortunately, all of the floorboards were sound. I didn't bother with the stretch of wood directly under the desk, because he would have had to push the desk out of the way whenever he needed access to the hidden material. I thought Ramsden, judging by his kitchen, was a lazy but pragmatic sort. The stuff would be hidden, but where he could find it when he needed it. I don't think he was a reader of Poe, so I wasn't going to find anything in plain view. Or so I thought then.

"Let's try that panelling next," I said, straightening up with more difficulty than I'd have imagined. Smiling at the absurdity of it all, Chris began to rap the panelling with his knuckles. I picked up a gavel with a brass plaque on it and started at the bottom end. I don't know what we were listening for, to tell you the truth. All I heard from the wall was the occasional dropping of plaster from the old lath behind it. When our rapping got to the same square, we gave up. The whole area sounded the same, but whether that meant there was or was not anything concealed behind it, neither of us could guess.

"We could rip it off," Chris suggested. After a moment, I shook my head.

"No sense in it, Chris. He'd have had to rip it off every time he needed it. I couldn't find a spring or button or release of any kind. There's no part of it mounted on hinges as far as I can see."

"Too many Saturday matinees when you were a kid, Benny." Chris patted his pocket to see if he had cigarettes, then thought better of it. "You think there's a hidy-hole behind those books up there?" I looked over at the rather pinched bookshelf, which leaned heavily to the history of the kings and queens of England. I didn't think that Ramsden would gut the text of these icons of his philosophy for his blackmailing needs, but a row of old legal tomes at the top looked like greener fields.

"Try those," I said, pointing. He moved a captain's chair to the bookcase and stepped up on it. That put him a little higher than top shelf. Above the books, he found something. It looked like an old-fashioned filing box, with a slightly rounded side to make it resemble a book about fifteen inches long. He handed it down so that he could continue his inspection of the law books.

On the spine end of the file was the name "Phoenix" and in capital letters, "Invoices." I could just make out the faded copperplate script: A to Z Orders 1918–1919." I tried to open it, like a book, but there was a catch to be released. When I did that, I could smell mildew and nearly eighty years of use as I lifted the lid. Inside was a set of files divided by tabs marked with the letters of the alphabet. I lifted one, *G*, at random and found a few letters to Ramsden from various people whose names started with that letter. There were business as well as personal letters bearing dates in the recent past, quite contrary to the information on the spine. Among the *G's* I could see no sign of blackmail. I looked further. Thinking of Orv and his problem, I dipped into the *W's*. Here I found a letter from Orv, dated three years ago. It was a request for a meeting on an unnamed subject. In pencil on the top of the letter I read: "put off to October. See Montgomery." I looked among the *M's* there was nothing with a Montgomery on it. "Montgomery" must be something outside the file, an *aide-mémoire.*

"These books are all solid," Chris complained from on high.

"I may be on to something," I said. "Give me a minute." I sat down in Ramsden's chair behind his desk and went through more of the files. Quite a few of the letters had pencilled notes on them. A few of these referred the searcher on elsewhere: "See French," "See Crerar," "See Horrocks," "See Bradley." In each case the file contained no letters from any of these named references.

Chris had come down off the chair and was glancing at the pictures on the wall. He turned a couple of these around to see if there was anything stuck on the backing. "He collected letters from a lot of famous people," he said, looking at some letters mounted between plates of glass.

"Shut up, Chris!"

"How long are you going to be? I think we should have a go at the cellar."

I knew I was close to some sort of answer, but I couldn't see it. I looked a little further, collected a few more dead-end references to McNaughton and Patton. As I closed the file, I asked Savas: "What do all these names have in common: Patton, McNaughton, Crerar, Horrocks, Bradley and French?"

"Horrocks is an English drink, isn't it? And French is mustard."

"You're cold," I said. "They're all top-ranking officers in the British, Canadian or US armies. Montgomery was a Field Marshal, Omar Bradley and George Patton were American generals."

"Never heard of French," Chris admitted.

"That's the First World War."

"So, what's that prove? He was a nut on the military, wasn't he?"

"Yeah, he was the official historian of the Royal Grantham Rifles. I only heard that last night."

"One of the people I was talking to said that he set up the regimental museum, which goes back to Butler's Rangers, whatever they are. He still has the run of the place, or did have, until he got run through with the Union Jack. Like I said, he was a nut on the military. I'm going to look at the basement. Wanna come?"

"I'll join you in a minute. First let me see where this stuff leads to."

"If you don't hear from me in ten minutes, stamp twice on the floor." And he was gone. I reviewed what I'd seen in the file and then got up and started wandering around. Maybe the evidence we were looking for was in the basement. Chris has as good a nose for evidence as I have and his was trained. Mine was just born that way. I looked at the empty socket in the flagstand. I remembered where

I'd seen the missing flagstaff last. I thought, irreverently, of shish kebab. I looked up at the pictures, more to clear my head than anything else.

Behind the flags hung a letter from General Sir Brian Horrocks. It was addressed to our friend and dated in 1960. It was about some action that had been fought around Arnhem in 1944. I turned the letter over. There was nothing on the back. I replaced it and began to notice other letters mounted in a similar way, between plates of clear glass. There was one from General Omar N. Bradley (retired) about General Patton and one from Patton to someone I'd never heard of. It had a stamp at the bottom showing that it had belonged to a collection. Above the small fireplace was the letter I was looking for: Field Marshal Bernard Law Montgomery. I moved the captain's chair and took the letter down. It was a single note from the field marshal, now retired, to Ramsden. It thanked him for his letter, the sentiments expressed in it, but offered no new information. It was the sort of letter that would drive a historian mad. It was a written equivalent of "no comment." Still, the ego of our friend was such that he preserved the letter and its envelope between the two pieces of glass. Even as an autograph, it would be a hard piece to brag about. I turned it over.

This is where I got a surprise. Fitted neatly behind the field marshal's note was a second piece of paper. It was about the same size as the note I'd just read, but the paper was newer and of a different quality. The two pieces of glass had been joined together with dark tape. I took my little red pocket-knife and split the panels apart. I was right: besides the envelope, there were two pieces of paper. The one I hadn't read began:

> The Beacon,
> 20 Queen St,
> Grantham, Ontario.

Dear Edge . . .

and ended:

> As ever,
> Yours sincerely,
> Harlan Ravenswood

The date was 1965. The body of the letter concerned the setting up of a trust fund for someone called Catherine Chestnut, who from the description was clearly a minor. The letter went into details of support payments to a woman called Renée Chestnut of Toronto. The payments to the older woman were to continue until the woman either married or died. The payments to the child were to continue as long as the child remained in an institution of higher learning or until she was twenty-five, whichever occurred last. Then, a lump sum of one hundred thousand dollars was to be paid to her from the investments made by the trust, giving her also at that time whatever assets remained in the trust or their cash equivalent.

The "Edge" in the salutation of the letter was Egerton Garsington, the manager of the Central Branch of the Upper Canadian Bank. He was cautioned to use utmost discretion in keeping the name of the benefactor secret. He was told that under no circumstances was Ravenswood's name to be mentioned to either of the beneficiaries. The letter was dated 2 February 1965.

"That would make her about thirty," I said, thinking out loud. There was much here for speculation, but I had no time to get on with it. There were all of those other preserved letters from famous military men to examine.

Quickly I pulled down all of the glass-encased letters and placed them on Ramsden's desk. I stamped heavily on the floor twice. It was easier pulling the plates of glass apart sitting down at Ramsden's desk. It didn't take me long to get a system going. There was a hidden document of some kind with each of the military letters. I placed each hidden letter with its soldier in a separate pile. One was a note from H. P. Kelmscott, a former member of the Ontario Legislature to a young woman who was addressed in language that could hardly be described as parliamentary. There was a cancelled cheque signed by the head of the biggest paving company in the whole district to a well-known Mafia figure in Hamilton. After looking quickly at the first three, I soon tired of the titillation. Let Savas worry about blackmail in the Niagara Peninsula. I stamped on the floor again. There was no immediate response, but in a minute I heard footsteps on the cellar stairs.

Savas had wisps of cobwebs spread on top of his hair. He looked suddenly aged.

"Take a look at this, Benny!" he said, smiling and panting at the same time. He put three piles of printed pamphlets on the desk on top of my recent discoveries. One was a stack of white supremacist garbage, the one in the middle made many allusions to *The Protocols of the Elders of Zion,* and the third appeared to be aimed at all groups except those who shared the guilt for burning the cakes with King Alfred the Great. "There's a mailing list that comes with this stuff, Benny. I'm glad I went down there."

"But it doesn't give you any names to put on your most-wanted list, does it?"

Chris wiped his face with a handkerchief. "I guess he could have been unpopular among the oppressed nations, Benny. I can't say I'd blame . . ."

"I can see where you're going, Chris. Forget it! This stuff," I said, lifting his pamphlets off my surprises, "is more to the point."

"What have you got?"

"You wanted to find blackmail? I got blackmail. What else can I do for you?"

"Lemme see!" He moved his big head around to look over my shoulder. I lifted the items one at a time and passed them to him.

"They were hidden behind the letters. I guess he read Poe after all," I said, addressing the last bit to myself. Chris let out a few long, low whistles: his way of showing delight and surprise. He couldn't help grinning.

"You know, Benny, this is great stuff! Just great!" He pounded me on the back. He meant it as a sign of praise, but his angle was bad, and I felt myself being nailed into Ramsden's chair.

"Glad you like it." I got up and tried to put the material into a pile so that Chris could slip them into a file he'd brought with him.

"I think you've hit the mother lode of stuff here, Benny. It moves your friend Kogan a lot farther down our list of suspects. That's what you wanted, isn't it?"

Chris was right. That's what I was after. But now, I was encouraged to think there might also be a lunch in it as well.

Chapter Twenty-One

Chris's cousin runs a kebab parlour on Academy Street where I'd eaten with both Chris and Pete a few years ago. It was usually a busy place because of the activity around the bus terminal, but that Sunday it was all but closed when we got there. I couldn't see anything hot on the stove while Chris was exchanging "Yahsoos" and bearhugs with his cousin and his wife, who'd been reading the weekend papers in back, but in a matter of minutes we were tucking into soft roast lamb and big potatoes and gravy. I declined the offer of shish kebab. Chris was in a great mood, joking with his cousins in Greek and with me in English, whenever he remembered that I wasn't fluent in his mother tongue.

The lunch was welcome, filling, but the conversation was not much help to me from a business point of view, although I learned a bit about spring-irrigated fields lying near the north coast of Cyprus. Even when I got him to talk shop, Chris, for all his dancing eyes and grins, was not telling me much I didn't know already. Temperley had been killed late Monday, some time after the grave was opened in the late afternoon. He'd been killed by two shots from an eight-millimetre piece of some kind. "Our guess is that it was a Japanese Nambu automatic, a handgun used in World War II," he said. That's when he reminded me that my pal Kogan had spent some years in the army and might have brought home a few illegal and unregistered souvenirs.

"So? We're back to Kogan, are we?"

"Just a remark in passing," Chris said breezily. "An observation, if you will. It's not the sort of piece you see every day."

"Tell me, Chris," I asked, just after Savas smiled at the good taste of roast potatoes in his mouth, "why was Newby trying to see Ramsden? What was that all about? And how was it Newby so conveniently had keys to let him in when Ramsden failed to hear him at the door?"

"That's a no-no, Benny. Let me just say that we were satisfied with his reasons. They had business. He had the keys from a while back when Ramsden had the house on the market, after his wife died. Newby had the key on his ring." All in all, Chris was feeling pretty good about himself, judging by his generosity with the information he had. Giving up information went against all of his inclination and training. Getting news from a cop is like trying to push a piece of string.

As I walked up Academy to St Andrew, I found time to ponder the other pieces of information that Chris had parted with. According to the post-mortem report, Ramsden had been killed between eight and ten in the morning. I was thinking about that when I stopped in the middle of the street. For a minute I didn't see the gaudy Christmas display in the window of a furniture store I was facing or hear the honking of a half-ton pick-up truck with a bent fender that had come to a stop less than five metres from where I'd suddenly rooted myself.

When the driver added his voice to the sound of the horn, I returned to reality.

Eight-thirty a.m. was the time of Cath Bracken's appointment to see Ramsden! Had she seen him? Had he cancelled? Had she run him through with a flagpole? These were a few of the things I had to find out. McStu, last night, hadn't hinted at anything wrong. I tried phoning Cath at her house from a pay-phone, without any luck. I tried McStu with the same result. I thought of phoning the station, but she didn't read the news on weekends. I wondered about trying to get hold of Wishart. I didn't want to run foul of Antonia, so I closed the phonebook's weathered pages and walked back to the office. At least on a Sunday, I might get a little peace and quiet.

Or so I thought. At the top of the steps I found the door to my neighbour's office ajar. Frank Bushmill, the chiropodist, was inside lying on his carpet. My heart shifted under my shirt: two bodies in two days! That's too much traffic for me. I checked to see whether the body was breathing. Thank God it was. I pulled back and eyelid and got a look at a pink eye trying to remember how to react to strong light.

"Frank!" I called out, slapping his face. "Frank!" I tried to pull him over to the waiting-room couch, where he had often slept one off in the past. With his heavy winter coat, it took all of my strength to get him into a sitting position with his back to the couch. He was groaning now, whenever I tried to shift him. "Frank, what happened?" I could see that his wallet was lying on the carpet, open and empty. There was a blue lump on his forehead.

With another effort, I got him on the couch and called

the ambulance from his phone on the other side of the partition. I found an open bottle of Jameson in his middle file drawer and poured a little into a glass beaker. This I waved under his nose until his eyelids twitched.

"Frank? Can you hear me?"

"Is that you, Benny? What are you saying at all?"

"Frank, you've been walloped on the head and robbed. Do you know where you are?"

"Hit on the head, was I? I remember, I remember, the house . . ."

"Frank, I've sent for an ambulance. I'm going to get the cops too."

"Don't trouble the constabulary. It's their day of rest. I'm thinking it's still Sunday, I hope." He was making a good recovery. I wondered how long he had been out. I had been away from the office since yesterday morning. But Frank can't have been lying there for any great time.

"Frank, do you know who hit you?" He pulled a hand out from under himself and took the beaker from me. He emptied it and looked at me for the first time.

"Damn it, Benny. I always get walloped when I do a favour for you!" He began exploring his forehead with his other hand. "That's a fair goose egg I've got in your service."

"What do you mean, Frank? You're not very clear."

"I heard some noise out here and found two young punks trying to break into your office. I surprised them and then they surprised me. There may have been a third one along the hall who came up behind me. Are you keeping your fortune in your office, Benny? Don't trust the banks, is it?"

"Frank, there's nothing in my office that anybody'd want. No money, nothing but my unpaid bills. I don't even have any interesting files. Nothing that would warrant this." Frank made an attempt to sit up. I helped him. I could see that he was weak, but he kept up a brave commentary until the ambulance people arrived and took him, under protest, down the stairs and off to the General. I put in a call to Niagara Regional Police and told them what had happened.

I waited around for the cops. The investigating officer was called Bedrosian. I remembered him from a long time ago, when I'd been discovered trying to replace a box of jewels that turned out to be a gun. There was no sign that Bedrosian recognized me, but it could have been his investigative style. He'd seen me often enough with Pete Staziak and Chris Savas.

I told Bedrosian what I'd seen and what I'd done. He wasn't as interested in my report of what Frank had told me. He'd have to get that from Bushmill himself as soon as he was feeling better. We walked down the office stairs together after he'd seen me turn off the lights and shut the door of Frank's office.

Out on the street, the chill wind slapped me in the face. I must have been sweating. I did up a few more buttons, then walked up past the intersection where St Andrew Street becomes Queenston Road to the old house with the widow's walk on the turret that housed the offices, mess and museum of the Royal Grantham Rifles. The offices were closed, but the museum was open, empty and warmed by overheated radiators that sounded off occasionally, as though they were being beaten by unseen hammers in the basement. The collection was an extension of Ramsden's office: flags mounted on the floor and photographs and framed letters on the walls. There were cases of flintlocks and carbines of all kinds, copper bugles and ancient mess kits. I went over to the case of side-arms and looked at them for a few minutes.

After a bite to eat, I slushed my way over the sidewalks that still hadn't been cleared. When I found that punks had not tried to force their way into my apartment, I ran a hot bath and spent the next hour in it trying to thaw out.

That night, I caught up on my television watching. Before going to bed, I tried to reach both Cath and McStu without getting answers. Those on the TV program *Mystery!* were all the answers I was going to get until morning and the beginning of Christmas week. I wasn't looking forward to any of it.

Chapter Twenty-Two

"Hello?" It was the phone and it was ringing in the dark and I hadn't answered it yet. My greeting was fakery, mere time-wasting until my hands could locate the instrument. When I had it, I repeated my rehearsed line with an excellent result. The clock on the bedside table told me that it was eight o'clock in the morning. In spite of the dark, I couldn't curse the intrusion and call it unreasonable.

"Hello, Benny?"

"Yeah? Who is this?"

"Cath. Cath Bracken. I just heard about Ramsden."

"Where the hell have you been for the last two days? I've been trying to raise you three or four times a day."

"I went skiing. I hadn't planned on it, but McStu couldn't get away. I just went off to enjoy the snow and the weekend. I heard about Ramsden on the seven-thirty news as I was driving home."

"So, you've been totally cut off from civilization since your eight-thirty meeting with the dead man. Are you sure you didn't panic and run for it?"

"Benny, if I'd panicked, it would have taken me further away than Fonthill! The hills were wonderful!"

"Ramsden is dead!"

"Oh, I know! *Now* I know, but I didn't know when I saw him that he was going to be murdered. The weekend's already making me feel bad. Don't you spoil it too!"

"Where are you?"

"At home. Where else should I be?"

"Well, one place might be in the cells on the basement level at Niagara Regional Police."

"What are you talking about?"

"Cath, the post-mortem report shows that he was killed between eight and ten on Saturday. You saw him in that period. Now do you understand?" There was a long pause, then:

"You better come over." She didn't even say goodbye. I heard the click and reached for the light switch.

About thirty minutes after I'd hung up the phone, I parked the Olds in front of Cath's house across from the snow-capped mountain of pulpwood on Oakdale Avenue. I recognized McStu's car parked next to a snowdrift in front of me. Cath's BMW was in the shovelled-out drive. McStu opened the door before I could knock.

"Morning," he said, waving a cup of coffee in my direction. I took it and he indicated the way to the kitchen. I followed and found Cath sitting at a plain pine table. She looked up as we came in.

"Hi," she said without any great enthusiasm. "What you said on the phone . . . You've got me worried."

"Have you ever been fingerprinted?" I asked. "For any reason?"

"Never. Why?"

"Well, the cops will have lifted prints from Ramsden's house. Some of them are bound to be yours, if you touched anything. But, if your prints aren't on file, then they won't bother you unless they find some record of your appointment in his date book, for instance. Your appointment may be recorded on his answering machine."

"He called me, Benny. He named the time and I agreed to come alone and without a camera crew." McStu came around behind Cath, sipping his coffee and putting his free hand on Cath's shoulder.

"What time did you get there? I mean was it before or after eight-thirty?"

"I was right on time, maybe a minute or two early. I was a little nervous about seeing him."

"Was he alone?"

"There was no one I saw," she said, drawing out the "saw" so that I wondered what her other senses told her. Cath was wearing faded blue jeans, a red, rag-wool sweater and glasses, which made a new Cath for me anyway. McStu was in heavy twill trousers. On top he was wearing a big white Irish pullover with a crew neck. There was a large loaf of brown bread on a cutting-board, to which he returned while Cath was telling me what happened.

"He answered the door himself and we went right into his office in the front of the house. He saw my cassette recorder and told me that he didn't want to be taped. So I put it away."

"What sort of mood was he in? Did he look harassed or bothered about anything? Was he preoccupied?"

"I suppose the fact that I was with him less than ten or fifteen minutes might be interpreted that way. I'd expected to stay longer, but he gave short answers — not very satisfactory answers — to my questions. Some he just shook his head at or waved his hand telling me to get on to the next."

"What was the gist?"

"Denial. He wasn't responsible for Oldridge's death. He didn't know of her financial difficulties. He hadn't seen her for a long time before her death, but stood ready to help, had she got in touch with him. In spite of the evidence brought out at the inquest!"

"Did he say anything about the property or Liz's will?"

"Just that he was surprised and delighted to accept the property on behalf of the Bede Bunch. Did he think I didn't know that he had helped her write the will?"

"And he was its sole executor," added McStu, handing me a sandwich. I took a peek at the filling and put the sandwich back on the plate.

"I asked him if there were any plans in the offing to sell the property. That was one of the questions he dodged."

"I asked you before whether you thought there was anyone in the house with you and you said that you didn't see anyone. Did you *feel* that there was another visitor?"

"Yes! Now you mention it. I can't place it exactly, but I felt that I was interrupting something. But I can't prove it. I honestly didn't see or hear anything."

"Ben," McStu asked, "is Cath a suspect at the moment?"

"No. To the best of my knowledge, we're the only ones who know about her appointment. But she was probably the last person to see Ramsden alive."

"Except the murderer."

"Yeah, except for the murderer. Did you tell anyone at the TV station that you were going to see Ramsden?"

"Orv Wishart knew I was trying to get to see him. He knew about the pocket-documentary I was putting together about Liz's death."

"Did he encourage you?"

"Orv is *all* encouragement. He can't do enough for me. He must be the last man on earth who still opens doors for women."

"But he didn't know the date and time of your appointment to see Ramsden?"

"It's written on the pad on my desk. If he looked he'd see it. It wouldn't be the first time that he's been into my things when I'm not there."

Orv bothered Cath. It came out in everything she said about him. She owed her job to him and she disliked the fact and the further disagreeable fact that she might have to put up with his familiarity if she wanted to hold the job. She'd been reading the news at the station for more than a year. When could she consider that the job was hers?

"You haven't touched your sandwich," McStu said, and I looked at the uneaten sandwich on the white plate beside me. But he'd been talking to Cath, who picked up her own sandwich and took a bite. I did the same, but I stayed on the crusts and didn't get into the part with the filling. It wasn't that I was Orthodox; it was just that I hate surprises. Virginia ham is a surprise that takes some getting used to. I went on nibbling and listening to catch anything Cath remembered about her meeting with Ramsden.

"You really scared me, Benny, when you suggested that the killer might have been in the house with us."

"Time of death is a pretty hard thing to pinpoint," I

said, catching the look McStu gave me. As a crime writer, he probably knew more about time of death and rigor mortis and lividity than I did. Why doesn't he try to get to the bottom of this business like the crime writers on television always do?

I managed to sneak my plate over to the wooden side-board by the sink and ditch my sandwich.

"Cath, how did you know I was following you? It's a matter of professional pride."

"Oh, Benny, I should have told you at your mother's. I got a tip by telephone."

"A tip? From whom?"

"It was a man's voice. Of course, he didn't give me his name."

"An anonymous tip! Just like that?"

"You want me to take a lie-detector test?"

"Benny, she told me about it," McStu added from the sidelines.

"Okay, okay! I believe you. What did you do about it?"

"I tried leading you all over the place, but then I just had to find out who you were. That's when I started tailing you. I am a trained investigative reporter, you know."

"It's the answer I was hoping for. I'm not getting feeble in my old age after all. Speaking of being a reporter, you once told me you'd started doing a documentary about Liz Oldridge." I began climbing into my boots and coat as I waited for Cath's answer.

"I'd made a start."

"You said you talked to Clarence Temperley. When?"

"A few days before the inquest."

"I've got to see that tape, Cath!"

"Sure. All that stuff is in the bottom drawer of my desk at the station. Just tell Robin who you are and he'll set it up for you. I'll call him now. You really think that the tape with Temperley's serious stuff?"

"I won't know until I've seen it, Cath. I'd better get over there." I finished getting into my things, while McStu and Cath watched.

"I'm staying around for a few days, Ben," McStu said. "Just to see how things go." McStu held Cath close as I struggled with the door.

"Benny!" It was Cath and her eyes were wide.

"What is it!"

"You know I had this feeling that we weren't alone? Well, I just remembered where it came from. There were two briefcases in his office. One near his desk and one near the chair I was sitting in. That's what gave me the feeling that I was in the middle of something!"

"You didn't tell me that!" said McStu.

"I just remembered!" she said grabbing his hand. "It was a big, hard-cornered briefcase, battered, old, but with good leather. I remember that I had to move it so that I could sit down."

"So, it was to the right of the chair?"

"Yeah. That makes the killer right-handed, right?"

"Cath," McStu interrupted. "This is serious. You're not on TV now." She made a face at McStu and won a smile in spite of the scolding.

"Any other last moment block-busters?" I asked as I opened the door. Cath and McStu were again occupied with one another as I went across the groaning frozen boards of the porch to the steps.

I was putting my money on the improbability that

Cath was herself the killer of Thurleigh Ramsden. This assumption lay outside the realm of evidence and proof; it was little more than a feeling in my bones, a hunch, coupled with the fact that I liked Cath and I didn't much care for Ramsden dead or alive. It was a perfect set-up for making an ass of myself. I'd better be right about her, I thought, as I fought to open my half-frozen car door.

Chapter Twenty-Three

As I went up the elevator, it hit me that this was the second time that I'd visited Frank in a hospital room after he'd been banged on the head. The first time was about ten years ago, but I could still remember his huddled form wedged behind my office door, as though it was last night. This second instance was almost forgotten already, although I didn't intend to tell Frank that.

Dr Frank Bushmill belonged to a fine old Irish family and had brought with him to Grantham one of the better-educated minds. While he worked with feet for a living, it was heads he was interested in. Mine, for instance. He kept telling me about the books I should read and when I made no step to get them, he presented me with copies, sometimes calf-bound and inscribed. He was a particular fan of the Irish writer Flann O'Brien, who had signed all of the books he lent me. In a way Frank was hiding out in Grantham, waiting for the tinkle of a mass bell in his brain that said it's all right to come home. All is forgiven. Frank was one of the saddest gays I'd ever met. He drank too much and he lived on the edge of suicide when the black depression hit him. There weren't many weeks that went by when I didn't at least once find him on the floor or on his couch in the faded past of an exalted moment. He was an easy drunk to deal with: he didn't get mean or amorous. When he was sober, he was a great fan of Anna Abraham and me. We sometimes went to the movies together.

When I saw that the door was closed, I wondered whether I shouldn't check back with the nursing station. I didn't want to wake him if he was asleep. But I decided to try it and take the consequences. As it turned out, he was in the middle of getting his clothes on. He had managed everything but his shoes when I came in.

"Shut the door behind you, Benny, for God's sake, or we'll have all the orderlies in the place coming in!"

"You must be feeling better," I observed.

"The fact is, they need the bed, and that's the truth. My X- rays aren't even dry and the little bit of a candy-striper comes in and announces 'You're out of here!' You're out of here! Just like that. I turn on the child and repeat an ancient Irish curse. 'Out of here?' says I. 'How are you!' And she says 'Give us a kiss' and closes the door behind her. What's the world coming to?"

"How's the lump on your head?"

"It'll do, Benny. I'm not looking to improve on it. 'Twill serve."

"Did you get a good look at the men who did it?"

"I told you at the time, Benny. Is it you or me who's been hit about the head? Two, maybe three young punks. I gave a description to that fellow Bedrosian. Now try to cheer me up while I try to remember how to tie up the other shoe."

"Where do you want me to start? I've been following a woman and got caught in the act by the woman herself. I must be getting old."

"She was tipped you were behind her, Benny. She was watching out for you."

"Yeah, it could be that. And it could be that that's what she wants me to believe. I don't think I understand this woman. She's as smart as hell, but she's still worried that her boss might be after her. She thinks he's one of those old-fashioned employers whose interest in his female employees runs into their private lives."

"This is the way the world ends, Benny, not with accord but assault."

"That's the way Cath sees it, but I'm not sure she's got it right. I think she's caught some of that show-business paranoia people in television get."

"Yes, Narcissus with a polluted pool; a cracked mirror gives a bad reflection. You wouldn't be talking about the face on the TV news, now, would you, Benny?"

"Forget I said it. See, I'm losing all my marbles at once. There goes another professional secret."

"Oh, it's safe with me, my lad. Just think of how many of my patients *you* know about! Bunions by the billions, corns beyond counting. But, Benny, you can't be serious about Cath Bracken's boss? That's Orville Wishart."

"That's right. So what?"

"Well, Benny. How can I put it delicately? There are those inclined to white wine. Some prefer red. Orv Wishart looks not upon the wine when it is red. No more than I do, if you follow my drift."

"You mean . . . ?"

"Exactly. For in the end it stingeth like the adder."

"I think you're giving it a bum rap, Frank, but we all have our prejudices and hang-ups. Most of us prefer red."

"There you are. There's no accounting for tastes."

"You're sure about that, Frank?"

"My boy, I'm not given to common gossip. You may take it as common knowledge within a small informed group."

"He's not maybe a fan of both red and white?"

"The taste for rosé is not well-developed in our friend, Benny. You may take it from me." Frank got up from the chair, wobbled a little, then straightened himself with a hand on the back of the chair. He glanced at the small mirror on the back of the closet door and gave himself a friendly grin. "Now, may I buy you a coffee?" he said, and we walked out of the room, past the nursing station, to the elevator.

It was close to an hour afterwards that I left Frank sitting in a booth at the Di. I'm not sure what we talked about. His earlier revelation had quite taken over my mind and made things that I thought were facts appear as the shams they were. I could now see why Orv's wife, Antonia, was interested in reclaiming Rupe McLay, the drunken lawyer from the Nag's Head. I could strike off Orv's amorous interest in Cath as the reason for my being hired by Newby in the first place. But he could still have some other interest in Cath, some reason I couldn't guess at. The more I wondered about this, the more I wanted to talk to Orv.

As I pointed my steps in the direction of the TV station, I began wondering about the three punks who tried to get into my office. What could they have been after? Who put them up to it? Were they hired by whoever got Newby to hire me? I stopped and stared at my reflection in the window of Woolworth's while I worked that one through. What could they think I had? If someone like Orv had hired me through Newby, why didn't he just send for me and make an offer? It was getting murky in my mind; I couldn't work it out. I pulled in my belly, readjusted my belt and continued down the street.

When I arrived at the station, Robin O'Neil was waiting for me. He didn't look too happy about it. "So, you've taken your young protégée to Catherine Bracken, have you? Bypassing your old friend?"

"What protégée, Robin?" Then I remembered the invented cousin I'd used in my last conversation with Robin. His nose was out of joint and he didn't care who knew it. "I've got the tapes you wanted here," he said as he took me to Cath's desk. There were half a dozen cassettes all neatly labelled. I found the one with Temperley's name on it and handed it to Robin. He said "Follow me!" as though it was a killer curtain line in a play he was directing. I followed and let him play with the fancy buttons on the electronic gear in an editing alcove.

Soon I was watching a well-lighted Clarence Temperley blinking as the lights were readjusted and the interview got moving. For a while he answered Cath's off-camera questions about Liz Oldridge without adding greatly to my knowledge. The key part of the interview was the following exchange:

CATH: You came to your present position in the bank on the death of the former manager? Is that right?

CLARE: Yes. Edge Garsington died at his summer place quite suddenly. I was brought in to hold things together.

CATH: And Liz Oldridge was one of your customers then?

CLARE: That's right. She was already an eccentric.

CATH: You were a party to the agreement between Thurleigh Ramsden and Ms Oldridge concerning her safety deposit box?

CLARE: I was there and tried to make bank policy clear to both parties.

CATH: You were also there when Oldridge tried to gain access to her box without Ramsden?

CLARE: That was an unfortunate scene. Yes, I was there.

CATH: Am I right in saying that she wanted to take money from the contents of the box?

CLARE: Yes, and I explained that in the light of their agreement, I couldn't let her.

CATH: She was quite upset, was she?

CLARE: Oh dear me, yes!

CATH: Did you explain to her that she could void the agreement?

CLARE: She couldn't void the agreement! Mr Ramsden would also have to sign.

CATH: Mr Temperley, I've talked to a number of bank managers and they told me that these arrangements are to a degree discretional. As bank manager, you could have bypassed the joint-access agreement.

CLARE: I would never have done such a thing. An agreement is an agreement!

CATH: But, according to the bank's rules and guidelines and traditional practice under similar circumstances . . .

CLARE: An agreement had been entered into. Mr Ramsden was not present.

CATH: But the money in the box didn't belong to Mr Ramsden, did it?

CLARE: I . . . ! You see, Mr Ramsden's instructions to me were . . . The woman was not in her right . . . I was within my powers not to let Miss Oldridge . . . Sorry, I'm making a muddle of this. I don't want to spoil your tape. I believe that I chiefly explained to Miss Oldridge the agreement as it had been set up and as it existed.

Clarence was now looking flustered and confused. There was a shine on his forehead. The interview broke off a few moments later.

"That's all there is on this tape, Benny. You want to see any of the others?"

"No thanks, Robin." I walked with Robin and watched him put the tapes back in Cath's bottom drawer. He accompanied me to the door, but I thought I might drop in on Orv Wishart for a few minutes and explained as much to Robin, who made some remark about my cousin soon becoming his supervisor and walked back into the TV part of the building. I went up the stairs.

Orv got out of his big chair when I came into his office. "Benny! I didn't think I'd be seeing you again so soon!" He kicked the open door closed as he shook my hand warmly and returned it to me numb. The pain quickly moved up to my shoulder. "Sit down! Sit down! Can I get you some coffee?"

"Yes you may," I said, recalling the proper use of "can" and "may" from my school days. I took a chair and moved it closer to the desk. Orv went out of the room to delegate someone to prepare the refreshment. Through the open doorway I could see men and women running back and forth with wire-service copy from one office to the next. When Orv returned, he again closed the big white door behind him.

"It won't be a moment," he said, taking that huge chair, which gasped at his weight. He let the chair swing around, so that I could catch a glimpse of the statue of the canal-builder through the window. He caught me looking and said: "Harlan Ravenswood's father once told me that *his* father had met William Hamilton Merritt, the canal-builder."

"Really?"

"He was cracking walnuts with a fire-poker. Funny how a thing like that makes history come alive."

When the coffee came, I let a moment go by and then spoke: "I've seen the letter that Harlan Ravenswood wrote to Egerton Garsington."

"What?"

"The police have it now. I suggest that you call Detective-Sergeant Savas and tell him about your interest in it. That way it won't get back to the old lady. That's who you're trying to protect, isn't it?"

"Wait a minute! This is going too fast! Where did you see this letter?"

"Ramsden's house. The cops asked me to assist them in searching the place for hidden documents."

"You bastard! They wouldn't have known there were any hidden papers if you hadn't told them!" Orv was literally getting red under the collar. Even in his involuntary actions he couldn't resist a cliché.

"The cops won't pass it around. Would you rather have some collector of rare letters get his hands on it? If I hadn't found it, it would have been sold off with the household furnishings. This way, you'll get a chance to give the cops a context to put it in. And, by the way," I added, to distance me from his temper, "I found other letters just as interesting. Ramsden had the bite on several of our fellow citizens." He seemed to be settling down; enough to drink some coffee anyway.

"You came here to tell me this? Why?"

"I hoped I could prompt you to tell me the rest of it. I've read the letter, Orv."

Orv began shaking his head. "Sorry," he said, "it's not my secret. I gave a promise. Figure it out as well as you can. You won't be able to say that I helped. I don't want innocent people hurt."

"Is that it? You don't want them *hurt?* I thought there might be an opportunity here for someone."

"I think you've said what you came to say, Benny, and now you've said it, I have a station to run." He had managed to tease a hurt smile onto his face, but he wasn't going to win an award with it.

"Will you answer a couple of questions that are unrelated to the letter?"

"That depends. Let's hear them."

"What can you tell me about the relations between Ramsden and the family?"

"They were terrible. Chalk and cheese on every subject. He thought that we're all Reds. It made him mad when the Ravenswoods wouldn't support him or any of his policies. Now, as you know, the family hardly counts as socialists. Hell, in the States they'd be Republicans, even conservative Republicans."

Orv had been demonstrating with his cup as he spoke. He now paused to drink from it and return it to its saucer. "Harlan always had friends in high places. Blame it on his class, his education, his — It was certainly more than money, although there was plenty of that. He called federal cabinet ministers by their first names and premiers would join him for fishing up at Go Home Bay, let their hair down and dig worms. That drove Ramsden mad! Ramsden with all his noisy flag-waving and 'Up the Empire!' nonsense appeared silly and beside the point when you're watching the prime minister select a trout fly."

"If he hated the family so much, why was he just blackmailing Harlan? Why didn't he use what he knew to disgrace the family name?"

Orv chuckled at that and scratched his chin. "I don't think he could get anybody to use it. I bet he tried. I *know* he tried to get to Gladys more than once. But the staff has always had orders where Ramsden is concerned. In general, he went away happy getting his mite first from Harlan and then, after Harlan passed on, from me. I think that Clarence Temperley, the bank manager who took over from Edge Garsington, kept an eye on Ramsden. They had a few deals together, and Clare had enough common sense for both of them. Not that I'd call Clare as sound a man as Edge had been. Clare always was a man to catch the nearest way, if you know what I mean."

"Do you think that Temperley might have seen the letter we were talking about in Edge Garsington's files when he took over at the bank?"

"I hadn't thought of that! Certainly he and Ramsden were always pretty close. Temperley must have been one of the few people who liked Ramsden. Harlan always called Ramsden 'Thoroughly Rotten Ramsden!' " He laughed thinking about it.

"Temperley wasn't Ramsden's only helping-hand, was he? Didn't he have other people going to bat for him?"

"Well, he had dealings with all sorts of unsavoury people. There was a Toronto printer who got into the headlines. Nasty piece of work he was. Luckily, they put him away. I think he's on a funny-farm someplace."

"Anyone else?"

"You knew that he was Steve Morella's brother-in-law, didn't you?"

"Steve Morella as in 'Frenchie's Fries'? I don't think I knew that. They married sisters? Is that it?"

"The Rudloe sisters from near Welland. Ramsden lost his wife in a car crash on the Burlington Skyway about two years ago. It was a year after that that Morella divorced Sue Ellen. If you want the details of that, you'll have to go to Morella or to Julian Newby. He handled the divorce from Morella's end. That drunk, Rupert McLay, handled it for Sue Ellen."

"But before the death and the divorce, Ramsden and Morella were chummy?"

"I wouldn't choose that word, Benny. Morella was starting as the newspaper on the bottom of the birdcage in this town. He knew nobody and nobody wanted to know him. I'm not going to make any excuses for it. That's just the way it was back then. From Morella's position, Ramsden seemed to stand for the steady old-time values. So, they were close for quite a time. But never chummy. Morella's a bright fellow, so it didn't take him long to see what a strange fake Ramsden was. So, he put some distance between them. There was the marriage connection and I think they had a few joint business deals, but Morella's name never appeared on Ramsden's petitions to deport the Chinese students up at Secord or to drive McKenzie Stewart away from his teaching post because of his odd lifestyle."

"What's odd about it? Shacking up in this day and age isn't enough to get your name in the papers."

"There are a few bigots around who objected to McStu's colour."

"I forgot about them. They won't go away, will they?"

"Don't I wish. Next question."

"Does Ramsden have any connection with Julian Newby?"

"Not that I know of. They're both members of the local bar association. But even Rupe belongs to that! Newby's Morella's chief legal adviser in all of his business dealings. When Ramsden's involved with Steve Morella, then Newby might get a Ramsden aftertaste. What I'm trying to say is —"

A phonecall put an end to our conversation. As he replaced the receiver, he explained that he was wanted in an important meeting. His almost painless handshake unaccountably reminded me of Julian Newby. I found my way down the curved white staircase and out into the street. The momentary reminder of Newby stayed with me as I turned my feet in the direction of my office. We'd had lunch at his club a week ago. I hadn't been able to tell him that I had screwed up my tailing of Cath Bracken — or had it screwed up for me. I had to officially resign from our contract. I was also curious to know how he was faring in the aftermath of finding Ramsden's body. There were lots of things to think about on a working day.

Chapter Twenty-Four

The call I'd been dreading from Chris Savas was the only call that my answering service had to report. I'd had my forty-eight hours, now Chris wanted me to come in for a little chat. During our lunch on Sunday, I'd hoped that he would refer to this deadline, hoped he'd cancel it in the light of the stuff we'd dug up at Ramsden's place. He was happy enough with what we'd found, all right. Maybe I should have brought it up at the time. I'm too much of the "sleeping dogs school" for my own good. How would I deal with Savas? I wasn't sure. If I told him he'd be crazy to lock up Kogan, he'd probably do it just to spite me. Kogan was nobody. There wasn't a body of concerned citizens who were going to protest about the violation of Kogan's civil rights. If I told him nothing and stood my ground, he might get nasty in my direction. There were even fewer concerned citizens who'd worry about me. I took a chance, picked up the phone, curious to hear what I was going to say.

As luck would have it, Chris wasn't in his office. I left my name and felt that my forthright intentions had earned me this temporary escape.

Since I was still holding the phone, I put in a call to Scarp Enterprises.

"M'yeah? Scarp. What can I do for you?"

"Martha?"

"That's the name. Who wants her?"

"It's Benny. I love your telephone technique, Martha, but I don't understand it."

"I didn't ask to be the chief telephone answerer, Benny, since you ask. What can I do for you, you little imp? Lunch is out; I'm being taken out by someone of quality."

"Who wants to pick your brains?"

"You're a suspicious rascal! Of course he wants to pick my brains, but over a good lunch! Not at the places you frequent."

"Martha, the last time we had lunch you said you didn't have time to be wined and dined. But blame Benny if it makes you feel better."

"What do you want this time, Benny? You want to take me to lunch tomorrow? I've got a last-minute cancellation."

"I may be in the lock-up tomorrow lunch, Martha, if I don't find out a few things."

"A deft parry, you little beggar. I forget the name of the fellow doing the cooking in the lock-up these days. I don't *think* he was a poisoner. What do you want to know?"

"What were the money and property arrangements when the Morellas split?"

"Ha! You don't want much for nothing!" she said, nearly piercing my eardrum. "Let me think. From what I heard, Sue Ellen got a bigger chunk of everything than anybody'd expected. She has a cotton-candy mind, Benny. No head for figures. Morella's loaded, right? But it's all tied up in small companies with numbers instead of names. You'd need a licensed pilot to steer a course through his holdings. From what I hear, he wasn't being all that cooperative, but somehow, she managed to dig up the names of most of his nearly invisible assets. She got a good share of these, adding a couple of million to what she would have gotten without the effort."

"Work conquers everything," I said. "That was the motto of our high school, only it was written in Latin."

"Yeah, Sue Ellen went there too and she took the motto to heart."

"Martha, where can I get all this stuff? I mean, where would it be recorded?"

"Try the files of the lawyers concerned. Who were they? Julian Newby's one —"

"And Rupe McLay's the other."

"Well, you won't get anywhere with Newby. You might as well try the other place, if you can find him above the table level."

"Thanks. I'll sweep out the drunk tank, while I'm at it. Martha, I want to thank —"

"Sure, Benny. Any time. B'bye." And she was gone before I had completely rounded out my gratitude in words. I held on to the phone for a couple of seconds after the line went dead, in case Savas was trying to raise me. In the end, I replaced the receiver and sat back in my chair staring at it. Sometimes a silent phone can be a lot noisier than a ringing one.

I was still running away from the sound of my quiet phone as I moved east along St Andrew Street. Snow from the sidewalks and the street had created a modest rampart in the gutter that made crossing the street hazardous except at intersections. I crossed over in front of the Lincoln Theatre. Christmas ornaments had been mounted on wires straddling the street. There was a lot of silver tinsel and coloured lights. The effect was as cheering as that of the plastic candy canes attached to the light standards. Either the decorations weren't in the mood for Santa or I wasn't. I couldn't decide which.

The sound of "Away in a Manger" coming over a pair of stereo speakers mounted outside Frenchie's Fries didn't help improve my usual denial that the season was once again upon us. I could already taste the familiar depression, the last gasp of the old year and reheated turkey. The feeling comes with the denial that I too will have to make a list and check it twice. I never suspected that this annual sensation had anything to do with my being Jewish. I got the same feeling when it was time to wind up all activity and get down to doing my income tax. Both were interruptions of normal activities. Both were inevitable, both wouldn't take "no" for an answer.

The plaque on the exhaust hood said: "FRENCHIE'S FRIES — No. 1." You could see it through the glass. I went in and sat down at a pedestal stool at the counter. The place was half-full. I recognized merchants my father's age sitting together in the centre and a group of kids from the high school trying to decide between ketchup and vinegar. Morella was standing behind the counter. His face had retained its youth although the blond hair had gone steel grey. He still wore it short and perhaps there was more forehead than there used to be. He was dressed in the standard white apron I'd first seen him in years ago. It was stained with oil.

"I know you," he said as I glanced at the menu, "You're Manny Cooperman's boy. Are you the doctor or the other one?" He still smiled with all of his face, not just with the corners of his mouth.

"I'm the other one, Mr Morella." He lifted a container of steaming French fries out of a vat and turned them out into a large sieve for draining.

"You know my name. That's remarkable. Around here people don't even look at my face. I'm just a pair of hands dishing out fries." To illustrate what he was saying, he dished out two orders and added gravy to one of them before delivering the plates to the two men seated at the other end of the counter. He talked to them for a few seconds then came back to the control centre of his frying vats. After he had filled another order, he returned to me.

"Your father's a great gin rummy player. You know that, I suspect. But I don't think he knows just how good he is. If he was a younger man, he could go anywhere, do anything with a pack of cards. It's a kind of genius. We call him 'the hammer' because he won't let up. He has an instinct for the jugular. It's an odd combination in such a friendly man. What can I get you?"

"Let's try the famous fries again. Are they still the same as they used to be at the corner of Queen and St Andrew?"

"Ah! You remember the truck, do you? You know, I've still got that truck. Can't make myself throw it away. And why should I? It made me my first dollar. In the end, it made me a millionaire. So I guess I can afford to give it room to rust in, eh? What can I get you to drink?"

"Coffee." When he brought it, I said: "I don't get this, Mr Morella."

"Steve, please."

"Steve."

"What don't you get?"

"Call me Benny. I don't understand what you're doing

here in an apron, up to your elbows in cooking fat. Isn't there a mountain of paperwork on the top floor of the Venezia Block waiting for your signature?"

"Let it wait! Let it wait! This is the important part of my job: talking to you, watching the faces, seeing what people eat and what they leave on their plates, seeing who comes in and who walks along the street to the next place."

"I see, but —"

"Look, anybody can buy three, four, half a dozen freight cars of potatoes. I've got people working for me who can tell where I should go to get the best deal. But who have I got to tell me why I should buy them and who am I buying them for?"

"You like a hands-on approach. I can see that that does very well here. But what about your other outlets?"

" 'Outlets': that's the kind of word my hired help uses. It turns them all into rubber stamps. They're all different, Benny. The one in Duluth isn't the same as the two in New Orleans. The three in Montreal aren't like the one that just opened in Paris. Each one has settled into its own community. But they all have my sign over the door." Steve Morella brought a cold cup of coffee to the counter and continued to explain.

"Just as the truck was right for the top of Queen Street, the new place in Paris has a zinc bar and serves good cheese and wine."

"You know your food!"

"Listen, Benny. Food is the study of my life. I was busy in the kitchens of big English hotels when I couldn't speak a word of English. I learned this racket from dishwasher and bus boy up through the ranks. I know all the angles."

"How are you going to deal with the death of your former brother-in-law, Thurleigh Ramsden?"

"Ha! They weren't kidding about you! You come right to the point!"

"After ordering a deck of fries, yeah."

"Ramsden's Newby's problem. I don't get in his way. Look, Benny, if Ramsden's death complicates things, I can live with it. I deal with the possible. Let Julian play games with making things happen. He knows Ramsden's business as well as I do. All I see coming out of this is delay. I can live with delay. I'm a patient man. Newby says there's a way to save the situation. I believe him. That's what he's good at. So far he's never let me down." At this moment, a man in white appeared holding a telephone.

"Steve, it's for you!" Steve Morella looked at me in a way that told me the telephone was the bane of his existence. He grinned and held his hand over the receiver.

"Look," he said, still smiling, "a fellow could get hurt messing around in a town like this. You know what I mean? Take it easy, Benny, and give my best to your father." A moment later he was deep in conversation on the phone. This too left no doubt about who he thought was in charge. I ate my fries, which were as good as I remembered them, paid my check and walked back in the direction of my office.

I hadn't really asked Morella any hard questions. I knew this, but he rose to the bait just the same. He didn't even know what cards I was holding. I was beginning to see what my father saw when he sat across from Steve Morella playing gin rummy.

Chapter Twenty-Five

Newby's office was located in an old house that used to be a doctor's residence in the last century. Most people knew where the brass speaking-tube ran from a former upstairs bedroom to the large veranda below. It simplified midnight interruptions on evenings when the doctor had to saddle up the horse and head halfway across town to attend a woman in labour. But that was history; for as long as I remember, this had always been a law office with the names Newby, Boyle, Weaver and Mendlesham on the small sign in front. To be perfectly honest, I remember when Newby was the second name on the sign, right after Trapnell. Of course, in those days, Stan Mendlesham hadn't been thought of.

I tried the door and found it open. There were large rooms both to the left and to the right of me. The one to the right was a waiting-room with an old piano standing against the wall, left over from some other age. The other room was a library in severe legal colours that included the dark, heavy boardroom table and all of those shelves of law books. Moving on through the central hall, past the stairway to the upper regions, I found myself in a reception area without a formal receptionist. There were two people there, sitting where the receptionist usually sits, but this couple was involved in private pursuits. They broke apart as I came in and the young woman began adjusting her blouse. The man, not abashed in the least, put on a friendly smile and told me that there was nobody about but themselves.

"We're really closed this late in the day," he explained. There was a drink of something balanced on top of a call director. He picked it up and took a sip.

"I was hoping to find Mr Newby in," I said.

"Julian's not been seen all day. I think he's taking a few days off. You heard that he found poor Ramsden's body, didn't you?"

"I was there when it happened. It wasn't any prettier being the second on the scene."

"Would you like a drink?" he asked. By now the young woman had vanished into the back part of the shop.

"Thanks, but I've just put one out," I lied. "Could I use your phone?"

"Sure. Just dial nine to get out. I'm Gerard Newby, by the way. I work here, Mr . . . ?"

"Cooperman. Ben Cooperman. Your father's a client of mine."

"Right! I've heard of you. Private eye, right?"

"Nobody calls me that. Nobody that knows me anyway." I began scouting around for a phonebook and found one on the floor, near a second glass with a drink in it. I looked up Newby without being able to find it. "Do you think I might bother your father at home?"

"Why not? Everybody else does." He told me the number and I dialled it. Young Newby vanished to the back, holding his drink but just.

"Hello, Mr Newby? It's Ben Cooperman." I could hear a pause at the other end. He then repeated my name, as though to recall who I was. I explained about how I'd been instructed to get in touch with him directly by Mendlesham. He said that the past two days hadn't been ordinary in any way for either of us. I agreed with him and shook my head at the sentiments he expressed about sudden death and its nearness at all times.

"The reason I'm calling, Mr Newby, is that the subject I've been attending to on your behalf knows that I'm on the job. It happens that way some times."

"She knows you are following her?"

"She caught me in the act. I didn't admit anything, of course, but I'm not much good to you from now on."

"I see." He took his time at seeing and, finally, thanked me for what I'd done and for letting him know. He would settle up with me later in the week if I could wait until then. I agreed and he was sure I would. He had that kind of assurance.

"Thanks for the use of the phone," I called to the back of the office after I'd hung up. In a moment both of the young people came forward to see me off the property, I thought, but in fact to invite me again to have a drink with them. A second invitation is supposed to be more serious than the first; it expresses a sincere desire for one's company, so I agreed to have a short drink.

"What'll it be?" I told him rye and ginger ale and the girl looked at her boy-friend with a special look. I'll have to sort out drinks one of these days. My old choices are getting dated. I could have tried out Orv Wishart's Campari and Perrier, but I didn't think that this establishment could provide anything but the serious basics. Gerard made up the drink and handed it over. "By the way," he said, almost as an afterthought, "this is Claudia Morella. Claudia, Ben Cooperman." We all said how do you do and sipped from our glasses.

"Was this the end of a Christmas party?" I asked. "I don't normally get a drink when I call on lawyers."

"Just some pre-Christmas cheer that we didn't want to cancel along with the party. The party's been canned because of what's happened."

"I didn't know that Mr Ramsden was so close to the firm."

"Mr Ramsden was doing some work for my father," Claudia volunteered, moving closer to Gerard.

"In a small town like this, Mr Cooperman, everybody knows everybody. For whom the bell tolls and all that," said young Newby.

"Well, I, for one, don't feel diminished at his passing," said Claudia to Gerard with a sly smile.

"He certainly had his share of enemies," I said, just fishing for any stray comments that might take the bait. "The police will have their hands full."

"I think it was that evil-smelling kook who was after Lizzy Oldridge's money, myself," said Gerard.

"Kogan?" I said, somewhat more loudly than I'd intended. "Kogan couldn't fix a toilet let alone Ramsden's hash, if you'll excuse me saying so. What makes you say he was after her money, by the way? I know he was trying to get some of it for Oldridge to spend while she was still alive. I doubt if he has any interest in the money or the property now she's dead. He wasn't named in the will, was he?"

The youngsters glanced at one another and said nothing. I waited but there was no flood of information. I tried priming the pump again: "Oldridge left everything to the Guild of the Venerable Bede, didn't she? Kogan wasn't mentioned as far as I know."

"You really should find the will and read it," Claudia said.

"Maybe I'll do that. Who was his lawyer?"

"Dad acted for him in some things — usually those connected with Steve's business," Gerard said. "I don't know who handled his personal stuff."

"I do," volunteered Claudia. "It's Rupe McLay. He's with Wilson, Carleton and Meyers on King Street, across from the market."

"That's right," added Gerard. "He used to be with Fleming, Harris, Irwin and Bartlett until they turfed him out."

"Oh?"

"Rupe's a well-known souse. Can't get his life together. He goes from one firm to the next and lasts about a year at each."

"And he's the lawyer that Ramsden got to draw up Liz Oldridge's will? When he was on close and friendly terms with this office? Sounds odd to me. Why would he do that?"

"I guess Thurleigh Ramsden took that secret to his grave, Mr Cooperman. He did a lot of peculiar things." Both my host and hostess were now standing shoulder to shoulder and I was suddenly feeling like a fifth wheel. So I drank up my drink, thanked them for their help and left the way I'd come in. As I walked along Ontario to King, I thought that Ramsden hadn't quite gone to his grave yet, he was still sharing accommodations in the morgue with a few other corpses including Temperley's. I wasn't sure what that did to the status of his secret. Maybe Rupe McLay could help me out on that one.

As I rounded the corner, the wind hit me in the face. It was uncompromising and icy. It cut through my clothes, making my knees feel numb against the cloth of my trousers. Mixed in with it were ice pellets which you couldn't see, only feel on your cheeks as they came at you from the direction of the old court-house. I tried to wrap myself more securely in my coat and save my hat from being whisked into Helliwell Lane. I was glad when I read the sign on the side of an old two-storey building on the south side of the street: Wilson, Carleton, Meyers and Devlin. Devlin I'd heard about from Rupe McLay. Devlin's name had been added since Claudia Morella had taken her last look at the sign in front of the building. But there were distractions for Claudia that made her mistake understandable.

There was no elevator, and the stairs creaked as I went up them. The building was about as old as mine, but the stairs weren't so steep. Nor were there so many of them. The first door on the right repeated the name of the firm again on frosted glass. In Toronto, this sort of office would be considered cute or trendy. Some businesses make a big deal of reproducing the look of the thirties. But this was the real thing. If business got bad, they could sell the front door and probably all the inside furnishings to a Toronto decorator and make a profit at the end of the year.

The door was locked, but there was a light burning inside, so I knocked. Soon I heard steps moving in my direction. Then the door snapped off the latch. It was the expected face that appeared in the crack between the door and the doorpost.

"Mr Cooperman! Well, well, well!" He opened the door and made an elaborate bow and motioned me to come in. I went in and caught a whiff of strong drink on his breath as I passed in front of him. What's the legal profession coming to in this town, I wondered. Was off-hours drinking part of the scene or should I blame it on the holiday that was fast approaching.

There was nothing festive on the other side of the frosted glass, only more doors with more frosted glass and a small empty reception desk with a call director standing out as the only recent piece of equipment. Even the typewriters looked like second-hand electrics bought from the *Beacon*'s sale ten years ago when they went to computer equipment in their editorial office. I won't even attempt to describe the effect of the plastic Christmas tree with grey cotton batting under it that had seen more Christmases than I had. McLay's long, triangular face topped by a thinning thatch of faded red hair had the look of a misspent youth and middle age about it. He was taller than I remembered, but most of my earlier sightings had been of him sitting down. His sloping shoulders gave him the watchful look of a meat-eating bird. Maybe he was bent over from his long years of sleeping on the briefs he should have been studying.

"Well, well, well," he repeated. I grinned at him, pretending I knew what the joke was. After all, was it so unusual that I should come up his stairs? Or maybe the world was a little distorted when glimpsed through the bottom of so many bottles.

"Mr McLay," I said. "I mean Rupe. You're working late." McLay looked at his glass, then back at me and decided not to comment. He opened the door leading into his private office and I followed.

"What may I do for you? Take a pew." We both sat down, he on the other side of a mound of paper that hid the wood of his desk completely, and me in a worn wooden chair that had the look of belonging to a different office suite than this one.

"You were Thurleigh Ramsden's lawyer," I said. I didn't ask; it saves time.

"One of them. He used Newby for the good stuff."

"I know. I was just over there. Place is being babysat by young Newby and Morella's girl, Claudia."

"They're both bright enough. In fact she's the better lawyer of the two. Top of her class."

"Interesting. I'll remember that."

"What's this about, Cooperman? You didn't come here to chat."

"I want to see Ramsden's will, if you'll let me see it."

"Ha! Anything else?"

"You drew up Lizzy Oldridge's will for Ramsden too. I'd like to see what's in that as well."

"You don't want much. How about my backside? Would you like a peek at that too while you're at it?"

"Look, Mr McLay, I'm just working at my job. If you show me, fine. If you don't, I'll try something else. But save the party talk for the people in the paper hats, okay? Neither of us likes to waste time, I'm sure."

"How the hell would you know? I like to waste time. Hell, it's the only fucking thing I'm any good at. In the inner sanctums of the legal circles of Grantham, Cooperman — what the hell's your name again? — I'm famous for non-productivity. Ben! No Benny. Yes, I remember you."

"Can we do business or not?"

"Your ass going numb? Sit still, I'm thinking."

"You know a fair amount about the Morellas," I threw in, thinking of Claudia buttoning up her blouse around the corner. "Sounds like a good place to start, if you want to stay away from Ramsden."

"Watched her grow up, Benny. I knew her mother, we were good friends in high school. Then I nearly spoiled it all by trying to act for her in the divorce. That soured things for a couple of years. But I kept up with Claudia. She used to play lawyer when she was a little brat. I forget where I was in those days. I move around a lot."

"I understand that Mrs Morella took Steve to the cleaners in the split. What more could you have done for her? She want his liver and lights too?"

"Sue Ellen wanted what was going. She knew he was loaded, so we got a fair share."

"Morella's a lot of people and companies. I understand you got a piece of everything he had. That must have taken a lot of research."

"That's what I'm good at, Benny. I love the library."

I knew enough about the law to know that nobody likes doing research. Research is only preferable to replacing pages in the monthly law report loose-leaf notebooks and going out to fetch coffee and sandwiches for the senior partners on a regular basis. "What about those wills, Mr McLay?"

McLay moved his long hand over his chin, checking to see when he had last held a razor to his throat. It was hard to tell how drunk he was. Sometimes he seemed quite sober, and then he'd begin sharing his stream of semi-consciousness with me. I heard about him not liking his name, his father's women on the side, his sister's teasing and the rat race in general. It didn't appear that there was one big tragedy in his life, just a lot of little ones. Unless he was avoiding it or saving it for dessert. He refilled his glass several times without inviting me to come into his magic sodden world. I figured I might get something useful if I could just sit still long enough.

"So you knew Sue Ellen Morella in high school. Was she older or younger than her sister, the one who married Ramsden?"

"Sue Ellen was two years older than Dora. Sue Ellen was the pretty one. Nice figure on her. Dora and I were on the debating team. She had a good head on her shoulders."

"What has Sue Ellen done since the divorce?"

"There's a little wood at the end of Lido Beach in Sarasota, Florida. Lovely white sand on the Gulf. She bought a place there. Sends me postcards. Got a Christmas card too around here somewhere. She's a good friend."

"Never remarried?"

"She says she has to fight off the suitors like Penelope in *The Odyssey*."

"You should pay her a visit."

"And bring the arrows of destruction with me? I've thought of that, but I'm not a good-deed-doer. I drink her health once in a while when I remember." He raised his glass and drank just in case I didn't catch what he meant. "But, you!" he said suddenly. "What are we going to do about you?"

"In what way? I'm not anywhere near the Gulf Stream."

"You want to know about Ramsden's will. Well, Benny, don't waste your time. His estate goes to three cousins he never met in the old country. They survive a sister, who died last year. His estate doesn't amount to much beyond the house, a registered retirement savings plan and a few good investment stocks. He wasn't a wealthy man. Did you think he was?"

"I didn't think he was on welfare. I don't know what I expected."

"I'll bet you weren't expecting that he would inherit from Liz Oldridge?"

"I know that the Bede Bunch gets Liz's estate and that the Bede Bunch was founded by Ramsden."

"But what you don't know is that the Guild of the Venerable Bede doesn't exist."

"What!"

"That's right. The Bede Bunch has always been Ramsden's back pocket. It isn't a legal entity."

"But don't they give away lots of money to worthy causes?"

"Don't you? Don't I, when I've got it? There's no rule that says a private citizen can't endow a scholarship or pay plane fares. You may find out that the guild has given away less than it likes to think it has. Ramsden didn't keep books. There was no reason why he should. The Bunch was just another arm of his own activities. I'm sure that he had a bank account in the Bede name, but he could add or subtract from what was there whenever he wanted to."

"So, what you're saying is that Liz's money and property went directly to her sole executor? Why didn't that come out at the inquest?"

"Nobody was curious enough to ask. The old girls in the Bunch trusted Ramsden. He gave them a place to meet and hold a singsong every week or so. He told them what good deeds their money was doing and, to a great extent, he wasn't telling fibs."

"But the Oldridge estate was a tidy sum of money with the potential of getting bigger."

"I don't see any of the old girls sending for the Public Trustee." That's the office that would make sure that Ramsden's right hand knew what his left hand was doing. The Public Trustee makes sure we all stay honest.

"How the hell did he think he could get away with it?"

"As long as the whole transaction was done in the name of the Guild, there would be no outcry. Don't forget that Thurleigh had an ally in Temperley, the bank manager. He could make Ramsden look whiter than white if he had to."

"So," I said, after letting this piece of news settle over me, "it all boils down to the fact that Ramsden's three cousins will inherit Liz's property and money."

"They would have, except for a little clause in the Oldridge will which will stop her estate from plunging into his." McLay lighted a fresh cigarette with an old-fashioned wooden match. "If Ramsden hadn't died so quickly after Liz, he would have got the lot, through the Bede Bunch. But the will is quite clear: in the event of his death, the estate reverted to one of the other minor beneficiaries."

I pulled out a pencil and a scrap of paper. "Can you give me a name?" I asked. Rupe looked at me and smiled. It was friendlier than saying no. I began to back-paddle to see what more I could learn.

"Wait a minute, if the estate was to go to the Bede Bunch, how could Ramsden's fate figure one way or the other?"

"Since I knew about Ramsden's relationship with the Bunch, I couldn't just put it in the will that way. Then nobody would inherit. The will clearly spells out Ramsden's relationship with the Bunch."

"Then Oldridge knew?"

"Of course not! She was well past reading anything by the time the will was written. And Ramsden accepted my explanation."

"So, the old woman never knew."

"I went around to see her, to see if I could explain it, but it was well beyond her. She said she trusted me and patted my hand."

"That's quite a compliment. I don't think she trusted many."

"I had no idea Ramsden was not allowing her access to her safety deposit box. That was arranged with the bank. That son of a bitch Temperley! I had no part in that."

"Why did you tell me this, Rupe?"

"No clients to protect any more. Better to serve the common good. You know. All that stuff. Sorry I bit your ear off when you came in. It's been a terrible day. The sun has not been seen. I've been invited to resign from the firm. I've only been here for ten months! Hell, Benny, look at this place! Damn it! Can you imagine that I'm not a credit to all *this*? I don't pinch asses and I don't bed the customers. Unlike some. I think the young, oh so young, Mr Devlin has ideas of taking this weary partnership into fast water. I'm being chucked overboard to lighten the load."

"I'm sorry," I said.

"You're sorry? Last thing in the world I need is your —!"

"You said 'Unlike some,' Rupe. Do you mean anyone in particular? This could be important."

"Young Devlin last week going off to have lunch with the great Julian Newby! Ha! When do they unveil *that* public monument? Oh, he was plenty discreet about his affair with Dora Ramsden. Wouldn't want that model of public virtue, his wife, to find out. Wouldn't do for the head of the Independent Foundation of the Women of the Commonwealth to have a husband in the divorce court."

"Who are you talking about? Newby or Devlin?"

"Joanne Newby is head of the IFWC, Benny; Tilly Devlin isn't up to much yet, but give her time. She's like her husband. Just give her time."

"Does that mean there was bad blood between Ramsden and Newby? They still did business together."

"Ramsden would have been the last to know. Head in red, white and blue clouds of past glory: that was Thurleigh Ramsden. No, he didn't know about them. Newby wouldn't allow that."

"This Julian Newby is getting more and more complicated."

"Julian has only one game. It's called control. He wants to manage everything. There can be no loose ends with Julian Newby. He never gives TV interviews, you know. You know why? The esteemed leader of the Grantham bar could not tolerate a situation where he isn't in charge of both the questions and the answers. That's why he stays away from the courtroom when he can; lets his partners do the criminal work and litigation. Newby stays close to business."

"I see," I said, maybe seeing about half of what he said.

"Newby takes Devlin to lunch. McLay gets his walking papers almost directly afterwards. Funny the way we all play into his hands."

"I wish I could do something."

"Like hell you do! Everybody suddenly wants to be Meals on Wheels for good old Rupe! I'll be damned if I seek your solicitude. Or anybody else's!" He had pulled himself up to his feet on his side of the mound of paper and teetered over it. A sudden gesture sent a score of documents to the floor.

"Rupe, I know some of the people who worry about you. I know who they are, I mean. I'd say you're damned lucky in your friends. Maybe luckier than you deserve."

"You can give me this place without you in it, Cooperman!"

"And leave you to soak up more of your self-pity. You know, Rupe, if I were you I'd stay drunk. It beats trying to figure out what's going on in this crazy place. And it hands people like Newby a fine set of illustrations for what he's always saying about you."

"Try the door and the stairs, Cooperman!"

"Sure, I'm on my way. And thanks, by the way. You've been a bigger help than most."

"The door's that way! Taste your legs, sir; put them to motion!"

I got out of there as fast as I could as his grip around the neck of his bottle tightened.

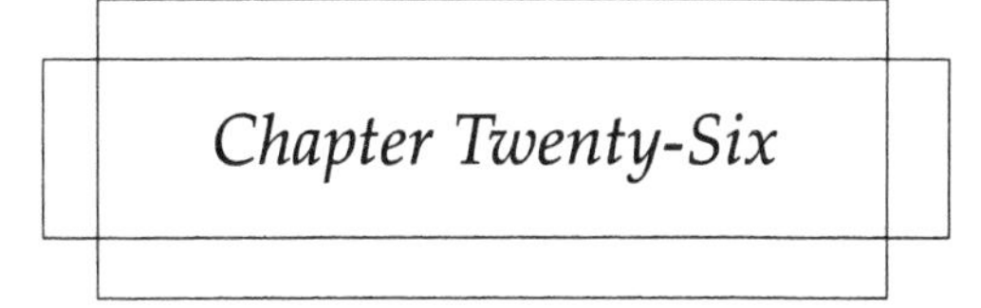

Chapter Twenty-Six

I was about to open the door that would let me back out onto King Street, when I heard my name called in a voice that was close to breaking. I turned and was looking into the frightened face of Antonia Wishart. She was haggard and, as I said, frightened.

"Mr Cooperman, may I talk to you for just a minute? You don't know me, but Rupe has mentioned you a few times. I've got to speak to somebody. I've never seen him so low. I'm scared for him."

"Mrs Wishart, you're not quite a stranger. Nobody is in a town this size. How can I help?"

"I can't reach him any more. I used to make a difference. I don't know what to say." I took my hand from the door and turned towards her. Before I had put a reassuring hand on her shoulder, she began to collapse into me. I grabbed her and held her close until the sobs that started racking her body began to subside. I heard myself saying: "There, there; there, there," and rubbing her back because I couldn't think of anything less futile to do with her.

"My friends call me 'Benny,' why don't you start there," I said in my most reassuring voice. When she grew calmer and I'd stopped my massage of her vertebrae, I pulled her out the door and into the coffee shop across the road next to the market.

It was deserted of all but the most stalwart of the Christmas shoppers. The rough, red faces of those with market stalls had long ago driven their trucks back into the hinterland, leaving the back tables empty for the likes of Antonia Wishart and me.

I couldn't get a good look at her for some time, because she was rubbing her eyes with a man-sized handkerchief. I got glimpses of red eyes and matching nose and cheeks. I helped her pull off the coat she had hanging on her shoulders. The waitress brought two coffees without being asked. They already had milk or cream in them. I couldn't wait to taste whether the sugar had gone in as well. I tried mine. The sugar was in place. All I had to do was to stir it until the desired degree of sweetness was achieved. I took my time and kept my mouth otherwise shut. By the time I'd finished my coffee and was waiting for a refill, Mrs Wishart was blowing her nose and trying to pull herself together. After she had replaced the handkerchief in her expensive leather handbag, she looked at me for the first time. "Thanks," she said. "I keep forgetting I'm not made of granite."

"Drink some coffee," I said and she picked up her cup, almost at once. Neither of us spoke while the waitress refilled my cup. When she'd returned to the dark front of the shop, Mrs Wishart let me see a whisper of a smile.

"Why do you care so much?" I asked, then wished I hadn't said it.

"The usual reason, I guess," she said, struggling with a cigarette and taking a deep drag when it was finally alight. "I don't suppose you'd understand."

"I think I know a little. But why is he taking this defeat harder than all the others?"

"He thinks this place is the last law office in town he hasn't somehow let down. Now he's as good as black-listed all over town."

"There are a few places up Niagara Street he hasn't tried. And there's always my cousin Melvyn. No, I think it's more than that. It's because he thinks Julian Newby has taken a personal hand in this. Do you think it's true?"

"Julian likes to pull strings," she said. For a woman who a few minutes earlier had been a moist handkerchief and a spasm of sobs, she had pulled herself together remarkably. The cords in her neck sometimes tightened as she fought to regain her composure. "I used to think he wanted to be the richest man in town, but I was wrong. It's power he's in love with, not money. He's happy making Steve Morella rich. He knows that he was the one who made it happen."

"Why does he dislike Rupe?"

"You really want to know?"

"Yes, I really want to know."

"I could tell you that he thinks Rupe is giving law a bad name in this town. And he'd be right; Rupe's had a hard life. But the reason Julian hates him is because of me." She paused before answering my unspoken question. "I was with Julian before I went with Rupe."

"I see. Julian Newby is quite the man. I just heard about him and Dora Ramsden."

"Dora? Oh, he knew Dora first long before she married. If Thurleigh knew about it, he was smart enough to keep his mouth shut."

"But you'll admit, he does get around."

"Dora and I were good friends. We were, I mean,

before Julian saw me coming home very late one night from the Byline Ball. I was with Orv, of course, and Julian told me I was like magic." I could believe Newby's assessment of Antonia Wishart. Of course, now she looked terrible, with her face blotchy from crying and her hair in a mess, but she had all the right makings. The good bones were there in her face; her figure was more than ample but she carried herself well. I could almost see glimpses of the magic Newby had noticed.

I didn't realize I'd been staring at Antonia until she began speaking again. I couldn't see whether I blushed or not. Maybe she liked it. Maybe there isn't enough magic in the world sometimes.

"Mr Cooperman, there's something that I should give you." I probably looked blank, because she said the same thing again in different words. While she was doing this, she rooted around in her bag and brought out a rather soiled and much-folded piece of paper, which she handed across to me. I opened it and read. It was a handwritten list of numbered companies, small companies and corporations. The list nearly filled the page.

"Where did you get this?" I asked.

"Rupe would never give it to you. It's his pride. He wants everybody to think that his handling of Sue Ellen Morella's divorce was all his own doing. But this is what made the settlement possible. It's all of Steve's shadowy holdings, the ones he didn't want her to know about."

"You took it from Rupe's files?"

"And he's never to know that."

"You want me to use it to get back at Newby? You want me to use it to smear him? You know I can't do that. Not even to please a lady." I tried to hand the paper back to her, but she held up her palm.

"Keep it anyway. I don't want it any more." I took it and stuffed it into my inside breast pocket.

"Can you tell me why Rupe is trying to kill himself with drink?"

"It's the wounds he got in Korea. His legs still give him a lot of pain. He drinks rather than take drugs. He came back from Korea with a morphine addiction. He replaced the one addiction with another."

"He could get help for all of that, you know."

"Sure, I know. Damn it, even he knows. But he won't do anything about it."

"You could help."

"I've been helping. I've tried. But I can't do any more as long as my mother's alive. I can't complicate that part of my life right now. It's bad enough as it is."

"And when your mother passes on?"

"'Dies,' that's the word. When she dies, I'll be able to write my own script, not follow someone else's scenario."

"Will Orv be able to swallow that?" I asked.

"Orv's married to a television station. And he's welcome to it. He's never been unfaithful to the station and never will be. I can't make myself jealous, Mr Cooperman. CXAN won hands down. I'm not contesting the decision."

"You're feeling a little better, I think?"

"Do you have to go somewhere?"

"No."

"Then just sit here with me for another minute. Okay?"

I sat with her without saying anything for another ten minutes. We sipped our coffee and when we had both finished we got up and left the coffee shop. For a minute, I thought it was snowing again.

I walked Antonia Wishart to her Volvo, parked behind City Hall. She held my hand briefly before shutting the door and I watched her back out of the space and drive out into traffic on Church Street. I'd been right about one thing: it was snowing.

Coming back to the office I tried to remember a thought that was only semi-visible in my memory. It had something to do with the list of Morella's assets. I'd seen that writing somewhere before.

Chapter Twenty-Seven

First thing Tuesday morning I wrestled with the blue pages at the back of my telephone book. I tried a number of government numbers and got lost in making electronic choices with my Touch Tone buttons, choices I had no interest in and choices that kept me away from what I really wanted, which was to speak to a human being. I finally got one at the end of an 800 number in Thunder Bay, Ontario. I explained my problem and was shunted about the freight yard until I came to the roundhouse known as Mr Stevenson. God bless Mr Stevenson. May his life be long, may his children honour him until he is overwhelmed by years and riches. I gave him some names and dates and, in return, he gave me information — some of which I had already guessed — that I wrote down for future reference.

Next, I phoned Joe Castaldi, an old friend who worked in the Hamilton Police Department's records department. I gave him the date of Dora Ramsden's fatal accident on the Burlington Skyway and he gave me — finally, after some minutes spent in the limbo called "hold" — the details of the accident report and the name of the garage that towed the car off the bridge.

I phoned the garage and confirmed that Stavro

Kouloukis, the owner, would be in all day. I looked at my watch after I hung up. I didn't want to take a long drive out of town, but what could I do? It would be too easy for him to put me off over the telephone. I had to talk to Kouloukis face to face.

The drive along the Queen Elizabeth Way to Burlington runs through flat beach country, studded with vineyards and orchards, where they haven't been displaced by industry. To my right, I caught glimpses of the lake, looking dark and treacherous. To my left, the snow-covered fields ran up to the foot of the escarpment that followed me all the way from Grantham. In general the roads were clear, but they were dirty and wet. I had to keep washing the windshield every time a truck went by in the other direction. It took about ten minutes longer than I'd figured; the directions I'd been given were sound, but I took a wrong turn and got confused somewhere under the Skyway bridge. At least the old canal bridge was down when I crossed and the garage, when I came to it, was well marked.

Stavro Kouloukis was a small man in grease-stained coveralls, who grinned at me like a matinée idol with teeth that were so real and well looked after they looked like cheap fakes.

"Sure, I remember that wreck! She was some mess! Red '89 Toyota. Sure, what do you want to know for?"

I explained who I was and what I was doing. He looked me up and down, searching for confirmation in my clothes, and finally took me into a small, dirty office with walls covered with pictures of soccer teams at rest and in motion. He flipped through a record book that looked cleaner than I expected and rested a dirty finger on the note he was looking for.

"Yeah! Here it is," he said, as though all I wanted was to confirm that it existed.

"May I have a peek?" I asked, and he moved out of the way slowly, like that hadn't been negotiated in advance.

The note recorded the damage done to the car, mostly to the front end from going through the bridge railing and coming up against the stiffer resistance of one of the girders that supported the central structure. Grill and lights had been smashed, the fender on the driver's side had been crunched, and the frame bent. Inside, the steering wheel had snapped, which gave me some idea of the speed she'd been travelling at.

"Thing about this is," Stavro said, as though he was elaborating on something he'd already said, "is that the brake cable broke."

" 'Broke'? Broke how?" I asked.

"Usual way, I guess. I don't know. Cables can only take so much and then they should be replaced. People never look after their cars. Don't know why there aren't more people killed than there are."

"So, you don't know for sure how it broke?"

"I don't remember looking all that close, to be honest. We had a three-car pile-up come in right after the Toyota. But, if you got half an hour, I could take a look."

"You've got the car here?"

"Sure. At the back. I use the parts when I need them."

I went to a cold, drafty café near the canal that looked as though it had seen its last dollar the day the Skyway opened, and ordered coffee, which turned out to be the best I'd tasted away from home in a long time. The woman who ran it was scanning the Hamilton paper, and making comments to herself about the operation of the Hamilton Harbour Commission. She said a few things to me that suggested we were both fully aware of some scandal that I'd never heard of. Harbours are always a problem. They breed trouble wherever they are.

When I got back to Stavro's Cross-Town Motors, he was holding two pieces of cable in his hands and grinning. "You gotta see this!" he said. I followed him into the office, away from the whine of the pneumatic wrench pulling off the nuts from the wheels of the Volvo on the hoist. On his desk he laid down the two pieces of twisted wire.

"You see these ends?" I nodded. "That's where I just clipped them free from the rest of the cable, just to show you." I nodded again.

"Now the other ends are the parts that separated." He held them up for me to get a better look. I saw the ends of two thick wires, nothing extraordinary. I shrugged. Stavro reached to the shelf above the desk and found a murky magnifying glass, which he passed over the two ends held close together.

"You see the jagged bits, where the separate wire threads are pulled and stretched? That's where the cable broke. But look on the other side. Here the threads are smooth and don't show no signs of stress. See, they don't even fit together snug. Yeah! This cable was filed more than halfway through before the lady put her foot on the brake." I thought of Dora, whose face I had never seen, with her foot on the brake on that downhill run off the bridge.

"Let me see!" I took the glass from him and turned the two cable ends around in my hands. I had to agree with him; less than half of each end showed the stress of being pulled snapping; the rest looked filed.

I got Stravo to put a note on the two pieces and to identify where they'd been taken from. To this he added what he thought they showed. He signed the note and put the whole works into a large brown envelope he rescued from his waste-paper basket.

My trip back to Grantham was slower than my drive out. I took a side trip to the Stoney Creek Dairy for an ice cream, where Pa used to take Sam and me when we were kids, but in the end I didn't get out of the car. The fact that Dora Ramsden had been murdered was too fresh for me to enjoy a sundae or milkshake. I drove home along the twisty Old Number Eight Highway, which I hadn't driven in years. The road was narrow and slow, but dry, even under the overhang of the escarpment. I stopped at an antique store in Grimsby, where I bought a few presents for people on my Christmas and Chanukkah list and accepted an offer of tea with the owner, who was well chaptered and versed in local history. It was a slow ride home because of the lower speed limit. I wasn't sorry. It helped give me time to take in the news Burlington had given me. I didn't like a lot of it, but it was making some things clearer.

Chapter Twenty-Eight

I was on my way back to the office, carrying a hot coffee in a brown paper bag, when I heard a shout from the street. It was Chris Savas. He called my name. There's a special sensation in hearing your name pronounced by an officer of the law. And to hear it shouted . . . I looked over at him, leaning his big head out of the car window. He was even smiling.

"Get in!" he ordered, "I've got to talk to you." I stood on the curb for a moment, probably looking as though I didn't understand the words, and certainly hoping that there would be a witness to the fact that I was getting into the car. They didn't lock people up and throw the key away any more. And Chris was a sort of friend when he wasn't being professional. Tonight, he looked professional.

The slam of the door of the car brought me back to St Andrew Street and the realization that the time had at last come to ante up. Chris had given me a day beyond his forty-eight-hour deadline. Finally I was going to have to make up my mind about what I was going to tell him.

"I've been trying to call you," I said, remembering my one half-hearted effort.

"Sure you have," he said with disbelief written all over

his face. It was an exchange in which neither side won the advantage. Chris was wearing a heavy trenchcoat, the kind with a zipped-in lining. He looked warm. The hands on the wheel were in good leather gloves.

"Do you have a destination in mind, or are we going on a tour of the city?"

"We're just taking a ride. That's all."

"Like Clarence Temperley. I hope I don't end up the way he did."

"Don't give me any ideas, Benny." I breathed out and tried to feel my back touching the car seat in several places. It was a relaxation test on which I wasn't making a passing grade.

Savas addressed himself to the road in front of us for a minute or so. It was snowing again and the wind was already playing games, blowing snow across the street and making vision beyond the headlights impossible. He switched on the wipers and the high beams. "There's a place I know where we can talk without being bothered," he said, flexing his fingers on the steering wheel. I sipped my coffee through a hole I punched in the lid with a ballpoint pen.

"Sure. Why not?" I said, pretending that it had been a question.

Savas drove down Ontario Street, after running back along King. Then we headed north, past my parents' turn-off, towards the lake. On the strip beyond the fast-food outlets and service stations, the wind got worse. Here there were accumulated drifts at the side of the road. The steady blast of wind threw a continuous white blind spot across the driver's path, so that he had to guess about what was coming from the opposite direction until he was hit by the full impact of oncoming headlights. He threaded his way through the twists and turns that led to Port Richmond, a former terminus of the Old Canal and now a summertime marina with seafood restaurants and beerhalls along the street facing the harbour. I had a lot of associations with Port Richmond and few of them were good.

Chris pulled up and parked in a lot across from Marie's Seafood Restaurant, which overlooked an abandoned lock of the Old Canal. I followed him into the place and looked around at the tank of lobsters whose time, like mine, had come. Chris was welcomed by the proprietor, who showed us to a table well away from the windows. Each window was decorated with a full-rigged ship model. Through the sails and rigging we could see little but the lights of the street. I remember Marie's from years ago. The ceiling had been strewn with fishnets and festooned with seashells and Christmas tree lights. Now all of this was gone, replaced by turning fans. Remaining were a few lobster traps and oil paintings of sailing ships in heavy gales and fishermen in oilskins battling the waves in a dory. The reassembled shell of a man-eating lobster was hung, plaque-like, on one wall.

"Will you join me in something to eat?" he asked.

"I take it that you're working?" Chris nodded. I sat down. I wasn't feeling talkative, but I wasn't sure what a good dinner might do to my tongue. Food could intimidate me where money couldn't. It was turning into my Achilles' heel.

Chris ordered "the usual," which the waitress seemed to know about. I took a chance and ordered the same. I hoped that whatever it was, it came cooked. I wasn't raised to eat raw things that didn't have stems. Savas ordered a bottle of white wine. When it came we watched the waitress open it. Chris sniffed the cork expertly and took the first sip. It's funny the way ritual leads people through the motions. As he put down his glass, he grinned and smiled at the waitress, who said, "Thank you kindly." I took a long sip from my glass and ended up coughing. As soon as that was under control, I was ready for the questioning to begin. But Chris said nothing.

In a few minutes bibs were affixed to our necks and all semblance of sophistication vanished. Then came the lobsters, red from their broth and huge. I'd seen them eaten before, but I'd never dared. At least they were cooked, I thought. They were the biggest insects I'd ever seen, except for the killer mounted on the wall.

"The time has come, Benny, for you to sing for your supper," Savas said, tearing a claw from his lobster. I winced.

"I'm no snitch, Chris. I've got clients and all that that implies."

"Christ, Benny. I'm not here to play silly games with your confidential sources, I want to hear what you know from your end. I can browbeat you for the names afterwards if I have to." He dug a little fork into the claw and brought out a piece of meat the size of a thumb, which he bathed in melted butter, then applied to his red tongue.

"This is going to take time," I said.

"I got all night. You're not eating!" I ate. I did that for a few minutes, idly scanning the room for a place to start. At last I thought I'd found one.

"We have to go back to Harlan Ravenswood's extramarital activities about thirty years ago."

"Ah, that letter Ramsden was holding under glass!"

"Yeah. He'd had an illegitimate child and made arrangements with his bank manager and good friend, Egerton Garsington, so that he would never have to think about his slip again. He was deathly afraid that Gladys would find out about it. When Edge Garsington died suddenly in 1967, his successor, Clarence Temperley, found the instructions and arrangements that Garsington had worked out along with the letter of authorization in a file. He made the mistake of showing it to Thurleigh Ramsden, who eventually took the letter from the file. He approached Harlan, who was by now getting close to the end of his life, and began blackmailing him. After his death, Ramsden went on with the blackmail. Harlan's son-in-law was willing to pay so that the old lady wouldn't find out. Maybe it had become more important after Ravenswood died. Orv saw himself as the keeper of the flame. He wanted to protect his former boss's memory at all costs. Gladys, as far as we know, never suspected a thing.

"When a client of mine asked me to follow the TV newsreader, Catherine Bracken, I went to see Orv Wishart, the son-in-law, about her, pretending to be making a credit report. He gave me Cath's date of birth and the place. When I checked it out with a man in Thunder Bay, I couldn't find a match in the records. However, I did find that a daughter had been born to a Renée Chestnut on the same date. Same town. Same hospital. The father was Harlan Ravenswood.

"You're telling me that Catherine Bracken, the TV news anchor, is Harlan's daughter?"

"That's right. But she doesn't know it. Only Orv knows and in his awkward way, he has been trying to get her into the business that she should rightly inherit a piece of one day.

"She's sitting on millions and she doesn't know it! But, hey, Benny, you're forgetting that whatever she gets will have to come out of the share of what's-her-name, the daughter."

"Antonia. That's right. But, for some reason, and I think that loyalty to the old man plays a part here, Orv is willing to make the sacrifice. In some way, I think he's getting a kick out of bringing her into the business, without anyone knowing that she might have a legitimate claim."

"But Orv isn't Antonia. We don't know how she'll take it."

"That's right, we don't."

"I'm beginning to like Wishart. Never did up to now."

"The trouble is, Cath hates him! She thinks that all his care and attention comes from seething carnal desires. When you're as good-looking as she is, it might be an easy mistake to make, Chris."

"Maybe his motives are mixed, Benny: a little boy scout mixed with desire. I've known it to happen."

"You'd be right, Chris, except that I discovered that Orv's natural inclinations might tend to you or me rather than to Cath or her kind."

"He's gay?"

"As a cricket. But he keeps clear of the mob. Even Robin O'Neil at CXAN doesn't suspect. Robin thought he'd been putting the moves on Cath. That's how observant he is."

"Benny, I don't mean to be unkind, but none of what you've just shared with me and Niagara Regional is going to tell me who did in Ramsden and Temperley. Nor does it do a thing for Kogan. Remember Kogan? Unless this has been a roundabout way of saying you don't know."

"Hold your questions, Chris, I've just got started. What's past is prologue as my father used to say."

"You must get your original cast of mind from him. Roosevelt said that!"

"He did? Well, what do you know. I wish I had your education."

"Damn it, Benny, get on with it! I'm getting to wonder whether you'll ever come to the point."

"So, we have seen that Ramsden was a blackmailer. Ravenswood and Orv were consecutive clients. So were some of the other people whose documents we found at Ramsden's last Sunday. It seems logical that he was murdered by one of his victims."

"You want me to dig through the dozen names that came out of those letters?"

"Well, not all blackmail is based on documents. I might know something about you, independent of any piece of proof, that you might find embarrassing for the world to know about."

"Cut out the compliments and get on with the story!"

"Okay! Okay! Let me catch my breath! According to the will left by Liz Oldridge, the Guild of the Venerable Bede was to inherit the bulk of her estate, including the property on Brogan Street. You may not have noticed this Chris, but Steve Morella has been buying up all of the property on the north side of that street for a project he calls 'Backstreet Revival.'"

"Remind me, where the hell is Brogan Street?"

"Runs between James and Queen. It's more an alley than a street. Has Foley Bros. at one end and the Nag's

Head at the other. Morella bought Foley's very quietly and also is acquiring the pub. The only piece missing is the Oldridge place, which, according to her wishes, goes to the Bede Bunch. Well, I've discovered that the Bede Bunch is in reality none other than Ramsden in fancy dress. It has no legal existence. The name's not registered. It's just a bank account that was set up by Clare Temperley for Ramsden. Ramsden can take out what he wants. He can buy and sell either in his own name or in the name of the BB. Morella wants that property bad, Chris."

"Are you saying that Steve Morella killed Ramsden for it?"

"He's smarter than that. I don't know whether he liked Ramsden or not, but he'd be a fool to run him through before he had control of the needed property."

"Okay, okay, I get you."

"Morella's legal work has always been done by Julian Newby, the senior partner in that old Ontario Street firm. Newby helped build Morella into the man he is today. Up from the curb-side fries at the top of Queen Street."

"I remember. Get on with it!"

"Morella wouldn't dare move without Newby. Newby's part and parcel of every dollar Morella ever made. On the private plain, they've seen little of one another until recently: Newby's son is taking out Morella's daughter. Both are lawyers and pretty bright. What else do we know? We know that Sue Ellen Morella, Claudia's mother, divorced Steve a few years ago and got a surprisingly large settlement. Was this because of the skill of her attorney, Rupe McLay?"

"McLay? That . . . that . . . ?"

"Okay, let's say that he is alcoholically challenged.

Okay, you smell a rat? So do I. Where does a bar-room lawyer get the inside information to make book on Morella? How does he even get to know about all of his holdings under different names and numbers?"

"There must have been an examination for discovery?"

"Sure, but Morella could still manage to slide over a few items, forget to mention things where his name doesn't appear but where he gets a share. No. The only person who knew exactly how much Morella was worth was Newby. Newby did all the deals, handled the taxes, the deferrals, the dodges, all the little havens that rich men are heir to. This was the best continuing lucrative client he had, Chris. Newby was more Morella than Morella was.

"So, how did Sue Ellen find out about all of these shelters and havens? Sue Ellen a great reader of the *Report on Business*? Sue Ellen a frequenter of the brokerage houses? Not that I know of. Sue Ellen shops. That's what she loves best, shopping and travelling. She can tell you more about Montego Bay than she can tell you about Morella's assets. Rupe told me that it was sister Dora who had the brains.

"So, where does she get her information? What else do we know about her? Sue Ellen's sister, Dora, was married to our old friend Ramsden. Could Ramsden have talked Newby into leaking a full list of Morella's involvements? Possibly. Could Dora? Could Dora Ramsden have been known to Newby? Do we know anything about them? Yes, we do. They were lovers for a time just prior to her death. I don't know for how long, probably not more than a few months. They'd known one another before she married Ramsden.

"Dora Ramsden's death was treated as an accident, Chris. It happened out of town, on the Burlington Skyway. What happened? Her car went out of control on the downward slope of the bridge and she crashed into the parapet at sixty miles an hour. Don't ask me what that is in kilometres. Was there a check done on her brakes? Has anybody ever asked what killed Dora Ramsden? Or who?"

"That's ancient history, Benny. Nobody can answer those questions. You're suggesting that either Ramsden killed his wife because she was carrying on with Newby or that Newby killed her to get her off his back? I won't buy either of those theories for a minute. Besides, you're the only one fool enough to call it murder. And damn it all, what the hell does it have to do with the here and now?"

"I spent a few hours digging around Burlington today, Chris." I reached down and dropped the manila envelope with the brake cable on the table between us. Chris stabbed at it with his fish fork.

"What the hell is this?"

"A broken brake cable taken from Dora's wrecked car. The wire was half-cut through before it broke." Chris frowned at the envelope, which he made no further attempt to examine. There was a time and place for everything.

"Before this happened, while Dora was still close to Newby, she got him to leak to her a list of Morella's assets so that her sister wouldn't starve to death with the half-million Morella had planned for her."

"You got proof of that in another envelope, Benny, or do you want me to take that on your say so?"

"You want paper? I can give you paper." I passed over

to him the list that Antonia had taken from Rupe McLay's files. I added that in my opinion the list was written in Newby's handwriting. Chris cracked open the second lobster claw with the tool provided. He did it thoughtfully.

"Later on, quite a while later, Ramsden got wind of this and was prepared to use it against Newby. Ramsden was a greedy man. He was already negotiating with Newby about the Oldridge property. Newby brought up the question of price. Both knew it was the centre-piece of Morella's Backstreet Revival project. Without it, the plan wouldn't work. Ramsden held Newby up for a lot more than he was offering. Newby threatened to bring in the Public Trustee. That would have delayed everything without necessarily killing the project. The Public Trustee could sell the property off at a fair price and hold the proceeds for whoever got them in the end. Time was on Newby's side not Ramsden's. He's been next to broke since his disastrous run for mayor. His law practice is all but dead. The only loot he had coming in came from the Bede Bunch and his blackmailing schemes. The only ace he had up his sleeve was to threaten to tell Morella of Newby's part in his wife's divorce — the part he didn't know about, that is. That would finish Newby with Morella forever. That couldn't be allowed to happen."

"Now you're saying that Newby pushed that flagpole through Ramsden, right?"

"That's the way it looks."

"But, damn it all, Benny, you know that Newby found the fucking body! You were there! You saw him do it!"

"Can you think of a better alibi?"

"Huh?"

"In these days of sophisticated crime, nobody suspects

the one who finds the body. That's too easy. Why would a killer go back to the scene of the crime several hours after the murder? Why would he put himself at risk? I can think of two reasons: one, to establish his innocence, as I've described, and, second, to carry something away from the scene with him."

"Benny, you know that's a load of crap!"

"You don't believe me?"

"You understate the case."

"Will you let me conduct a little experiment that will test my theory?"

"What's it going to cost?"

"Nothing. All I want you to do is to call Newby and tell him to come to your office. Tell him that Cath Bracken will be there with some new evidence. Tell him to bring a couple of lawbooks with him, books on evidence: *Forensic Evidence in Canada, Modern Scientific Evidence,* and a couple of cases about big take-overs. Could you ask him to do this to assist the investigation, Chris? Set a time, say tomorrow at three. Be your persuasive self. Get Cath Bracken to be in your office too."

"I hate these little charades of yours, Benny. You keep dragging me out of the real world and into some cockamamy movie script!"

"I know the feeling."

"How does Cath Bracken fit into this? There's a detail you haven't gone into. Well?"

"Bracken had an appointment to see Ramsden the morning he was murdered, Chris." I said it as simply as I could, but I knew there was no way of passing on that news without detonating an explosion. He managed to smother most of the fireworks; I could hardly hear the earth shake.

"Oh, well, I can see why you didn't mention it." Chris was sucking on one of the smaller lobster legs. I couldn't help taking it personally. The look he gave me was hard coming from an old friend. It was only mitigated by the fact that tied around Chris Savas's neck, beneath the anger in his eyes, was a ridiculous white bib with a red lobster printed on it.

Half an hour later, I'd told Chris the details he had to know to carry out our charade and the waitress said, "Thank you kindly."

Chapter Twenty-Nine

Three days before Christmas, I presented myself at Chris's office. It was five minutes to three. Savas looked spiffy. I mean for *Savas* it was spiffy. He had run a wet comb through his remaining strands of hair and appeared with less daytime beard than I'd seen him wearing during the week. A beard grows quickly on a working man.

The morning had dragged on interminably. I tried to imagine the meeting in Chris's office. I tried taking all of the parts. I tried to hear in my head what people were going to say. When I began to feel a little smug about the way it was all running as smoothly as a play on its last night, I began to get worried. There had to be a snag somewhere. I went over it again carefully. Then I saw the flaw.

If things went that way, I thought, I'd look ridiculous. But that was the least of it. Chris Savas could get into serious trouble. I backed up my thoughts again to Chris's office at three. As I listened to the distant murmur of running water down the hall, I worked out a contingency plan.

After that, the time went more quickly. Frank Bushmill stuck his head around the door to tell me that our landlady, Mrs Onischuk, was thinking of putting our building on the market. I tried to put that news out of my head. I like a settled life without domestic surprises. Maybe that's why I work at trying to tidy up other people's muddles. I pondered this while drinking cold coffee from a styrofoam cup.

Cath Bracken was the next person to arrive in Chris Savas's office, just on the stroke of three o'clock. I introduced them and Cath took the best seat in the room without demurring. We spoke of the coming holiday season and the snow-clogged streets. We were all glad when Julian Newby came into the room, escorted by a guiding constable and carrying a briefcase. Pleasantries were exchanged and Chris offered me the remaining chair. He perched on the corner of his desk or stood with his back to the venetian blinds.

Newby, even within the bowels of Niagara Regional Police Headquarters, looked unflappable. He took up his briefcase from the floor and opened it on the well-ironed creases in his trousers. From inside he removed the bundle of books and a file with Xerox copies of the cases Chris had requested. Chris took these from him and placed them on his desk.

"This is a lot of help to us, Mr Newby," Chris said. "Saves no end of time." He joked that it was unusual to see counsel in his office that was unattached to a client.

"Perhaps you've invented a new category, Sergeant, comparable to *amicus curiae*."

"Maybe, Mr Newby, but a 'friend of the court' will always get a better press than a 'friend of the cops.'"

"Perhaps," Newby smiled.

To fill time, Chris led Newby through his statement about finding the body last Saturday. Then he compared this statement with small points in what I'd said in my statement. While these small matters were being cleared up, I moved the briefcase to the right side of Cath's chair. She looked down at it. I held my breath. She looked up at me and slowly shook her head in the negative. I tried to smile, but I could see that the briefcase that Newby had brought into the room with him was not the one Cath saw in Ramsden's office. Chris looked over at me and I shook my head. Chris smiled his superior smile. It made a fine contrast with the sad look on Cath's face. I don't think Newby was aware of any of this.

Chris picked up his cue, and began asking some questions about court rulings on admissible evidence. This was when I excused myself to make a phonecall from the empty office next door. When I got back, Newby was holding forth on what judges had ruled and what had been thrown out in a higher court. He hardly looked up as I took my place again. Chris asked him a few questions about a big property take-over that I missed catching the name of, and then he asked Newby a few questions about the fiduciary regulations regarding access to safety deposit boxes. Newby gave full answers to all these questions, and there was just a hint in his voice that he was slowly losing patience with Savas and his scattered barrage of questions.

Soon, there was a knock at the door and Claudia Morella came in. She was carrying a briefcase in a business-like way. "Here is your briefcase, Mr Newby," she said as soon as she had been introduced to Cath and Chris. "Mr Cooperman's call caught me just as I was leaving the office." Newby looked ruffled; he wasn't used to sharing space with a very junior partner in a small room. He didn't question Claudia on what she had said. He took the briefcase from her and set it down by his chair. His face betrayed nothing. Claudia appeared to be looking for her cue to get out of there. Like a lot of juniors in law offices, she was getting used to ducking into and out of private meetings. But this one was going to be different.

"Claudia," I said, after getting the nod from Savas, "will you answer a couple of questions for us?"

"Yes," she said slowly, her round brown eyes looking over at Newby, who was seated straight in his chair, not moving. "But may I ask 'Why?' "

"It will assist our investigation of Mr Ramsden's death," Chris said. She looked at Newby again. Newby was staring straight ahead of him. Claudia turned to me.

"Is this Mr Newby's briefcase?" I asked, pointing at the one Newby had brought with him.

"It's one that has been around the office. It's not the one he usually uses."

"And where is that one?"

"Why, that is," she said, indicating the briefcase she had brought with her.

"May I see that?" Cath asked. Newby passed it to her without a word and she examined it for a minute. I could hear a clock ticking somewhere. "This is the case I saw in Mr Ramsden's office the day he was killed," she said.

"Mr Newby? Do you have anything to say?"

"Say? Why should I say anything? Memory is a fallible commodity, Detective-Sergeant Savas. I carried this briefcase with me to the house, but that was later, when Mr Cooperman saw me."

"I saw you carry a briefcase *from* the house, Mr Newby. I don't think I ever said I saw you with it before we were in the house together."

"You see, Mr Newby," Chris said, "Miss Bracken had an appointment some hours before you discovered the body and gave the alarm. She says that that briefcase was standing beside her chair, giving her the feeling that there was someone else already in the house, perhaps the murderer."

"This is highly melodramatic! It's worthy of television! Just suppose for a moment that it was me. What possible motive could I have for killing poor Mr Ramsden?"

"Benny?" Savas looked at me to field all the questions from now on. If anyone was going to be made to look ridiculous under the pounding of Newby's famous glare, it wasn't going to be him.

"Ramsden knew about the list of Morella's assets that you leaked to Dora Ramsden, which she passed on to her sister."

"That may well be, but how does it signify? What could I do about it? Killing Ramsden would have cut me off from completing the Backstreet Revival project. Ramsden alive was our link to the Oldridge property. Dead, his estate would go who knows where."

"The Brogan Street project was only one item in your work with Morella. There would be others, but not once he knew of your double-dealing through Dora Ramsden."

"Sergeant? Are you going to listen to any more of this twaddle? We both know about the laws of evidence, I think, somewhat better than Mr Cooperman."

"That may well be, sir, but I would like to hear from you in some detail where you were at the time of Mr Ramsden's death."

At a nod, Cath Bracken, Claudia Morella and I were

dismissed from the office. In the hall, I could see that Claudia's face was white with rage.

"You tricked me into coming here! You tricked me into being a witness against the kindest, dearest man I know! I wouldn't have believed people could sink so low." Having said this, she started to leave, but Cath caught her by the sleeve.

"If Benny's wrong, then Mr Newby will be able to explain how it is that he didn't want me to see his usual briefcase. He knew I would be here. He also knew that I may have seen the one he left at the scene. Why did he change briefcases before coming out to this meeting?" The woman looked confused. She bit hard on her lower lip.

"Have you ever seen him switch briefcases before?" I asked. "Was it something he generally did?" Of course, she didn't answer. We didn't expect her to. Newby in many ways was a local great, good man. He endowed charities, took on bright young students, fought the good fight in may ways. But he did all of this because Morella's business made him independent. In the union of his family with Morella's, through the probable marriage between Gerard Newby and Claudia, Newby was cementing a continuance of these good offices. It didn't seem to be the right time to mention this, so I kept my mouth shut.

After about twenty minutes, Pete Staziak went into the office without seeing any of us waiting in the hall. A few minutes later, a stenographer joined them with her dictating book. Nobody seemed interested in coffee. The smokers weren't even patting their pockets or bags.

It was nearly an hour later that Chris stuck his nose out his door long enough to say that he was booking

Julian Newby in the murder of Thurleigh Ramsden. He wasn't singling any of us out when he said this. He particularly kept his eyes clear of Claudia's tormented face. He had already closed the door again before a choked "Oh, no!" escaped her pale lips. I looked at Cath and she looked at me. Together we took an arm each and led her from Niagara Regional. We ended up in The Snug at the back of the Beaumont Hotel, where so many of the joys and tragedies of Grantham are enacted. We were with her, listening to her reiterations of disbelief, until Cath had to leave for the TV station. I offered to drive Claudia home and she let me. When I got home myself, I called Gerard and told him what happened. All in all, he took the news better than Claudia had.

Chapter Thirty

There's really not a lot more to say. The town did its best not to make a circus of the five-month-long trial, and failed. One of Toronto's top criminal lawyers spent his leisure hours in a room at the Eastbank Hotel. When the trial ended, the hotel management held a small ceremony in which they retired his room number and made him a present of the door. Of course Newby went to prison. Even a defence that put most of the blame on the villain Ramsden couldn't get Newby off the hook.

Old Mrs Ravenswood at last allowed herself to get the help she needed with her drinking problem. At these church basement meetings she sometimes encountered Rupert McLay, whose attendance, she boasted, left a good deal to be desired. But, she allowed that he was a well-spoken "young man with a gift for wry humour."

One day while the trial was still going on, the old woman sent her car for me. As usual my answering service got the name wrong, so that it wasn't until I was ushered into her presence in a big, sunny room that I realized who it was.

"Sit down, Mr Cooperman," she said. "You'll find that the tea on the coffee-table is still quite hot." I settled myself and went through the motions of playing with the cup and saucer. The biscuits were oatcakes and not brought out of the Highlands by any rapid means.

"I brought you here to listen to an old woman ramble. I intend to pay you for your time, but I don't mean to hire you. So, you may put that out of your head." I nodded and she went on. "You know this trial of Julian Newby is most distressful for me. I knew his people, you see. Thank God they're long dead! What interests me — concerns me, really — is that the name of one of my employees has been repeatedly brought into the proceedings. You know to whom I'm referring, I think?"

"Catherine Bracken," I said.

"Yes, Catherine Bracken. Is there any way that you can see to eliminate her name? It comes up day after day."

"Short of Julian Newby changing his plea, no."

"I see. I believe you, Mr Cooperman. My son-in-law holds you in high regard. And I seem to remember you myself from somewhere."

"May I ask why you wish to spare Cath Bracken? The Crown's case depends upon her recognition of Newby's briefcase at the scene of the crime."

"Yes, yes, yes! I know all that. I hate publicity, especially when it comes close. I loathe it."

"A news reader is news, Mrs Ravenswood."

"I don't care about that. I'm thinking of the girl, you silly man! I've become fond of the girl and I hate thinking of what this is doing to her."

"I think you underestimate Cath, Mrs Ravenswood. She's made of tough material. She won't break."

"Yes, I'm rather counting on that. One has to count on something and it's a comfort to know she's tough."

"I didn't say unbreakable."

"No, I know what you mean. She comes of tough

stock, you see. I have every confidence that she'll get through it."

"I didn't know you knew her family."

"Did you not? Yes, I knew her father rather well. But that was a long time ago. Will you be going back to the court-house?"

"Not today. But I'm due to testify before the end of the week."

"I see. Well, I won't keep you any longer, Mr Cooperman."

The interview was over and there were still oatcakes to be returned to their box for another five or ten years. My last sight of Gladys Ravenswood was a mauve smile as she gave me her hand before I gave myself up to her driver to be returned to my office.

The old woman lived to celebrate her eighty-ninth birthday. After her death, Orv and Antonia split their marriage without splitting up their working arrangements. Antonia went to the *Beacon*, where she introduced some overdue changes. She enjoyed being a "hands-on" publisher. She continued, changes notwithstanding, to employ some alcoholic friends of mine. Orv Wishart, left with a free hand to run the broadcasting centre, brought Cath Bracken into the management team, which gave her an important voice in how the broadcasting wing of the Ravenswood media empire was run. Her official title was Head of Radio, but she was elevated to the board of directors, while continuing to read the evening news on TV, to my father's secret delight and mine.

Cath and McStu got married quietly in the new year, shortly after McStu's new book came out the day before Christmas Eve. The book did well. I bought an armful myself at the launching party in Susan Torres's book store on Queen Street. I was behind in my Christmas shopping and the book made a great choice for friends and family. The antiques I bought in Grimsby also found favour with some very special people.

I remember at the book launching, with Anna and Cath getting to know one another and Anna listening to Cath go on and on about the pleasures of a skiing holiday at Fonthill and Susan Torres trying to maintain some order around the cheese and crackers, that McStu took me over to one side of the store, leaned me against the wall of books and asked: "Why did Newby get you to follow Cath, Benny?"

"To get me to stop snooping around Ramsden."

"Who was he fronting for? Who was his client?"

"McStu, there wasn't a client. Newby was doing this for himself. It was a way to control me, he thought."

"And what about Cath? Why her?"

"He wanted me to hinder her getting the Oldridge documentary on the air. That's why he tipped her off that she was being tailed. He wanted to add confusion, just to slow her down. He needed quiet to complete his deal with Ramsden. And Ramsden wasn't making it easy. Newby knew that once the papers got hold of the Bede Bunch flimflam, the Public Trustee would swoop down on the whole enterprise, delaying things indefinitely. Of course, that became irrelevant as soon as Ramsden threatened Newby. Quite simply, Ramsden had to be killed. Newby was like that about people. He dealt with them unsentimentally. Just as he did with poor Dora. As soon as their little affair threatened the course of Newby's planned future, Dora had to be eliminated."

"Brilliant! Just brilliant!" said McStu.

"He hasn't explained away Temperley yet," said a voice I knew. It was Chris Savas chewing on some orange cheese.

"Yes," said McStu, "what about Temperley?"

"Cath's interview with Temperley frankly scared him. Maybe it was his conscience or maybe it was the smell of prison, Chris. He told Ramsden he wasn't going to cover for him any more. So, Ramsden took him for an old-fashioned ride in the cemetery just before closing time on Monday night. He popped him with that Japanese piece you haven't been able to trace and dumped him into a freshly dug grave. He kicked some loose dirt on top of him, but by then it must have been getting too dark to see. Six feet down, Temperley must have looked gone forever."

"That's just talk, Benny," Chris said.

"Try the little museum Ramsden set up for the Royal Grantham Rifles. The gun is in their collection. Ramsden took it, used it and had it back in the collection before it was even missed."

"What if it is? That still doesn't make it Ramsden."

"You can tell quickly enough if the piece was used recently or not. And, hell, Chris, since Ramsden's dead, I didn't think you'd need an airtight case. But, for what it's worth, have a look at the muddy shoes Ramsden was wearing the night I had my tussle with him. They can compare the mud on his shoes with the mud in the grave, can't they?"

"You bloody well know they can!" Chris said, biting down hard and sending chips of biscuit into McStu's hair.

Trying to change the subject, I turned on McStu, who was now being pulled by Cath back to his autographing table. "Tell me," I said, "why do you change the names of some of the Hamilton streets and not change others? You change the names of some of the places near Hamilton too and not others. Why is that?"

"Ah," said McStu, pouring red wine into a plastic glass, "that's a secret known only to me, my editor and God almighty."

"What's going on here?" said Frank Bushmill, pushing a book under McStu's nose for signing. He had made his way through a growing crowd of admirers. He looked completely recovered from the bang on his head. "Benny, did you ever figure out who it was who was trying to get into your office that night?"

"What's this?" Chris demanded.

"Oh, it's just one of those loose ends. You get them at the end of every big case," I said. "It may have been Mendlesham trying to see what I had on Ramsden. It might have been Newby himself, but I doubt it. We can't lay everything at the feet of our villain, can we?" I looked up at McStu for support, but he broke up and started laughing. Savas joined him and so did Cath Bracken. But Frank shouted his way through the laughter.

"Benny," he said. "When are we holding a tenants' meeting?"

"Meeting? What meeting?" I asked.

"We have to find a replacement for our old friend Mr Kogan."

"Kogan? This all started with Kogan. Has he finally eaten a bad can of cat food?"

"Not a bit of it,' Frank said. "I was talking to Rupe McLay over at the Nag's Head. He tells me that Kogan has just come into a lot of money. Turns out he was Liz Oldridge's heir in the hole. He's inherited everything! Rupe says he plans to buy our building on St Andrew Street from Mrs Onischuk. Damned if he isn't threatening to turn our offices into a hostel for vagrants. We're going to have to move, Benny! As Kogan says, 'How do you like them apples?' "